ANOTHER COLORADO KILL

I0587224

Bob Doerr

TotalRecall Publications, Inc.
www.totalrecallpress.com

TotalRecall Publications, Inc.
1103 Middlecreek
Friendswood, Texas 77546
281-992-3131   281-482-5390 Fax
www.totalrecallpress.com

Printed in the United States of America with simultaneous
printings in Australia, Canada, and United Kingdom.

FIRST EDITION
1   2   3   4   5   6   7   8   9   10

To my wife, Leigh.

About the Author

Bob Doerr grew up in a military family, attended the Air Force Academy, and then had a career of his own in the Air Force. It was a life style that had him moving every three or four years, but also one that exposed him to the people and cultures of numerous countries in Asia, Europe and to most of these United States. In the Air Force, Bob specialized in criminal investigations and counterintelligence gaining significant insight to the worlds of crime, espionage and terrorism. In addition to his degree from the Academy he also has a Masters in International Relations from Creighton University. Bob now lives in Garden Ridge, Texas, with his wife of 38 years, their pet dog Skyler and ornery cat Cinco.

To my wife, Leigh.

About the Author

Bob Doerr grew up in a military family, attended the Air Force Academy, and then had a career of his own in the Air Force. It was a life style that had him moving every three or four years, but also one that exposed him to the people and cultures of numerous countries in Asia, Europe and to most of these United States. In the Air Force, Bob specialized in criminal investigations and counterintelligence gaining significant insight to the worlds of crime, espionage and terrorism. In addition to his degree from the Academy he also has a Masters in International Relations from Creighton University. Bob now lives in Garden Ridge, Texas, with his wife of 38 years, their pet dog Skyler and ornery cat Cinco.

Bob Doerr turns up the heat in his latest thriller, *Another Colorado Kill*. It's a tale packed with suspense, keeping readers on edge as they try to keep pace with Jim West yet again. Hold on tight as Doerr takes you along on a plot twisting read that will turn you topsy-turvy.

-- John M. Wills, Award-winning Free Lance Writer / Speaker

Creator of the -- **Chicago Warriors™** *Thriller Series now available in print and eBook*

www.JohnMWills.com

Chapter 1

Parked under the lone tree in the Lowes' parking lot, I had the top down on my Mustang to take advantage of the beautiful spring morning in New Mexico. I knew it would take Perry a long time to return his circular saw. Not because Lowes was slow, Perry simply couldn't do anything quickly.

In fact, I had already started to regret that I had agreed to go on this golf trip with him, and we hadn't even left Clovis. I could have easily worked myself into a real sour mood, right then and there, if it hadn't been for the bird. A large crow or grackle had center stage in front of me. It had staked out a small section of the parking lot and expertly picked dead insects off the bumpers of parked cars. The bird paced back and forth inspecting the vehicles and made quick work of any dead bugs it discovered. If any other birds landed on its turf, it immediately chased them away. I would have to remember the next time I have a lot of dead bugs on my car to bring it here for a free pre-wash.

I saw Perry come out of the store, take about five steps, and then turn around and go back in. I just shook my head. It would only be four days, I told myself. We'd drive up to Colorado Springs today and meet up with Steve and Mike. Play 36 holes at the Air Force Academy tomorrow, another 18 holes at the Broadmoor on Thursday, and return on Friday. I would survive, and the golf would be fun.

Perry exited the store for a second time. This time he carried a small plastic bag and had a dumb grin on his face like he had just drawn the last card to an inside straight. Perry's actual name was Edward Mason, but, for obvious reasons, everyone called him Perry. If I were him, I would've pursued a career in law, but he became a realtor. He was overweight and out of shape, but it didn't seem to bother him. He was much more concerned about his receding hair line. He had married one of the sweetest women I had ever known, so why he worried about his hair and not his health bewildered me.

"Hey," Perry shouted as he approached the car. "I picked us up something to hold us over until lunch."

I figured if he needed to make another stop before we left town, it would be lunch time. I was already frustrated that he had waited until this morning to return the circular saw.

He squeezed into the passenger seat. I had often wondered if my black Mustang with its grey interior was too colorless. But, this morning, any other color would have seriously clashed with Perry's XXXL flowered shirt. I put the roof up and we headed north. We hadn't even passed Grady, heading north on State Highway 209, when Perry tore open his family-sized Baby Ruth. He took a bite and then, looking at me, remembered his manners and took a second huge candy bar out of his bag. He tore the wrapper open and handed it to me.

Thanks to the light traffic, we passed through Logan in no time. The next leg of the trip took us through some beautiful country and to Springer, where we connected with I-25. We stopped for lunch in Springer. Perry surprised me by lasting as long as he did, but the second large candy bar must have done the trick. He had offered me a second Baby Ruth, too, but I declined.

"Tell me, Jim, does the golf ball really travel further at the Academy?"

"Yes, Perry, especially if you're hitting it down-hill."

Perry laughed out loud. He had a lot of faults, but, at least, he liked my sense of humor. He was actually a pretty good golfer and easy to play with. I had agreed to come on this trip only after a lot of forestalling the inevitable. I had played with Mike and Steve on a few occasions when they had come down to Clovis to visit Perry and his wife, Claire. They were related in some way to her. Cousins, I thought, but they had grown up like brothers and sister. It was Claire who finally talked me into making the trip with Perry.

"Jim," she had said, "they've been inviting Perry up to Colorado for years to play golf. He has never gone up to play with them despite the few times they've come down here to play with him. He'll go if you go with him." There was more to the conversation, of course, and Mike, Steve, and Perry had already been on me to make the trip, but it was Claire who talked me into it.

Some time ago, I had decided that there were actually two Perrys: one on the golf course – the good Perry, and one everywhere else – the aggravating Perry. The latter now sat across from me at the Fiesta Grande Restaurant.

"Hola chica!" he half screamed at the twenty something year old waitress as she approached us.

She smiled back at him but took up a position of safety partly behind my right shoulder. I didn't blame her.

"Guapa, how about giving me the large enchilada plate with a taco on the side?" He held up his menu for her to take but kept it close, so she would have to approach him to retrieve it. I saved her the anguish by taking it from him and giving it to her.

I ordered three tacos, a la carte, and we both had iced tea.

"She's a looker," Perry said after she was gone.

"Certainly is," I concurred. I figured Perry was simply having some fun at her expense, but I also figured that in her eyes, Perry was just a creepy old man.

"So, Jim, if I can drive the ball two hundred and fifty yards in Clovis, how far will it go at the Academy?"

"Longer, I guess, but I don't know the specifics. Clovis is just over four thousand feet above sea level and both Academy courses are over six thousand feet, so the air will be thinner. You know, though, our problem has never been distance. It's been keeping the ball in the fairway. Not to mention chipping and putting." I added with a smile.

"You got that straight," he laughed.

We continued to talk golf as we left Springer and all the way to Raton pass. However, by the time we entered Colorado, Perry had dosed off. I turned the radio on, kept the volume low and found a station playing jazz.

I had driven this highway a number of times in the past but not in the last fifteen years. The cities were all where they used to be, just bigger, but the traffic still moved quickly to the north. We were past Trinidad, Walsenburg and Pueblo in no time, and I started watching for Pikes Peak in the distance. The ground rolled around a lot here, just east of the foothills. The taller peaks stood farther to the west. This part of the drive was surprisingly treeless. Still, the landscape appeared beautiful in its own way.

As Perry slept and the terrain flew by, I had second thoughts whether I had locked the back door to my house. It didn't really matter. I had left Chubbs, my fearless mutt, in the care of my neighbor's kids. He was crazy about them, and they enjoyed being responsible for him whenever I was away. They appreciated the extra money they earned by watching him, too.

Perry coughed and sat up straight. "Where are we?"

"Almost there, maybe thirty miles out."

"Wow, I slept that long?" Perry asked as he rubbed his eyes.

"Unless you were just pretending."

He tried unsuccessfully to stretch out his arms in the car.

"You need a bigger car."

"We could've brought yours."

"Yeah, I know, but like I told you, Claire needs the good car and my old Dodge wouldn't make a long drive. Luckily, it's paid off and good enough to get me back and forth in town."

I did have to stuff our luggage onto the Mustang's back seat. The clubs and shoes fit snugly in the trunk. But, I was glad to be driving. I wouldn't have felt comfortable with Perry driving all the way.

"If you see a gas station or a rest stop, I need to take a leak."

"I think I saw a sign a few miles back that indicated we're close to a rest area. So, if we don't see a gas station first, we can stop there."

"How are we on gas?"

"We've got enough to get to the Springs. But if you're buying, I can stop anytime."

Perry laughed, but didn't offer. I had wondered early on if he would help out with the gas, not because of the cost, but simply because I was curious if he would. Most of me hoped he would chip in, thereby proving to me that he wasn't a total loser away from the golf course. However, there was that small, outspoken part of my inner mind that hoped Perry wouldn't spring for any gas, thus substantiating his loser status.

In less than a minute, another sign appeared, telling us we

were only one mile from a rest stop.

"Don't pass it by, Jim. It wouldn't be funny."

I grinned at his remark. Until he made the comment, I had no intention of driving by the rest stop. Now, the thought did creep into my mind. Fighting the urge, I turned onto the exit and steered the Mustang to one of the vacant spots closest to the lone building. There were no other cars in the lot.

"Looks like we have the place to ourselves," I said, as I turned the engine off.

Perry hurried out of the car and trotted to the covered porch area at the front of the building. He looked right, left and then entered the door to the left. I opened both front side windows, got out of the car and stretched by the driver's door. The small grey concrete building looked like it could use some sprucing up. The handful of concrete picnic tables, set off to the north, also had that rundown appearance. At least it was functional, I thought, and that was all that really mattered.

A muffled scream came from the building in front of me, almost immediately followed by Perry running out of the men's room.

"Aaaagh! We gotta get out of here! Jeez!" Perry dashed to the car. "Don't go in there! Dead guy! Let's get out of here."

I pride myself on my ability to quickly assess a situation and take appropriate action. However, at the moment, my initial state of concern had been ambushed by the sight of Perry running at me. The crotch area and one leg of his tan shorts were soaking wet, and the shorts were still unzipped. Fortunately, there was nothing else exposed to make the sight even more ridiculous. I wanted to laugh, but I knew something had terrified Perry to the point that his desire to flee overcame all other rational behavior.

"Hold on! Don't get into my car like that. If someone is dead inside we need to call the police." He didn't slow down. As I spoke, I reached inside my open door and pushed the lock button. He reached the car and pulled at the handle. "Slow down big guy. Now what's going on?"

He looked at me. At first, his eyes didn't seem to focus. He looked back at the building and then back at me.

"Jim, there's a guy in there. I think he's dead. I was standing there taking a leak when I happened to look over toward the stalls. I saw a guy lying there staring at me. There was blood all around him. I guess I panicked and just ran."

"Stay here, Perry. Don't get in the car. Let me go see, then we'll need to call the police."

I pushed the door to the men's room open and saw nothing. I had to walk a few steps and turn right. That took me around the privacy wall and into the large latrine area. I instinctively stopped to study the scene. Three sinks appeared to my right, fastened against the wall. A bunch of urinals hung next to them. Directly ahead of me I saw the wall to the first of the toilet stalls. A large trash can stood by my side. I didn't look inside it and from where I stood, nothing out of the ordinary appeared on the floor.

I walked further in, past the wall to the first stall, and looked left, down the front of the stalls. The body of a man was in plain view. I should say from the waist up the body was in plain view. The rest of the body appeared to be inside the stall. Perry, in his hurry, must have rushed straight to the urinals, not noticing the body.   I approached the body, being careful I didn't disturb the scene. Other than the blood on the floor and on the man's white dress shirt, I couldn't see anything else that I needed to worry about, but I still took my time. I reached down to his neck and felt for a pulse. I couldn't find one.

The body was cool but not yet as cold as it would get. The blood had stopped flowing out of the wound, no - make that two wounds in his chest, but it wasn't dry. The hairs on the back of my neck stood up. This guy hadn't been dead very long. His killer, or killers, could still be close by. I stood up and hurried out of the building.

Chapter 2

When I came out of the building I saw Perry bent over, leaning into the passenger side back seat, and rummaging through his suitcase. As I approached, he emerged with a fresh pair of underwear and shorts.

"I need to change my clothes."

"Do it in the women's room," I instructed, and he waddled off. I watched him to make sure he didn't go back into the men's room.

I dialed 911 on my cell and went through the lengthy process of reporting our discovery. I could've simply told the operator what we had found and hung up, but we weren't going anywhere, so I remained on the line while she went through her checklist of questions. As we talked, I leaned against the Mustang and watched the traffic on the Interstate. With any luck, this would only delay us an hour or so.

I happened to look back at the building just as Perry came out the men's side of the building.

"What the....." I mumbled to myself.

"Is there a problem?" the 911 operator asked.

"No, no, but I have to get off the phone. Don't worry; we'll stay here until the police get here." I hung up the phone.

"Perry, why did you go back in there? I asked you to stay out."

"I only wanted to take a quick look. I never really got a good look last time."

"Well, the police are on their way. They want us to stay out and to keep anyone else who shows up out of the men's room, too."

"Okay, no big deal."

Perry opened the passenger door and put his wet clothing on the floor mat behind the passenger seat.

I'm going to have to buy a new floor mat, I thought. The sound of approaching sirens interrupted my concern for my car. A vehicle, lights flashing, rapidly approached from the north. As it came even with the rest stop, it slowed, crossed the grass median and the north bound lanes and pulled up close to us. The lone trooper inside the Colorado State Patrol vehicle got out but stayed adjacent to his open door. He was young, and he looked nervous. His gun hand stayed down, close to his side.

"Are you the guys that called in the dead body?" He looked suspiciously at the two of us. Homicides weren't really the state patrol's cup of tea. I figured he was closest to the scene and therefore requested by the sheriff's office to help secure the crime scene until they arrived.

"Yes. The body is inside the men's room," I answered.

He continued watching us, apparently trying to decide if he should leave us alone.

"Show me."

"Sure, this way," I turned and led him into the men's room, wondering if he hesitated simply because he didn't want to go in by himself. Maybe he had never seen a dead body. Perry stayed outside as we entered the building.

"Stay over there," he said, once the body was in full view, and pointed toward the sinks. The trooper was tall and thin. He carefully avoided the blood on the floor when he approached the body. He leaned his tall frame over to check for any vital signs.

"Do you know who he is?" He asked as he stood up.

"No idea. I checked him like you did to see if he was alive. He wasn't." I took a couple steps toward him, looking back down at the victim, as I spoke. Something didn't look right. I didn't know what, and I was about to ask the trooper if I could take a closer look at him when we heard the sound of approaching sirens.

"Let's go back outside and leave the scene for the experts." He motioned for me to go first.

I walked out, troubled by something about the body, barely noticing that another vehicle had pulled up. Something had been moved or was missing. The dead man wore a blue blazer with the white shirt. The blazer was different, not a different blazer but something about it. The more I thought about it, the less certain I became.

"May I see some identification?" A voice interrupted my train of thought.

I took my New Mexico driver's license out and handed it over. The man talking to me wore an El Paso County Deputy Sheriff uniform. His nametag had the name Gray inscribed on it. He looked as young as the state trooper, just not as tall or thin.

Another deputy, one who looked like he had more experience, had arrived with Gray. He was conferring with the trooper by the entrance to the men's room. Two more county vehicles pulled up. One of them belonged to the El Paso County medical examiner. I could see an ambulance rapidly approaching. This place would soon be crawling with people.

"Thanks Mr. West," Deputy Gray handed me back my driver's license. "Just stand over there by your car for a few minutes. Someone will be by to take your statement."

I strolled over to the car and leaned against the side. Deputy Gray went over to talk to Perry. I wondered if he was going to pass on all the details surrounding his discovery and reaction to seeing the body.

Gray sent Perry over to wait with me.

"Why can't we leave?" Perry asked me.

"I'm sure they want an official statement from us."

"What can we say other than we found the body?"

"Not much, but they'll want the complete picture. Who we are, why we're traveling up I-25, why we stopped here, what we did when we saw the body, did we notice anyone else in the area, and did we know the victim – all those sorts of things. But like you said, Perry, not really much."

"How long before we can leave?"

"I can't imagine it'll be much more than an hour."

I was wrong, way wrong. For the first thirty minutes, no one seemed to take any interest in us. I didn't mind as it was fascinating to watch them go through the steps of processing the crime scene. Not the immediate area inside, but how they checked, inspected and searched everything within a hundred yards outside the building.

Deputy Gray approached us again, but rather than ask us any questions, he asked us to get in and stay in the car. Someone must have thought we might be contaminating the scene, but as we'd been into the immediate crime scene before they arrived and by the car ever since, we'd already done what contamination we could do. However, we did what we were told and climbed back into the Mustang.

The smell hit me immediately. Perry's shorts and underwear had been enclosed in the car, in the sun, for the last thirty minutes or so.

"Damn, Perry."

"Whew! I know. I know. Sorry about that."

I worked the windows and the top of the convertible as he was talking. In just a few seconds the fresh air let us both breathe again. Despite the bright sun, the air felt cool. It was getting late in the afternoon. In a little while the sun would be setting behind the mountains to our west.

"Why can't we just drive off?" Perry whined.

"We've been through that. Whoever's in charge of this will want a statement from both of us."

In the rear view mirror, I noticed one of the uniformed deputies behind my car scrutinizing us and the interior of my car. I turned my head around to him.

"Can we help you?"

"Oh, excuse me," he responded and walked off toward the building.

"I was wondering what that was all about." I asked Perry.

He didn't appear to hear me, as he had focused his attention on finding the last Baby Ruth.

"Want half?"

"No."

He began eating his third large candy bar of the day and had barely finished it when he said, "I need to go to the bathroom. Do you think they'll let me?"

"Of course, but you'll probably have to use the women's. Ask that cop over there." I pointed to the uniformed deputy that had been positioned at the front of the building. "I think he's been given the job of controlling who goes in and out of the crime scene."

Perry had just disappeared from view when the deputy who had been studying us a minute ago from the back of my car came back in view. A tall, slender woman in civilian clothes accompanied him. She had red hair pulled back tight and big, green eyes that grabbed mine as soon as they met. I knew it wasn't polite to stare, but this time it wasn't really my fault.

The male deputy addressed me first. I knew this because I could hear him speak. The sound of his voice allowed me to break the lock the lady's eyes had on me and look his way.

"Mr. West," he repeated, "can you step out of your car, please."

I climbed out of the car wondering why I hadn't seen the female arrive.

"What can I do for you?"

The woman walked on by, slowing by the rear of the car, and then circling back around to us. She moved with an air of confidence and authority.

"Where's your friend?" the male deputy asked.

"He had to use the bathroom."

"Do you mind if we look inside your car?" This time she asked the question, and, in doing so, she broke whatever advantage she had over me. Maybe the request was routine. After all, I had never discovered a body in a rest stop before. However, I knew something was up. I could feel it in my bones. He had gone in, brought her out, and now they wanted to search the car.

I had nothing to worry about. I knew that also, but it made no sense. We'd been there for at least forty minutes, and all the while no one seemed to have the least amount of interest in us. I had lowered the top of the Mustang exposing the contents to the world. Would I have done that if I was hiding anything? I looked back at the car. I couldn't see anything of interest.

I looked back at the male deputy.

"Why the sudden interest?"

Rather than wait for an answer, I walked slowly to the back of the car. They both followed me. I noticed a third officer approach the car. I didn't like this.

I saw it when I stood beside the rear wheel on the passenger side of my car. It was easy to spot with the sun reflecting off it, despite being partially concealed in the top, unzipped pouch of Perry's suitcase.

"You've got to be kidding me," I said to myself. Both of them heard me.

"What is it?" she asked.

Of course she knew. We all did, and it came to me right then -- the reason the victim's blazer looked different. Perry, Perry, what an idiot!

"Please take it. It's not mine, and I didn't put it there."

The uniformed deputy didn't need to open the door. He just leaned over the side of the car and, using a ball point pen, extracted the small, semiautomatic pistol. He held it up for us both to see. It was actually very attractive, for a pistol. Its grip looked like a coral shaded pearl, and the rest of the gun seemed to be a deep, dark, metallic navy blue. It glistened in the sunlight, looking more like a collector's item than a gun used for its intended purpose.

"It's his," the uniformed deputy said.

I wanted to ask, "Whose?" I wanted to ask, "How do you know that so quickly." I wanted to say a lot of things, but I just stayed quiet.

"Bag it," she told him. "Anything else in there you want to tell us about?"

"I didn't know the gun was there. So, please, to make us both feel better, look to your heart's content."

Just then Perry emerged from the building. He stopped when he saw the deputy with the pistol. The panic registered clearly in his eyes. He looked around and for a second I thought he might try to run. Even Perry had to see that he had nowhere to go. Besides, I doubted if he could've outrun any of the dozen or so personnel still at the scene.

"Come here, Mr. Mason," she instructed, and Perry did as he was told.

She turned back to the uniformed deputy, "Cuff him and see if he has anything else of interest on his person."

I just started to feel sorry for Perry, when she turned those beautiful eyes back at me.

"Turn around West, and spread 'em."

Normally, I would've been my jovial self at a time like this, and would've had a dozen funny comments to keep things calm. After all, I knew I hadn't done anything to be concerned about and here was this great looking dame running her hands all over my body.

Instead, I was furious, and I rarely even get mad. This day had spiraled out of control, and all because of a jerk whom I didn't want to be with anyway. Good thing she had me cuffed, because I had the strongest urge to jump over my car and bust Perry's head apart.

"Why did the two of you take the pistol? Theft of a handgun is a serious offense. Not to mention tampering with a crime scene, concealing evidence, obstruction of justice, possession of a stolen gun, and who knows what else we'll find?"

I hardly listened to her. I didn't need to. I knew what laws Perry had broken as soon as I saw the pistol. The question of why he did it would get essentially the same answer as why the proverbial knucklehead couldn't resist licking the frozen metal signpost. It was like God had put that gun there in front of Perry just like a fisherman might put a pretty, shiny lure in the water to attract a fish. Perry was that dumb fish.

Through the clutter of angry thoughts that I focused at Perry, something clicked in my mind. Nowhere in Miss Colorado's diatribe of offenses did she mention the possibility that the pistol could have been the murder weapon.

She finished with her pat down of me.

"Turn around," she instructed. "Let's walk to the tables over there so we can talk."

She led the way and I followed, my hands still cuffed. They were all empty so we grabbed the nearest picnic table.

"West, I'm going to be easy on you."

She paused but I remained quiet.

"You really didn't know that the pistol was in your car. Is that right?"

"Yes."

"So how do you think it got there?"

"As a matter of principle, Detective...."

"It's Lieutenant, Lieutenant Michelle Prado."

"Lieutenant, I'd rather Perry explain everything to you. I never laid eyes on the pistol until I saw it in the car. I don't mean to be obstructive, and if he doesn't come clean, I'll get the information from him. It's just that I think it would be better for him to come clean, and it would do my conscious good to not tell you what a total jerk he is, at least not at this point."

Prado looked over to where the other deputy was interviewing Perry. "Well, your friend's talking. Hopefully he's explaining this whole thing better than you have."

"I hope he is, too."

"What brings you up here? I noticed your car has New

Mexico tags."

"A golf trip. How did you know the pistol wasn't the murder weapon?"

She looked at me inquisitively, "Did you know the victim?"

"No, never saw him before in my life."

"Why'd you stop here?"

I didn't get to answer because the deputy talking to Perry started shouting. Perry, who had been leaning against the far side of the Mustang, was no longer in sight.

"Man down! Medic! Now! Medic!" the young deputy waved his right arm up in the air as he shouted.

Instinctively, we both started moving in Perry's direction. I felt stupid wearing the cuffs, but any concerns about myself, evaporated when I saw Perry. He had collapsed onto the ground in an oddly twisted shape. He didn't look like he was breathing.

"I think he had a heart attack!" the deputy said to all of us. Seconds passed, and it seemed to me everyone was just going to stand around and do nothing. Fortunately, the ambulance that had responded to the scene had not left, and two men jumped out of the vehicle and ran to where Perry had fallen. A third person, whom I later learned was an assistant county medical examiner, almost immediately joined them and things started moving fast.

I felt a hand on my arm. "Come on back to our table. I have a few last questions to ask you. We can't do anything here. Your friend is in good hands."

I wasn't reassured. Not because of my distrust of the people now treating him, but because he already looked dead to me. If Perry had had a massive heart attack, there might be very little anyone could do for him.

I let her lead me back to the picnic table. The issue with the gun seemed like nothing now. I lost all interest in the dead body in the men's room. Someone would have to call Claire. I didn't want to, but I knew I would have to. Jesus, I wished I hadn't agreed to come on this trip.

"Hey!"   Lt. Prado's voice finally penetrated my own thoughts.

"Sorry."

"Stay here for one minute. I'm going to go talk to Ray."

Ray was apparently the deputy who had been talking to Perry, as that was whom she approached. They talked for about one minute. Ray looked a little shaken up.

"Okay, West. It's your lucky day."

Dumb thing to say, I thought.

"Your friend admitted right away that he took the gun and hid it in your car. He said you knew nothing about it."

"Did he say why he did it?"

"No, although he did acknowledge that it was a stupid thing to do. He said he went back in to look at the body while you were on the phone. He started to say something more, but then just collapsed."

"Poor, Perry. I can't imagine why he would've taken that gun."

"West, why did you ask me how I knew it wasn't the murder weapon?"

"The way you listed all the offenses that had been committed by removing the pistol. Believe me, I don't mean to downplay them, but if you thought that gun was the murder weapon you would've been in the right to treat us like a couple of murder suspects."

"Are you a cop?"

"No, but for a long time I did something similar."

She let that ride.

"Turn around."

I did. She removed the handcuffs.

The ambulance pulled out in a hurry, heading north.

"Is there someone who should know about your friend's situation?"

"His wife, but I think I better wait until we know for sure."

"I wouldn't wait long."

She made sense. I knew I was just stalling.

"Where are they taking him?"

"I'll find out. Before I do, I need you to stick around for a day or two. Do you have a place to stay tonight?"

"Yes, the Town Plaza in the Springs."

"Good, I need to see you tomorrow morning at nine. We'll want to get an official statement."

"Not tonight?" I wanted to get this over with.

"No, tomorrow morning. Is that going to be a problem?"

"No."

She handed me her card. I just glanced at it and stuck it in my pocket.

"Did anyone get your cell phone number?"

"I don't remember." I gave it to her.

Chapter 3

They had taken Perry to the closest major hospital, Southeast Methodist Hospital in Colorado Springs.

Despite all the commotion, the police still had found time to go through my car. Not much to it, since there wasn't much to inspect. I did have to finish zipping shut my suitcase, and Perry's soiled shorts now sat on top of his suitcase. As delicately as I could, I made sure there wasn't anything in the shorts' pockets. Next, I found the plastic bag that came with the candy bars Perry had purchased earlier that day and dropped the shorts and underwear into it. I then walked over to a nearby trash can and dropped the bag into it. Perry had bigger things to worry about now, and I didn't need to be lugging his soiled shorts around with me.

I drove off, heading north to Colorado Springs. I hadn't gone a mile when I realized I had no idea how to get to the hospital. I knew my way to the hotel, but I wanted to go to the hospital first. I decided I would head to the hotel and watch for the hospital as I drove. If I saw it, I would go there first. Otherwise, I would check in, get directions and then go directly to the hospital.

I had barely passed the city limits sign when I saw the tall façade of the hospital clearly marked and shining bright. The mountains to my left had already hid the setting sun from those of us at road level, but above three stories the walls of the hospital still reflected its light. After parking in the closest visitor slot I could find, I ran into the hospital.

It was a huge complex and the doors I entered led me into a series of hallways, offices, and the urology unit - not where I wanted to be. I stopped a man in a white smock.

"I had a friend who was just brought in here suffering from a possible heart attack. Where would they have taken him?"

"At first, most likely to the emergency and trauma bay. It's on the north side of the building on this level." He hurried off without giving me a chance to ask about the best way to get there.

I decided to keep moving towards the center of the building. I had come in from the south parking lot so if I just kept going straight, I should be getting closer. As luck would have it, my hallway ended and I had the choice of right or left. I didn't see any signs, other than those on the doors and walls identifying the offices and wards that were in my immediate area. People were walking all around me, so I decided to ask another person for some help.

This time I selected a short woman in a smock, wearing thick glasses and an identification card hanging from a chain around her neck.

"Excuse me, ma'am. A friend of mine was just brought in by ambulance suffering from a heart attack. I'm trying to find where they have him…"

"That's probably cardiology. It's on the third floor. You can get there by taking the elevators at the end of this hallway behind you."

"Thanks," I turned and started walking fast in the direction she told me. I figured that I was now heading east. The hallway came to an end and there were no elevators in sight.

"Are there any elevators around here?" I asked a passing

pregnant lady.

"I don't know," she responded without slowing down.

"Right over there," a man who was also passing by pointed to an open space in the wall about twenty feet to my left.

I walked over to find an alcove with bathrooms secluded on one side and the elevators on the other. The door to the elevator was just opening. Two people got off and I jumped on, pressing the button for the third floor.

My luck didn't appear to be improving, the elevator stopped on the second floor and a maintenance man wheeled in a large trash container. He parked it in the middle of the elevator and stood opposite it from me. He didn't make eye contact, and I knew why. Whatever was in the container stunk like a mixture of ammonia and sour milk. If I was back in my car, I'd be popping the roof open again. As it was, I simply had to suffer as the elevator made its slow way to the next floor.

When the door opened, I hurriedly squeezed by the bin to reach the fresh air beyond. The door had no sooner closed than I realized something from the outside of the bin had rubbed off onto my light green golf shirt. A dark smear about four inches long and an inch wide ran across my shirt mid-way between my belt and my left armpit.

"Damn!"

"Pardon me?"

I looked up to see the oldest looking woman I think I had ever seen in my life. She stood there alone dressed in a faded, floral print bathrobe and slippers. Behind her I could see double doors with a big sign that read, "No entry." I looked back the other direction and saw that I was in another alcove, with a hallway a few feet away.

"Excuse me. It's just that….."

"Young man, there are no excuses for swearing."

"I'm sorry. By any chance, do you know where cardiology is?"

"In there," she pointed with her thumb to the door behind her.

"Are you sure?"

"Of course, I'm a patient. I just snuck out to get a breath of fresh air and a candy bar."

"How do I get in there?"

"Not through there, young man. You see the sign, don't you?"

"Yes."

"You have to go around. But you can't do that from this floor. You have to go down to the second floor and walk to the other side. Then come back up by the stairs or the elevator."

She must have seen the look of frustration on my face.

"Do you know someone in there?"

"A friend of mine had a heart attack today. They just brought him in by ambulance."

"Well, I doubt if your friend is in there. If she just had the heart attack, she's probably in intensive care. That's where they keep us until we're stable."

"It's a he."

"What's his name, I have connections in there. I'll find out where he is."

I told her. She turned around and slowly shuffled through the doors. I hoped her "connection" wasn't too far away, she wasn't moving very fast. I imagined she was pushing the century mark. She stood slightly stooped, barely five feet tall, but had impressive, sharp blue eyes. They shone despite being surrounded by a sea of wrinkles and very stringy, white hair.

I walked out from the alcove to the hallway to look around. To my left was another set of doors that also displayed a "Do Not Enter" sign. To my right the hallway extended about ninety feet before it appeared to end at the intersection with another hallway. That one looked busy, but no one else occupied the hallway in which I now stood. To my right just a few feet down the corridor stood two vending machines, one for soft drinks and the other filled with candy and snacks.

The doors to the cardiology unit opened and the woman appeared again. She had a twinkle in her eyes and a smile on her face.

"Your friend, Mr. Mason, is in intensive care. He's not listed as deceased, so he'll probably pull through."

"Thanks, Mrs.?" I paused to get her name.

"Doris, I just go by Doris."

"Well, Doris, thank you very much for that good news. Now, can I treat you to that candy bar?"

"That would be nice of you, Mr.?" It was her turn to pause for a response.

"I'm Jim West. Now, how about that candy bar?" I led her around the corner to the vending machines.

"A Snickers, please."

"I thought hospitals didn't share information about patients to non-family members. How were you able to learn about Perry so fast?"

"If you can keep a secret, Jim, the nurse' station is just inside that door, and my niece has this shift."

She took the Snickers, and I escorted her back past the elevators.

"You wouldn't happen to know where the intensive care unit is, would you?"

"Down the hall from the emergency room. They actually have a couple of areas your friend could be moved to, depending on his status, before he would end up here. It just depends on his recovery status. But, from what June said, I think he's still down on the first floor."

"The best way to get there?"

"Take the hallway past the vending machines to the next hallway then turn right. That hallway runs the entire length of the hospital. If you go all the way, you'll run into stairs that will take you right down to the emergency room. But, about half way down you'll see a large open foyer on your left. That's the main entrance. If you want to stop there, admissions and reception can give you the latest on your friend."

"Thanks, Doris. You've been a lot of help."

I turned and quickly followed the directions she gave me. I felt like I was back in the maze of the Pentagon. The people who worked here even had the same wearied look on their faces. They just wore a different uniform.

The large, impressive entrance foyer appeared on my left and below me. I hustled down the stairs to join the crowd below. I saw one smaller counter that for some reason had not drawn a crowd and approached it. A lone man wearing a nametag that identified him as a volunteer sat behind it. A name plate that said "Information" was sitting on the counter top.

"Afternoon, I have a friend who was recently brought here by ambulance. I'm trying to find out where he is at the moment, and his health status. Can you help me?"

"What's your friend's name?" the man asked without actually looking up to make eye contact.

"Perry Mason."

"Are you serious?" This time he looked up at me.

"It's actually Edward Mason, but he goes by Perry. I guess they could have him registered under either name."

"I don't see that he's been assigned a room. That usually means that they still have him in the emergency room or in one of the pass through intensive care operating rooms. However, I don't have access to that specific information. Sorry, but your best bet is to go to the emergency room and talk to someone there."

"Thanks. Best way to get there?"

"Take that main hallway to the left," he pointed to a hallway that ran underneath the one I was on. "It'll take you right to it."

It did. The emergency room was a mad house. Saying it was crowded would be an understatement. People filled all the available chairs and at least a dozen others sat on the floor along one of the walls. Kids cried, and a man and a woman were yelling at a lone official behind the only counter. Four other people waited in line behind the two for their turn to yell at the man. Other medical staff moved in and out the room without making eye contact with those waiting.

"Excuse me," I called out to a nurse as she shot by. She either didn't hear me or chose to ignore me. My frustration had climbed close to the overload level, when I saw Lieutenant Michelle Prado walk through one of the interior doors, alone, and head for the exit.

I hustled over to her and caught up with her just as she reached the exit doors.

"Hey, Lieutenant."

She turned, looked at me, but continued through the doors to the calm outside. I followed her.

"I don't like hospitals, especially emergency rooms," she

explained, stopping a few steps later. "What can I do for you, Mr. West?"

"I was hoping you were in there checking on Perry's status. Since I've been here, I've had no luck learning anything about him."

"He's still alive and they expect him to pull through. The doc said it was a severe attack, and he'll need to be closely monitored for several days. He's sedated right now. Have you called his wife?"

"No, I wanted to find out if he had any chance before I did. I'll call her in a minute."

"Do," she instructed. "Nine a.m., tomorrow, you won't forget?"

"I'll be there. Ask for you, right?"

She nodded, turned and walked away. No goodbyes. I watched her walk for a while. Interesting woman.

I sat down on one of the metal benches which were spread evenly over a large concrete patio adjacent to the emergency room entrance and opposite the ambulance arrival bays. A handful of outdoor pole lights were on, keeping the area lit in the growing darkness of the evening. Claire answered on the first ring.

She had tried to call Perry a few times in the last hour, and when he didn't answer had become worried. She had tried my number, and I hadn't answered. On average I receive about one call a month, so I normally leave my phone turned off. Claire had contacted Steve and Mike, but they had not heard from us either. Finally, she called the hotel and was told we hadn't checked in. She was debating calling the police to see if we were involved in an accident when I called.

I let her ramble on for a minute before she finally paused. I broke the bad news to her.

"Claire, Perry has had a heart attack, but the doctors believe he is going to be okay."

"What, a heart attack?" I could hear her voice crack.

"Yes, but he's now in the hospital. The doctors have him stabilized, but I think you should come here as soon as possible."

"I'll drive up first thing in the morning."

"Good," I gave her the name of the hospital and the exit number I had taken off the interstate to get to it. I also suggested she call the hospital as soon as possible to get more specific information. I imagined the hospital would want to talk to her, too. We talked for a few minutes more. I tried to give her the reassurance she wanted to hear, whether it was accurate or not. I didn't tell her about the dead man or our run in with the police. That part could wait until after she arrived.

Chapter 4

I woke up hungry and tired. By the time I had checked in the night before, and informed the hotel that Perry wasn't going to need his room, it was getting late. The hotel restaurant had stopped serving, and I lacked the motivation to go out. I had grabbed a small bag of chips and a diet coke from a vending machine and called it quits. I didn't even watch television.

I checked my phone and noticed that at some time during the night I had received a text message from Steve, asking me to please call him. If people were going to start calling me, I guess I would just have to leave my phone on. I put it on vibrate as a compromise. It was too early to call Steve, so I went for a walk to think and get some fresh air – thin as it was. My walk soon turned into a search for coffee and some breakfast.

I didn't have to go too far. I located a Schafli's Donuts just a few blocks from the hotel, ordered a large coffee and a couple of cinnamon cake donuts and sat down to figure out how to handle the rest of the day. For one thing, golf was out. I would have to talk to the police, but hoped that after this interview, I would be free to go. My preference would be to return to Clovis, but I felt obligated to stay through the day to do what I could for Claire. Tomorrow, then, unless the police played hardball with me, I should be able to return home.

My phone started vibrating in my pocket. It was Steve. Claire had told him about Perry's heart attack. He wanted to know what was going on and sounded a little miffed that I hadn't called him. I told him that I was sorry, which I wasn't, and that the golf would have to be cancelled. Steve wanted to know the details behind the heart attack, but I side-stepped his questions and said that I was in heavy traffic and would have to call him back. It undoubtedly further irritated him, but I didn't want him to be passing anything on to Claire. He could hear the whole story later.

The phone was barely back in my pocket when it started vibrating again. This time I found Claire at the other end of the line. She had gotten an early start and wanted me to meet her at the hospital when she arrived. I told her I would.

I planned to be early for my appointment with Lieutenant Prado, but I had problems finding the sheriff's office and then finding a parking spot. By the time I checked in at reception it was a couple minutes past nine. Another five minutes passed before a uniformed deputy, whom I did not recall seeing the day before, came out to escort me in.

Rather than take me to an interview room, the deputy took me to Lt. Prado's office. A good sign, I thought. She stood up when I entered, we shook hands, and when we sat back down the uniformed deputy stayed in the room with us, but back off to the side.

The next thirty minutes that passed were surprisingly dull. Everything appeared to be by the book and reminded me of the old Dragnet phrase, "Just the facts, nothing but the facts, sir." We rehashed everything I had already told her the day before – nothing new. She politely, but firmly, brushed off all of my questions. By the time she concluded the interview, I considered the whole experience a waste of time for both of us.

She surprised me then when I stood up to leave by telling

my uniformed escort that she would walk me out. At first she didn't say anything as we walked down the long corridor. When we approached the exit, though, she slowed and turned to face me.

"Can I buy you a cup of coffee? I need a break and there's a diner right across the street that serves a decent cup?"

I accepted her offer. Hopefully, over a cup of coffee she'd be more talkative, and I could get answers to a few questions that I had. We left the building and jay-walked across South Cascade Boulevard to the Foot Hills Café. It was bigger inside than it looked from the outside and populated by a dozen other customers scattered around the dining room. I saw that most of them wore a deputy's uniform.

"Let's go sit over there," Lieutenant Prado said, leading me to a table by the front window.

"Is Perry going to be charged with anything?" I asked as soon as we were seated.

"Yes, he has to be charged with something. I've already discussed the situation with the DA's office. Luckily for your friend, his heart attack will likely bring out a very lenient misdemeanor charge - something that carries a fine and maybe some probation or community service."

"Thanks, Lieutenant."

"Call me Michelle, please."

"Then I'm Jim, no more Mr. West. You make me feel old."

"Okay, Jim."

"Michelle, I have a few more questions about yesterday if you don't mind my asking."

"Fire away, but keep the answers to yourself."

"The pistol, why didn't you think it might have been the murder weapon?"

"Too small of caliber. Plus we knew the gun and its owner."

"The victim?"

"Yes, his name was Phillip Garibaldi. He's, or at least was, a fairly flamboyant character here in the city. He was friends with a lot of cops. He was a P.I., and he was always passing out business cards with a big eye on it. Yet, as far as any of us knew, he never really did much investigating. A few missing people cases, a divorce or two, but nothing else. His parents are wealthy, and most of us believed that's where the real money came from to keep him going."

"What kind of pistol was that?" I asked referring to the one Perry took.

"A Walther PPK, a 32."

"It looked pretty fancy. Was it custom made for him?"

"I think a brother or sister had it customized for him as a gift."

I thought again about the fancy lure and the dumb fish. I also wondered why Michelle had invited me over for the coffee. I doubted it was my woman-killer good looks. Something was up.

"Jim, what do you think happened to Garibaldi?"

"You mean other than being shot twice in the chest at fairly close range."

"Yeah, what's your take?"

"He was there to meet with someone. My guess, he was either set up or the meeting went bad."

"A rendezvous in a remote men's room. Think it could've been a homosexual thing?"

"No. Although, I could easily be persuaded to change my guess if you all found some forensic evidence I don't know about."

"We haven't. It's just a theory a couple of the guys came up with."

"Say, Lieutenant….."

"Michelle."

"Michelle, why are you asking me all this?"

"You ever do an internet search on yourself, Jim?"

"No."

"One of my team members did so last night. It's routine. We can learn a lot about some people that way. With you, he hit a gold mine of interesting stuff. He called me up at home and told me to check you out for myself."

"Believe me, my life isn't that interesting. Most of the time -- that is."

"Well, from my viewpoint, Jim, you're the closest thing to a Sherlock Holmes I've ever met."

"Michelle, I'm sorry if you think I can do something to help you with this investigation. I would love to be able to, but I really don't know anything. I'm not a psychic, or a profiler, or even up to date with the best ways to process evidence. I absolutely have none of the skills of observation that Holmes had, nor the I.Q. I've just had the terrible luck to fall into the middle of a few bad situations and the good luck to make it through them alive. The press may have over-glamorized my involvement a bit."

She looked at me doubtfully.

"Luck plays its hand in many ways," she said. "True luck is winning the lottery, or conversely, getting hit by lightning. In most situations, you make your own luck. It's more a factor of an individual's intuition and action than simple luck. People do certain things, in a certain way, and things happen. I believe less in luck and more in fate."

I looked at her face while she was talking. It was a nice face. The skin, the greenish-blue eyes, the lips, even the nose flowed together in a natural perfection. Part of me wanted to tell her I'd do anything to help her solve the case as long as I could stay close to her. However, my more rationale side yelled out at me that my finding this guy dead was my bad luck, and because of it, my subconscious now flashed a large neon sign to my conscious brain warning to me to get away from this investigation and Colorado Springs as fast as I could.

"Michelle, I wish there were something I could do to help, but I don't have any idea what that could be."

"I don't either. At least not at the moment."

"Are you in charge of the investigation?"

"No, Bob is. He's the senior Lieutenant in homicide. We operate with two teams and his team is in charge of this one. It's normal to help each other out, especially in the first forty eight hours. Your interview was the last official task I had in the case. I guess after reading about you last night, I just had to talk to you. I don't know. It seemed like fate that you were there at the scene."

Yeah, bad fate, I thought.

"Not much good came out of our being there," I said. "Perry nearly died, and we nearly ended up in a lot of trouble. That being said, I do appreciate your leniency toward Perry."

"It's the heart attack as much as anything else. Plus, the gun had not been fired. Other than the fact that it was at the scene and not used, it tells us very little."

"Still you could've thrown the book at us."

"Bad PR to do so, and the DA here is sensitive to her PR," she explained.

"What made you decide to go into law enforcement?" I

asked, more interested in her than the investigation.

She smiled, "I've been asked that question a thousand times in the last dozen years. I'm still not sure I know what specifically drew me to it. Maybe one of the cop shows I used to watch on television. I remember that I thought it would be a lot more exciting and glamorous than it's turned out to be."

"Either of your parents cops?"

"No, nobody close. In fact, in college I majored in psychology. Didn't join the Sheriff's office until a couple years after I graduated. Maybe it was 9/11. I heard a story right afterwards about one of the cops who went into one of the towers, you know, to help people get out. He helped this one elderly woman get out of the building and turned to go back in. The woman said she yelled at him, told him not to go back into the building. She told him the building was going to collapse. He turned to her and with a gentle voice told her not to worry about him. She said he just looked at her and said, "Don't worry about me ma'am. My job today is to help others out of the building." She said the way the cop said the word "others," she knew he wasn't talking about himself."

I wanted to say something but didn't know what. I had no doubt the story was true. Many, many first responders of all types sacrificed their lives that day to help others.

"Being a Sheriff's deputy is not bad. I guess I'll stay with it 'til retirement," she said.

"Worse things to do. You made Lieutenant. You must be doing something right."

"I try."

"Michelle, Perry's wife will be arriving later today. I need to make sure she gets in and settled, and that Perry's condition is improving. By tomorrow, though, I hope to be heading back home. Is that going to be alright with you and Bob?"

"I think so. We have your number and your address. I'll double check and let you know. Sure I can't talk you into staying here for a few days longer?"

I wasn't sure if the remark was purely personal or made because she still thought I had some magic karma that could help solve the case. She wasn't wearing a ring, but her body language unfortunately implied to me that it was the latter.

"Sorry your golf trip got messed up," she said as we stood up to part ways.

I didn't have a response, so I just nodded. We shook hands. She had a good grip and I was still thinking of it as I left the diner and headed toward my car. Too bad I hadn't met her under different circumstances.

Chapter 5

"Jim!" Claire shouted as she saw me in the hospital main entry foyer. She ran over to me and gave me a hug. "Where is he?"

"They still have him in an intensive care unit." I took her by the hand. "Come with me. I can get us to the general area." She followed close to me. I let go of her hand. "Last I heard, he was stable, but they still had him knocked out. Unfortunately, the only visitors he's allowed are immediate family members, so I haven't been able to see him. You should have better luck."

"How'd it happen?"

"He was talking and just collapsed to the ground." I didn't want to get into the whole story yet.

"That doesn't make sense."

"There's more to it, but let's get you to him first."

She didn't ask any more questions. The large double doors at the entrance to the Intensive Care Unit were closed when we arrived. A big sign on the doors stated that all visitors had to check in at the nurses' station, which could be found immediately inside and to the right.

I let Claire do the talking, and, in just a few moments, we were led down the hallway to Perry's room by one of the nurses. The nurse cautioned us not to touch any of the equipment and told us that a Doctor Melbourne would be by in a few minutes. She then took a quick look at Perry and the monitors, before leaving us alone.

"He looks peaceful," I said in an attempt to be positive.

"A little pale," Claire responded as tears began to roll down her face.

I pulled a chair over close to the bed.

"Claire, why don't you sit here?"

Once seated, she placed her hand over Perry's left hand. There was no response from Perry, and while I didn't expect there would be one, it reinforced the graveness of the situation he was in. With her free hand, Claire wiped at the tears now running fairly freely down her face. I handed her my handkerchief.

I stood there watching the two of them, feeling out of place and impotent. I wanted to leave them alone. I guess mainly I just wanted to leave.

True to the nurse's prediction, after only a couple of minutes, the door to the room opened and Dr. Melbourne entered. He took a quick look at Perry and the monitors before he spoke to us.

"Mrs. Mason?"

"Yes," Claire responded to him.

He looked at me but didn't ask who I was. Rather, he knelt down near Claire and addressed his comments to her.

"Your husband has suffered a major heart attack, but he's going to pull through just fine. He needs to rest and we'll need to monitor him closely for a few days, but he's in the best hands that he could be in right now. And, I'm not talking about me. We have the best nursing staff of any cardiology unit in the state. With you here now, well, that's just the icing on the cake."

"What exactly happened to him?" Claire asked.

Odd question, I thought, since I had already told her Perry

had suffered a heart attack and the Doctor had now confirmed it for her. But I guessed she wasn't in a normal state of mind. Melbourne took the question in stride and spent a few minutes to further elaborate on what a heart attack actually was and, in a generic sense, what could have caused it.

After spending about five minutes talking to Claire, he stood up, cupped her free hand in both of his and reassured her again. He then nodded at me and walked out of the room. Classy guy, I thought.

His visit had a positive impact on Claire, too. She followed the doctor's departure with a smile aimed at me and then Perry.

"When you get home, dear, you are going on a diet. And, we're both going to start walking in the evenings. No arguments." She looked back at me. "I guess it's partially my fault for letting him get so far out of shape."

"No, Claire. Don't go blaming yourself. The hotel is holding Perry's room for you tonight and tomorrow night. If you need it longer, you'll need to let the hotel know tomorrow. I'm going to leave you alone now with Perry, but when you get to the hotel tonight give me a call. I'd like to know the latest, and there are a few things I'd like to discuss."

She looked at me inquisitively, but I told her that it could wait. I left the hospital and headed back to the hotel. It was late afternoon and the sun would soon be setting on another beautiful day in Colorado. Too bad I didn't get to play some golf, I thought for the first time since arriving in Colorado Springs.

At the hotel I asked the concierge where he would recommend I go for a couple of beers and a light dinner. He suggested a place that had recently opened north of town called the Colorado Mountain Brewery. He said it was located just east of I-25 and provided outstanding views of the mountains. Good enough for me.

The drive only took a few minutes, and I easily found the restaurant. The hotel concierge had correctly described the views. They were magnificent. The hostess took me to an open table outside on the patio. The menu claimed the place brewed six different beers, and I wondered if I could make it through all six.

One of the waitresses, a tall, slender blond approached me and introduced herself as Tasha. I ordered a house brewed, amber ale and dinner. When she returned with my beer, she stuck around and we chatted for a few minutes. She described herself as a transplant from Bryan, Texas. She had come to Colorado Springs after two years at Texas A&M to be with her fiancé, at that time a senior at the Air Force Academy. The relationship turned sour, but by that point she was already sold on life in Colorado. I liked Tasha's chatty and friendly personality. Before long I had forgotten the stress and turmoil of the last two days.

I had just finished off a very tasty bowl of their bison chili and the amber ale, when I noticed a lady sitting with two men at a table on the far side of the patio. She looked at me, but when I looked back she immediately turned away. She had dark brown hair, pulled tight behind her head and was wearing a dark pants suit. She appeared like she may have just come from work. I knew her from somewhere. I was sure of it, but I couldn't place her. I even started to wave at her before she had looked away.

Tasha brought me another beer, the Rollercoaster Red this time, and the bison burger I had ordered but shouldn't have. The chili had filled me up. I ate a couple bites of the burger while trying to remember why I recognized the woman. She knew I was watching her because a couple of times she briefly glanced my way.

I'm good at faces, always have been. Names I forget, but as I said, I'm quite good at faces, and I knew I had met this woman before. It would come to me. It wasn't that important anyway, but I couldn't help but try to remember why I knew her.

She sat there, talking and laughing with the two men. Occasionally she would scribble something down on a small note pad that she had placed on the table. The two men didn't look familiar. The three looked like they were skipping dinner and just having drinks and appetizers. The lights on the patio came on as the evening light faded away.

Tasha returned and tried to talk me into a third beer. Normally I would have liked to try their stout, but between the two beers, the chili and the two thirds of the bison burger I had already put away, I felt bloated. I thanked her and asked for the bill. Once I got the bill, I planned to walk slowly by my mystery woman and, if she gave me any sign of recognition, stop and talk to her for a minute. I knew if I didn't, she would be on my mind all night as I tried to remember why I knew her. Some people get tunes stuck in their head, I get people.

As Tasha approached me with the bill, in my peripheral vision I caught my mystery woman watching me. I tried not to look at her, but I knew she was studying me. Maybe she had the same difficulty in remembering my name.

I turned my attention back to Tasha and my bill. She wanted me to take the rest of my burger home, but I explained my home was a long way away. She then wanted to know at which hotel I was staying, and the conversation drifted in a direction I would have normally appreciated. But tonight I needed to get back, make sure Perry was still alright, and talk to Claire.

When I turned away to leave, my mystery woman had disappeared. The two men still sat there, so I walked over to their table. One held a draft beer, just inches off the table, and the other had a little bit of red wine in a glass in front of him. Whatever food they did have had been cleared away.

"Is your lady friend returning?" I asked.

They both looked at me like I was someone from outer space. Neither spoke.

"Sorry," I continued, "but I thought I recognized her from somewhere. Could you tell me her name?"

"Get lost," the one drinking the beer snarled.

I looked over at the guy drinking the wine. He was no help. He just sat there with an aggravating smirk on his face.

This would have been a perfect scene for my old, fictional hero Travis McGee. He would have smashed one guy's face into the table and then repeated the question one last time for the other guy. But, this was real life and I didn't think such a stunt would go over very well with the restaurant. Nor did I kid myself into thinking it might be as easy to do as it appears in the movies. So, I simply sucked up my pride and walked away.

I paused inside the restaurant by the women's restroom in case she was there, but after five minutes I gave up and left.

The return drive to the hotel only took fifteen minutes. Claire had not yet checked in, and the clerk wanted to know if she still needed the room. Although I knew it was possible she might spend the night at the hospital, I told the clerk that she would be arriving later in the evening. That seemed to pacify him.

I really didn't want to go back to the hospital, but the two times I tried to call Claire she didn't answer her phone. If she was in the room with Perry she might have it turned off. Despite the strong tug of the shower and the king sized bed in my room, I gave in to doing the right thing and headed off in the direction of the hospital. Traffic this late in the evening was light, and I was parked and out of my car by eight thirty.

It took me no time to find the right unit, but once again the hospital had my number. Despite the big sign that limited visitors to immediate family members, I entered the unit and approached the nurses' station.

"Hi," I greeted the sole gatekeeper as I approached the counter. "I need to speak to Claire Mason. She's here visiting her husband, Perry Mason, but you may have him under Ed Mason."

"Are you a family member?"

"No," trick question, I answered too quickly.

"Then I'm sorry, sir. You're not allowed in here." She recited her response as though she had said it a thousand times before. Her dark eyes held no pity.

"I understand. I can wait out in the hallway, but I have no way to get in touch with Mrs. Mason and it's very important I talk to her."

She stared at me. She was probably hoping I would disappear, but since I didn't, she finally responded. "What is your name?"

"Jim West. She knows me."

"Please wait back out there in the hall. I'll go see if she's here - the first chance I get."

"Thanks," I really didn't like the way she said "the first chance I get," but what choice did I have? I obviously wasn't the first person to be sent out. A well-worn couch sat against the wall.

I plopped down on the couch and prepared myself for a long wait. The silence and the tranquility in the waiting area almost overwhelmed me and I contemplated a quick nap, but to my surprise Nurse Hatchet appeared in the doorway. She leaned out but kept her feet fixed to the floor inside the unit.

I stood up smiling. This wasn't going to be that hard after all.

"I'm sorry, sir, but Mrs. Mason is sleeping. I didn't think I should awaken her."

"Are you sure? Maybe she's just half asleep," I said hopefully.

Her expression didn't soften. "Sir, I'll be happy to relay a message, but I'm not going to disturb her at this time."

"Okay, okay. Please let her know that Jim West, that's me, came to check on her and Perry. Make sure she knows that she has a hotel room at the Town Plaza here in the city. It's important because I'm not sure she knows that they have held a room there for her."

"I'm sure she will want to stay here with her husband tonight."

"That's okay. Just let her know so she can tell me in the morning if she wants to keep the room or not. Could you do that?"

"Certainly," she responded as though I had insulted her. "Anything else?"

"No, that's all. Thanks."

She disappeared behind the doors, and I traced my steps back out of the hospital. Unfortunately, it appeared that getting an early start back to Clovis was not going to be possible. Too frustrated to go directly back to the hotel, I headed into the city center to find a place to get a drink.

For a Wednesday night, it surprised me that so many people were still out on the streets. With nowhere special in mind, I tried to get a feel for which place seemed to be a crowd favorite. I saw a group of people milling around in front of a place called Jack Quinn's and decided to give it a try. An open parking spot directly across the street reinforced my decision.

The place had booths along the wall and table seating further in. The aromas that wafted in from the kitchen teased me with the thoughts of eating again. A female vocalist on a small stage sang a song that sounded familiar, something Sade had done. Her audience moved their heads and swayed to the rhythm. She was good. I looked around but didn't see a single open seat and turned to head elsewhere when a waiter walked by and mentioned to me that additional seating existed upstairs.

I went upstairs to a large open room with a long, attractive, wooden bar. Unlike the room downstairs, only a few people occupied this floor. A couple guys played pool in one corner of the room, and a middle aged couple snuggled close together at a table in the opposite corner. I grabbed a stool near the center of the bar.

One of the beer taps identified its contents solely by the number 5. I couldn't remember ever having a beer named 5 before, so I ordered a sixteen ounce mug of it. The beer came out really cold and tasted just fine.

"How is it?" The woman working behind the bar asked.

"Very good. They make you work this floor by yourself?" I asked.

"When it's slow like this, yes. If it picks up, I can always buzz for backup."

"Are you a native Coloradan?" She looked more sexy than beautiful. I don't mean to imply that she looked bad either -

maybe the correct word to describe her would be attractive. I could definitely see where she might attract men, yet never be described by them as a real looker.

"Been here for twenty years, but I'm originally from Minnesota. My Dad moved here with the Army and then retired here. How about you?"

I placed her around thirty years old. She had short blond hair, that I thought might not be her natural color, and wore a tight white shirt which accentuated her breasts.

"I'm from New Mexico, just up here a couple days."

"I love New Mexico. I've been to Santa Fe, Taos, Albuquerque and to Angel Fire. It's a fun state."

"You've got better skiing up here."

No one else ever came upstairs, so Sidney - that was the name she gave me - and I spent the next forty five minutes discussing the most irrelevant things in life: the weather, the changes in the Springs in the past twenty years, famous movie stars that she had seen at the restaurant. I even learned that the building had an interesting history, and that some people still claimed it was haunted.

Without my asking, she let me know that she got off at eleven, but that her boyfriend was picking her up. However, he was going to be out of town for the weekend. If I wanted to come back on Saturday, she'd be free after she got off. I told her I'd love to, but that on Saturday I'd already be back in New Mexico.

Later when I left the bar, a heavy set, grungy-looking guy in biker attire walked by me on the stairs. He gave me the once over as we passed. If he was her boyfriend, I was glad I would be out of town and would not be tempted to get anywhere near his bad side this Saturday night.

Chapter 6

While I slept in my hotel room that night, for some unknown reason, I dreamt about Sidney, her biker friend and me. In my dream, Sidney and I had just crawled into bed when I thought I saw her boyfriend staring at us through the window. The apparition of his face in the window startled me. As though that wasn't enough, he started banging on the door. I remembered thinking this was no good while I struggled to move. My arms and legs felt numb and refused to move on command. The pounding on the door continued.

Sidney kept calling out my name. Slowly, I realized that I was dreaming and that the voice was coming from the other side of my hotel room door.

"One minute," I mumbled as I got up trying to shake off the cobwebs in my mind.

"Jim," the voice sounded like Michelle's. I involuntarily smiled.

"What's up?" I asked, still not fully awake when I opened the door.

What happened next was neither expected nor friendly. Michelle was there, but when I opened the door she immediately stepped back, and two uniformed policemen stepped in and grabbed me. I was awake enough to know not to resist. They spun me around and cuffed my hands. They had no need to search me, since I was only wearing my boxers and a Rhodes College tee shirt.

I looked back inquisitively at Michelle, whom I now assumed had become Lt. Prado again.

"What's going on?"

As I asked the question a grizzled, older looking man walked in front of Michelle from the side. I didn't recognize him, and I would've if I'd met him before. He had more hair in his eyebrows and ears than he had on his head. The hair trying to escape his nose wasn't far behind.

"I'm Detective Doyle with the Colorado Springs Police Department. We have a few questions to ask you. If you think you can be open and answer them, we may be able to handle this here. If not, we have some nice rooms downtown."

Again, I looked inquisitively at Michelle.

"I'm here at Detective Doyle's request. This is his investigation," she said in response to my look.

"Help him sit over there on the bed," Doyle instructed his two men.

They took me, none too gently, to the bed. I sat there looking at them, my anger slowly building.

"Detective," I addressed Doyle this time, "what's going on?"

"Do you know a Lynda Ball?" he asked, ignoring my question.

"No!" I said too quickly.

"Why would……"

"Hold on." That's who she was -- Lynda Ball. I did know her. Not well, I'd only met her a few times. The last time I saw her we had sat next to each other at a charity gala in Santa Fe. I recalled that she was married to someone in the state legislature. "I do know her. In fact, I saw her last night. She was having dinner with two men at Colorado Mountain Brewery. I couldn't remember her name at the time, and she left before I had the chance to say hello."

"What time was that?"

"Between seven and eight. I ate dinner there by myself."

"Did you see her after that?" Doyle was focused, but I was fully awake now. The back of my mind began sending warning signals to the rest of me. I had a pretty good idea where this line of questioning was going.

"No."

"Where did you go after you left the restaurant?"

"First, I came back to the hotel to talk to Claire Mason. She hadn't checked in, so I went to the hospital."

"Can anyone else verify your movements?"

I described the hotel clerk and the nurse I talked to at the hospital.

"Those two people should be easy to identify. I'm sorry I don't know their names, but they can corroborate my story. Their security cameras should also be able to show my coming and going. After I left the hospital, I stopped by a place called Jack Quinn's. A waitress named Sidney was working the second floor and can verify my presence. I left there just before eleven and came directly back to this hotel. Again, the security cameras here at the hotel can verify that."

Doyle walked over to Michelle and spoke to her briefly. She left, and he returned his attention to me.

"If you never spoke to her West, why would she have your name written down in her notebook?"

I thought about that for a few seconds.

"Let me take a guess at this Detective. Was my name written in ink on a page by itself, with maybe a question mark next to it? There may be other doodle marks on the page."

I realized I was close by Doyle's reaction.

"She looked at me a few times from her table last night. I didn't know if she remembered me or not. When I tried to make eye contact or wave, she immediately looked away. She had a notebook on the table and was jotting things in it during her conversation with her two male friends. If she remembered who I was, one plausible thing for her to do would have been to write my name down in the notebook. It's an act of confirmation, not uncommon when paper and pen are right in front of you."

"What's your relationship with Ms. Ball?"

"None, other than the one or two times we have met. Ms. Ball can easily confirm that information."

I wasn't dumb to the probability that something may have happened to her. Doyle wouldn't be here asking me all these questions if he had already had the chance to talk to her.

"Did you know she was in the city?"

"No. I mean I saw her last night, but I didn't talk to her and couldn't even remember who she was until you said her name a minute ago."

"Do you know why she might have been here in Colorado?"

"No." Doyle didn't follow up with another question, so I broke the silence,

"What happened to her, Detective?"

He didn't answer my question.

"Describe the two men she was with at the restaurant."

"Neither was too friendly. They both had dark hair, probably dyed as they looked old enough to have some grey. Both had dark complexions, maybe Greek or Italian backgrounds, no glasses, no distinguishing marks on their faces. Both were about average weight. They were sitting down so I can't tell you height."

"Would you recognize either of them if you saw them again?"

"I think so. I got a close look as I was leaving."

Doyle reached into his inside coat pocket and pulled out a couple of photos. He selected one and handed it to me. It looked like an enlargement of a driver's license photo. He looked younger in the picture, but I recognized him immediately as the man who told me to get lost.

"Yeah, that's one of them."

Doyle turned away from me, put the photo back in his pocket, and said nothing. I also remained silent and let him think. He looked like he had been doing this for many years, and by my not being an easy fall guy, he would have to start anew at solving whatever crime had fallen in his lap.

He finally turned and instructed one of the uniformed cops to take a look around. I felt like asking him if he had a warrant, but I knew nothing of any interest would be found in the room. I once found two hundred dollars someone had left behind on top of an armoire in a hotel room, and, in my past career, I had stayed in rooms overseas that had been bugged. Ever since, I do a quick search of any hotel room I check into - just a harmless habit.

Michelle returned while the room was being searched. She pulled Doyle outside the room and the two of them talked. As I watched them, I could sense that the news wasn't what Doyle wanted to hear. It would make things a lot simpler for him if he could just hang whatever crime had occurred on me. I wondered what did happen. I didn't know Lynda very well, but she seemed like a nice enough person, and whatever happened to her couldn't be good.

"Remove the cuffs," Doyle half-snarled at his two assistants.

The shorter of the two did the honors.

"What happened to Lynda?" I asked.

"You don't really need to know that."

I started to make a caustic, witty comeback, when Michelle's eyes caught mine. I remained silent. She and Doyle talked some more in the hallway, too softly for me to overhear. Doyle then signaled the others and the three of them left.

I walked out to Michelle. "Not even a goodbye?"

"I told them I'd smooth things over with you. First, though, I think you may want to go back into your room and get dressed. Standing out here in the hall like this," she gestured at my boxer shorts, "may yet get you arrested."

"Want to come in?"

"No, better not. Done that before and nothing good came from it, but I'll buy you a cup of coffee downstairs, if you're interested."

"I am. I'll be down in five minutes."

I threw on my jeans, a new, red golf shirt, brushed my teeth and was out the door. I took the stairs and was in the dining room just as the waitress was walking up to the table Michelle had selected. We both ordered coffee and I ordered a cinnamon roll.

"Now, Michelle, please tell me what in the world is going on. I've never been handcuffed before this trip, and, in the last 48 hours, it's happened to me twice."

"Lynda Ball and Frank Grazzard were both shot last night. Grazzard died immediately. Ball was still alive when they found her but is in critical condition. She has not been able to say anything and her prognosis is poor."

"Was Grazzard the guy in the picture?"

"Yes. We think the gun used to kill Garibaldi was also used

on these two."

"That was quick."

"It's only preliminary, not positive. Anyway, you can only imagine that when the police detective saw your name in her notebook and discovered you were also at the first crime scene, well, let's just say it was too good to be true."

"I don't blame them."

"They're rushing the forensics on the rounds today. If the bullets do match, then we have a killer out there who's killed two, maybe three people, in as many days."

"Find the gun and you have your man."

"Or woman," Michelle said.

"True. Do you know of any connection between the three victims?"

"No, not yet anyway. It shouldn't be hard though, both the Sheriff's office and the city police department have these killings as their top priority now. The state is lending a hand, and I just found out a few minutes ago that the FBI has sent us a query. There'll be a lot of pressure from the mayor and the press to get this solved."

"Where were the two shot?"

"You mean location?"

"Well, I guess both. Where did the shooting take place and where did the bullets enter their bodies?"

"The two were shot in his hotel room."

"Anybody hear the shots?"

"No, and that's the interesting part. The hotel is full of people, but no one reported hearing any shots being fired."

"Think the shooter used a silencer?"

"It's likely, but it's also not very common. In fact, it's damn rare."

Although I didn't immediately comment, I knew it was extremely rare. While silencers are a favorite prop for the movies, in real life, they are normally only used by the most sophisticated, professional killers.

"It does fit the pattern," she continued. "If the shootings were planned ahead of time, and I bet they were, I could see a pro using a silencer. Just like executions - two shots to each of the guys and one headshot for her. No emotions, just business."

"See any significance to the two shots to each of the men but only one for her?"

"No, do you?"

"Just a thought," I said, "but, continuing with our professional assassin theory, she may not have been the target. The two men were. The killer has a habit of using two shots to ensure the victim is dead. He's thorough. She may have simply been there. Something he couldn't -"

"There you go with the "he's" again."

"Okay, something he or she couldn't tolerate. So she shot Lynda, with the intent to kill her and probably thought she had. But, Lynda wasn't someone that she had been instructed or paid to kill. The killer could take the risk, a small one in her eyes, even more so if Lynda never got a good look at her."

Michelle thought about my theory for a few moments before smiling. "I knew there was a reason I wanted to keep you close to my side on this case."

"What piqued the FBI's interest in your case?"

"I'm not sure. There's going to be a meeting this morning. It's at the DA's office and the police chief, the sheriff and the FBI will be there. I think it's at the FBI's suggestion. So, I imagine we'll all know more after the meeting."

"Are you going?"

"No. Bob is, and he'll keep me in the loop. We have a good relationship." Michelle sounded confident.

I finished the last of my cinnamon roll and looked at my watch. It was just seven.

"Need to be somewhere?"

I felt like replying, "Home." Instead I answered, "No, although I still need to talk to Claire about Perry taking the gun, the dead guy and the trouble Perry is in."

"You haven't done that yet?"

"No, but it's not for lack of trying. I don't even know if she's checked into the hotel yet. I'll talk to her today."

"By now, Jim, Perry may have already told her everything."

"That's all right by me. Especially if it means he's improving."

Just then Michelle's phone rang. She answered it and acknowledged to the caller that she was still with me. After a moment, she rolled her eyes and elaborated that we were having coffee in the hotel's restaurant. She then looked back at me and smiled while responding to her caller that she would be happy to tell me.

"What was that about?"

"The office – appears that you aren't completely off the hook yet."

"And that made you smile?" I asked.

"Oh, it's just the DA's office. They're being stubborn. You're the only connection to both shootings so they want you to stick around for a while." She tried to suppress her smile but I knew she was getting a kick out of my having to stay.

"Not really much of a connection," I responded, despite knowing that any connection is better than none. I didn't blame the DA's office. I just didn't like getting tangled in the DA's web while she searched for someone to blame for the murders.

"One more question," I said.

"What?"

"Do you know what Lynda and the male victim were doing in the hotel room?"

"You mean were they in bed?"

"Yes."

"No, they were both fully dressed. The bed was still made up. Does that mean something?" Michelle asked.

"No. It might have if there was specific evidence indicating they were lovers. Might help us with a possible motive."

Michelle smile at my unintended use of the word, "Us."

Chapter 7

As I drove back to the hospital for what seemed to be the umpteenth time since my arrival in Colorado Springs, my thoughts weren't on the murders or Perry. I was thinking of Michelle. She was growing on me, and I found myself enjoying our time together. Although I had only known her a couple of days, she was already getting past the defensive wall I had erected around my emotions to keep me safe from being hurt again. That wall, I thought, was becoming more and more like the Maginot Line.

It had only been a handful of years since my divorce. Emotionally, that divorce had hit me like a freight train. I never saw it coming – one of the reasons it happened in the first place. I retired from my job in the military and moved back to New Mexico to lick my wounds and avoid life. I hadn't had much luck in doing either, but fortunately my life was getting better. I was getting better. Not long ago, I would've avoided any entanglement with Michelle. Now I found myself happily thinking about her. She had agreed to call me once she discovered the results of the meeting with the FBI. I looked forward to that call, and not because I really cared about the meeting.

Too many people had crowded into the hospital again this morning. I weaved my way to the wing of the hospital where I had last located Perry and, once again, made my effort to talk to Claire. The hotel had not heard from her, so I figured she had remained with Perry at the hospital. I was surprised, but pleased, to hear that Perry had already been moved to the cardiology unit. It meant his condition had improved.

After getting lost twice, I found the main entrance to cardiology. The sign on the main doors indicated that "non-family" visiting hours hadn't yet started. I didn't want to leave and come back, so I entered anyway with hopes of getting Claire to come out and talk to me.

As I approached the nurses' station, a woman's voice called to me.

"Jim, Jim, your brother's room is over here. He and Claire have been waiting for you."

I looked up and was surprised to see old Doris in her same tattered nightgown waving at me and grinning from ear to ear. Glancing over at the nurses' station, I saw one of them motion me on. I hurried to Doris.

"Jim, I hope you don't mind. I thought it would be easier for you this way."

"I appreciate it, Doris. Do you know what room Perry is in?"

"Sure, I've been down to visit them this morning. He's doing fine, and what a sweet young wife he has."

Doris led me about halfway down the corridor and knocked gently on a door.

"Come in," came the soft response from inside.

I opened the door, and Doris grabbed me by my arm and led me inside. Claire stood up and came over to hug me. Perry, awake, simply raised an arm and waved.

Over the next hour, the three of us talked and Doris listened. Perry had warned Claire that there was something he needed to talk to her about, but he wanted to wait until I arrived before he did. Claire had told him not to worry about whatever it was, she just wanted him well and home again.

However, once we got into the story about the rest stop and the dead body, Claire became very interested. She asked a lot of questions. As the conversation evolved, I sensed that her looks at me became more accusatory. At one point she even asked me how I let this happen. To Perry's credit, he told her that I hadn't caused anything to happen. Still, I felt Claire held me responsible. Like she said, "finding dead people" is what I do, not what Perry does. I was in no mood to argue with her and didn't.

No one seemed to care that Doris stayed in the room for the whole conversation. She only added a "My, my," on a couple of occasions. When I finally got up to leave, though, she left with me.

"Jim," she said once we were in the hallway, "it seems a little obvious that Claire blames you for her husband's heart attack and the problem with the police. It's normal for her to want to blame someone. Don't you worry; I'll talk to her later."

"Thanks, Doris, and how have you been doing?"

"Good. I had my eye out for your friend. I remembered his name. People new to the unit like to be able to talk to someone other than the staff. I imagine my doctor will be trying to send me home again soon. I like it here, don't want to go home."

I said my goodbyes and left her there. An interesting woman, I wished her luck.

While I didn't mind Claire's desire to blame me, I didn't like her comment that finding dead bodies was what I did. It reminded me too much of Michelle's remarks yesterday, that fate put me at that rest stop. Finding dead bodies is not what I ever wanted to do. However, I knew that over the last few years I was likely closing in on the record, if there was one, for dead bodies found by someone who wasn't looking for them. And, I didn't like it, fate or not.

I left the hospital a little more depressed than when I arrived. I checked my cell phone to make sure I hadn't missed a call. I hadn't. It was almost ten. The meeting between the FBI and sheriff's office should just be getting started.

After returning to the hotel, I decided to go for a three mile walk to get in some easy exercise and remove any lingering cobwebs in my mind. It was trying, without much success, to rain, so I put on my wind breaker just in case. As I walked, the breeze picked up a little and more clouds filled the sky, but the rain held off.

Reentering the hotel lobby, it surprised me to find Michelle sitting on a sofa and doing something with her phone. I still only used mine to make and receive calls. She looked up as I approached.

"Hey, Jim, long time, no see. What's it been, three hours?" She appeared to be in a good mood.

"Info on the meeting?" I asked.

"No, not yet. Should be starting at eleven thirty."

"What brings you here then?"

"I was actually following up on something from a different case nearby when I got a call from the office. A man called in anonymously to report he saw a woman throw something that he thought was a pistol or a revolver into a ravine near Green Mountain Springs, a town a few miles west of here off Highway 24. Since Bob and his number two are tied up with the meeting, they asked me if I would send someone out to look."

"Is the caller going to meet you there?"

"No, he claimed he was afraid to become any more involved. Anyway, I figured I'd drive out there. He gave us a good reference point."

"You're going out alone?"

"Not if I can talk someone into accompanying me."

"Me?" I asked.

"And you said you weren't as good as Sherlock Holmes," Michelle said with a big grin. "Are you up for it?"

"Sure, but shouldn't you be taking another deputy with you?"

"Not necessary. More than likely there won't be anything there. However, if we get out there and something doesn't look right, we can always call in the nearest patrol car for backup. But, I can't imagine we'll need it."

Chapter 8

Once we got on Highway 24, we started a slow and steady ascent deeper into the foothills that serve as a buffer between the flat lands and the real mountains. Michelle drove her own car, a fairly new Jeep Wrangler. I liked it. Painted a deep, dark blue with a dark grey interior, the Jeep had a detachable soft top. She kept it clean, and the dash had been recently scrubbed with Armor All or one of its competitors.

"Let's hope this place is still in El Paso County," she remarked just after we passed the exit to Manitou Springs and the cog rail up to Pikes Peak.

"How high up will we be going?" I asked, not sharing her concern with the jurisdiction.

"Well, Green Mountain Falls is approximately eight thousand feet. I'm not sure if the spot we're going to is higher or lower. I've only been out to it a couple of times."

"How will we recognize the location?" I asked.

"It's actually an old Indian site. The Ute Indians used to consider it a sacred location. Now it's more of a nature spot for hikers and lovers." She glanced over at me with one of her devious smiles and a wink this time.

It didn't take us long to reach the intersection where we turned off the main road onto a narrower one. At least it's paved, I thought to myself. We wound back and forth for about two miles until we came to a spot where the pavement ended, and then drove onto what looked like a dirt parking lot about the size of a major league baseball diamond's infield. Michelle pulled the jeep over close to the edge of the lot. Railroad ties had been placed on the ground as a makeshift curb. A smart idea because about five feet past the wooden curb, the ground dropped off sharply.

"Isn't it beautiful up here?" she asked as she climbed out of the car.

"Sure is," I responded, taking in the scenery. Looking out over the valley in front of the car, the landscape reminded me of my time in Austria. To our left, the valley narrowed quickly in a few hundred yards until it was no wider than the small stream that ran down and out of the steep hills. To our right the valley widened considerably until it ran into more hills about two miles away. The view right in front of us fascinated me the most. The edge of our hillside appeared to have been broken off from the rest of our hill centuries ago. It looked as though Mother Nature had taken a meat cleaver and chopped away a portion of the earth. A wooden bridge that extended for twenty to thirty feet had been built to connect our piece with the piece that had broken away. The far side of the bridge looked to be about four feet lower than where we were standing.

"Come on out here on the bridge," Michelle instructed.

I followed her. As I did, I looked back and down, and saw that the side of the hill sharply dropped for about a hundred feet. To my left and right I saw the same sharp drop off, at least for the couple hundred yards that I could see.

"Look over here, Jim." She was pointing across the bridge at a large rock slab that made up most of the top of the hill. "That's what makes this place special." She continued across the bridge and walked out to the center of the rock slab.

Once I was next to her I could easily see how this place had become a favorite of the Ute Indians and still remained popular today. There was virtually no shrubbery or trees to block a person's view in any direction. Admittedly we were only some twenty five feet from the other side of the bridge, but from this spot, even the view back toward the parking lot took on a totally new look. A steep, mostly rock-faced hill, just on the other side of the parking area from where Michelle had left her jeep, climbed a few hundred feet into the sky.

"What do you think?" Michelle asked.

"I think it's beautiful out here. I really do."

"Over the centuries, the rain has eroded a lot of the hill away. This rock platform has protected this piece of what at one time was a larger hill that extended in both directions." She smiled, "At least that's what the tour guide told me."

"Makes sense to me."

"The caller said he saw the woman toss the handgun down there." Michelle pointed down to the rocky stretch of ground at the base of the mini-gorge that was directly below the bridge.

"How do we get there?" I asked.

"It's not hard from this side. There are a number of trails that lead down to the valley below. One doubles back around to there." She pointed to a spot below. "I think we can find it."

Michelle's memory turned out to be correct. We had little trouble getting down to the ground level under the bridge. Here, only about eight feet separated the steep rock walls and the ground consisted of a jumbled mix of rocks. Dozens of large boulders, some three to four feet in diameter had fallen here over the years and sat quietly among thousands of smaller rocks of all shapes and sizes.

"This might not be so easy," I said.

"I thought it might not be as easy as it sounded. If we can't find it in one or two sweeps, I'll call in the cavalry."

"I'm in. How do you want to do this?"

She studied the narrow passage that extended about a hundred yards.

"Jim, why don't we go through it together, side by side, with you on my left? Once we get to the other end we turn around and come back. You'll still be on my left side. You search your side of the trail and I'll do mine. That way the whole stretch gets two sets of eyeballs on it."

"Sounds good. We won't be able to move very fast through there anyway. And, I suggest we keep an eye out for falling rocks."

"Falling rocks I'm not too concerned about, but this looks like a perfect spot for rattlesnakes." She looked at me. Her eyes appeared to be suggesting I could always back out.

"I ain't afraid of no snakes," I blustered, taking the art of lying to new heights.

"Then let's go, tough guy," she chuckled.

We made slow progress. It seemed like every two to three steps we had to stop to look between or behind rocks. When she stopped, I waited for her. She did the same for me. It wasn't part of the original plan, but it seemed the right thing to do. It took a good fifteen minutes to reach the other side. We didn't see the pistol, or, thankfully, any rattlesnakes.

We turned around, and after about ten more minutes, had approached a spot below the bridge when we heard a sound that resembled breaking branches and falling rocks - probably because that's exactly what was happening. We both looked up and instinctively jumped back as Michelle's Jeep Wrangler came rolling off the side of the hill and directly onto the small pedestrian bridge. The Jeep appeared to perfectly balance itself on the small bridge as it skidded to a stop not even half way across it. But then, while we watched, the jeep slowly tilted toward the driver's side, in what appeared to be a slow motion creep, leaning more and more precariously. I was amazed that the little bridge was able to withstand the weight of the jeep. As soon as the thought entered my mind, I heard the loud crack. Something was about to give.

"We need to get to that side," Michelle shouted at me. We still had about ten yards to go just to get directly under the bridge.

"Michelle, that's going to give any second -"

"But -" she started to interrupt me. Another large pop interrupted us both.

Although everything at that point happened quickly, the separate events remain very clear in my mind. First, the near hand railing snapped, and the jeep turned in the air as its creep to the side accelerated into a tumbling fall. As it turned, it twisted the bridge with it until the bridge itself broke apart. The whole tangled mess came down, bouncing off one side above us to the other side and back.

I grabbed at Michelle and she grabbed at me. I wasn't sure who grabbed who first, but we both leapt backwards together. I felt a sharp pain in my left shoulder as it struck the corner of a large rock.

"Oh, damn," Michelle muttered rubbing the back of her head.

"You okay?" I asked.

"Yeah, I think so." She sat up rubbing her head and then looked at her hand for any blood. I looked, too, but didn't see any. "My poor jeep," she said while she sat there staring at the pile of rocks, wood and jeep that created a ten foot high wall in front of us. "I know I put on the emergency brake."

I looked up and studied the area where the bridge had been.

"Michelle, it wasn't your brakes. There was a railroad tie in front of your tires. Someone moved it and rolled your car off the edge."

"Why?" Then, as if to answer her question, "It was some stupid punks having fun. If I get my hands on them, I'll kill them."

Something in the back of my mind whispered to me this wasn't simply juvenile vandalism, but I kept my thoughts to myself.

"I'm sorry about your jeep, Michelle. Are you sure you're okay?"

"No! I'm pissed!" She looked back up at where the bridge had been. "I just need to shoot somebody, and then I'll feel better."

"Not me, I hope."

She finally grinned. "With a little luck I'll be able to resist the urge until it goes away."

"I think we can get over the pile of rocks and the jeep without too much trouble, but I don't like those." I pointed to the large swarm of yellow jackets that were around and above the car. As the jeep fell, it must have carved off enough earth and rock at some point to expose a yellow jacket hive. We were far enough away not to have attracted their interest.

Michelle appeared less concerned about them than I was. She stood up and took a few steps toward her jeep. She got close enough to peer through the broken and warped passenger window closest to us.

Turning back to me, "I can smell gasoline. It's quite strong."

"You may want to step away."

"Damn," she swatted at the back of her neck, her hair flying to her left as she instinctively swung her head. I could see sand and dirt flying from her hair as she did so.

I realized then that we were both covered with dust, dirt and other debris that had showered over us as the jeep came crashing down. I stood up and dusted myself off as Michelle walked back to me. I was impressed. Despite being stung, she wasn't going to let the yellow jackets intimidate her.

"Bee sting?"

"Yes," she answered, staring at the jeep.

"How did that happen?" Michelle asked again. "I can't believe it. We've only been away from it for twenty, thirty minutes."

I didn't say anything. I stared up to where the bridge had been. I didn't know what I thought I might see, but I saw nothing.

"I think we'll have to get out by going that way," she pointed to the opposite end of the path from where we had entered. "The problem is, unless we want to do some serious climbing, we'll have even a longer hike going that way."

"I'm up for it," I responded, not really knowing how long of a hike either way would be. I took out my cell phone. No signal.

"Any signal out here will be pretty much hit and miss," Michelle said.

"Should we wait here? Your office knows we're out here and will send someone out later to look for you when they don't hear from you."

"I doubt if anyone would come looking for several hours. Once they get out here, they would still have to figure out how to get us across. The bridge is gone. We could easily find ourselves stuck all night. It should only take us four or five hours to get back to Green Mountain Falls, or at least to the highway where we can wave someone down."

She made sense. We had six or seven hours before it would get dark, and it looked like we were going to have another warm spring afternoon. Doing something would be better than doing nothing at all. I had on good shoes for walking, but not for hiking or climbing. Michelle was more prepared. She had on what looked like hiking boots and was wearing a lightweight jacket. Not much to keep her warm if the weather changed, but more than what I was wearing.

"Do you think you can find the way back to the road or to the town?" I had to ask.

"That's the million dollar question. We really just need to head east to northeast. If we can, I figure we'll be fine. We can also try to find a spot further down where we can get back up there." She pointed up to where we had left the jeep. "Then we can simply hike back down the road."

"If we could, that might be the best way to go."

"I hate to leave my jeep." She pursed her lips into a pouting expression. "Hell, let's go."

We stumbled out of the narrow confines of the ravine and found ourselves in a small valley. The rock face of the hillside to our left remained almost vertical. The ground to our right had a subtle climb for twenty or so yards before it began its real ascent. The last ten feet of the side of the hill ended in a sheer rock face. Water in large puddles marked the center of the small valley, but no water flowed through it.

We walked in silence for a while. Until we could find a spot to climb or walk out, we were obliged to keep moving ahead. Michelle and the loss of her car concerned me more than being stuck in the woods. I had little doubt that we would find some aspect of civilization before dark, and this was a lot better than the last time I found myself lost in the mountains. That time someone had been shooting at me, it was snowing, and I was lost. This would be a cake walk, and I had a very nice looking guide.

Besides, the idea that Michelle might have been set up preoccupied my thoughts. There only seemed to be three possibilities to how the jeep may have been sent rolling over the ledge and almost on top of us. First, it could have been sheer accident. Michelle may not have set the brake and, despite being in park, the jeep simply rolled forward, bounced over the wood curb and went over the cliff by itself. No way, I thought, I saw her put on the brake.

The second possibility was that some punks had, by sheer chance, arrived at the parking area just moments after we did and saw us go across the bridge and to the ground below. Then, simply as a vicious prank, they moved the railroad tie, broke into the car, and disengaged the brake. They could have even taken it out of park, but that would have taken some skill. The jeep wouldn't have needed much of a push. However, I put this possibility in the unlikely category, too.

The third possibility was the one that seemed most probable to me and was the one I liked the least. Whoever made the call about seeing the woman toss the handgun might have hung around to see what the police response would be. That wouldn't surprise me, but why mess with the jeep? That's what worried me. It was personal, and that made no sense. How would anyone know that Michelle would be the one to respond to the scene? Why would anyone care?

Chapter 9

"Cat got your tongue?" Michelle asked after we'd been walking for a while.

"I've just been thinking about your jeep."

"Me, too. I've been thinking about what I'd like to do to the jerks that pushed it over the ledge."

"It makes no sense," I said.

"Vandalism never does," she replied.

I didn't respond, but I didn't think this was vandalism, either.

"Have you spent much time hiking out here?" I asked.

"If by out here you mean in the mountains and foothills, the answer is yes. If you mean this specific area, the answer is no, but we aren't very remote here. It shouldn't be hard to find a house, a road or something. Look! Right there," Michelle pointed at a trail that worked its way up the slope on our left. "Looks like others have hiked back here."

It wasn't much, but it was definitely a path that appeared to take us up and out of our isolated, small valley. We took it and, after some huffing and puffing, found ourselves on fairly flat terrain about thirty feet above where we had been moments before.

"This trail continues on straight ahead. I think we should be going a little more to our left, but I suggest we take it, at least for a while, and see where it leads us."

"Okay," I thought she was correct in saying that we should

be heading slightly more to our left. However, going left would take us directly toward a steep wooded hill a couple hundred yards away. Straight ahead and to our right, the terrain stayed fairly flat a lot further.

We had only taken a few more steps when I heard a dog barking in the distance. It sounded like the dog was somewhere in front of us.

"Not a wolf, I hope." I said jokingly.

"There are some out here," she said playing along. "But I'm not worried, I can run pretty fast."

"Think you're fast enough to outrun a wolf?" I asked.

"Don't need to; just need to outrun you."

"Oh," I groaned, "I can't believe I fell for that one."

A twig snapped in the distance, breaking the relative silence around us. Michelle's hand instinctively went to her holster. We both looked around but saw nothing.

"Now who's getting jumpy?" I teased her, despite the noise startling me, too.

We walked on, talking about the mountains, skiing, hiking and outdoor activities in general. I got the impression that Michelle was pretty much a tomboy growing up. After about twenty minutes, the trail opened up into a wide open field. Across it, somewhat hidden in some trees, I saw a parked trailer. It looked like a fifth wheeler that you might see in a KOA campsite or being pulled down the highway behind a big pickup truck.

"Think anyone is there?" I asked.

"Let's go take a look."

A dog, chained to a tree next to the trailer, started barking as soon as he noticed us.

"It's a lab," Michelle said, referring to the dog.

We crossed the field and walked up to the front of the trailer. The dog continued barking at us and strained on his leash to get closer to us.

"Good watchdog," I said. "I'm glad he's on a leash."

"Doesn't seem like anyone is here," Michelle said. Then to my surprise, she walked up to the dog.

I started to tell her to be careful, when I realized she was already petting the dog's head, and the lab, in return, had stopped barking. I moved in behind her, closer to the trailer, and turned to peek through a window. In my effort to see what was inside, I was surprised when I saw a face peering out of the window at us. Surprised might be understating my reaction at that moment, since I jumped back and gasped loud enough for Michelle to ask what's up.

"There's someone in there. A woman, I think." The face was gone when I looked back.

"You think?" Michelle asked.

"Looked kind of scraggly." I took a step away from the trailer.

"What?"

"Never mind, but there's at least one person inside."

What I really wanted to say was let's leave and find some other place. I felt we had just entered into the middle of one of those B movies – you know, one of those movies where people go hiking and get lost in the woods, only to be discovered by a crazy, backwoods family of cannibals. I kept my thoughts to myself.

Michelle walked up the two metal stairs and knocked on the door. The lab followed her, but was more interested in getting petted than defending the trailer.

"Are you coming?" she asked. "The dog won't hurt you."

My hesitation had nothing to do with the dog. Instead of saying anything, I walked up next to her. The lab moved over to me, so I scratched his head to show I could be a friend too.

"You sure you saw someone?"

"Yes, someone is in there. Maybe they don't want company. Let's find another place to be rescued," I suggested.

Rather than take my advice, Michelle tried the door knob. It turned and the door opened with a loud squeak.

"Oh, great," I said quietly to myself. This was getting creepier by the moment. The inside of the trailer was darker than the bright sunshine outside. It took our eyes a few seconds to adjust as we stood in the doorway and peered inside. The lab had come up next to us and was straining on its leash to come inside, too. At least it wasn't growling.

"My God!" Michelle exclaimed, her young eyes adjusting quicker than mine. She moved inside, and I saw what she'd seen. A woman was crouched as though she was hiding in a corner of the kitchen. That wasn't what drew the exclamation from Michelle. Rather, it was the chain running from the collar around the woman's neck.

"Are you all right?" Michelle asked as she hurried over to her. "Who did this to you?" Before the woman could answer, Michelle was leaning over and pulling her by her hands to a standing position. "Who are you? Are you hurt?"

The woman looked from Michelle to me. I got the impression my being there frightened her.

"Michelle, reassure her that I'm not here to hurt her."

"I'm Lieutenant Prado, with the sheriff's office. This is Jim West. We're here to help you, not cause you any harm."

The woman looked back and forth between us, and then her hand went to her hair in an attempt to fix it.

"Sorry, but you startled me. Would you like a coke or maybe some coffee?" She asked as though we were a couple of neighbors that stopped by to visit.

"Ma'am, what's your name?" Michelle ignored the offer. For my part, I wouldn't have minded a Diet Coke.

"Louise. I'm sorry I was a little frightened. We don't usually get visitors."

"We?" Michelle asked.

"Carl and me. We don't get visitors."

"Who's Carl?"

"My husband, but he's not here right now. Went to town to get some beer."

"Louise, did he do this to you?" Michelle asked.

"Do what?"

I was beginning to think that Louise was in some state of shock.

"Where is the key to get this off?" Michelle asked, holding a small padlock that locked the end of the chain to a link that kept the chain snug around Louise's neck.

"Over there," Louise pointed to a nail on the wall over a small television.

"Jim, can you bring it here?"

I retrieved the key and gave it to Michelle. She promptly unlocked the padlock and removed the chain from her neck.

Louise rubbed her neck nervously. "Thank you. I hope Carl doesn't get mad at us for taking it off."

"Let him get mad," Michelle responded.

Michelle had held onto the chain, and I took it from her hand. I walked with the chain in my hand to the door. It was long enough to allow Louise to get to the door and a few feet beyond, but not long enough to reach the wall where the key hung. Michelle was still trying to determine Louise's condition, so I followed the chain back to the bedroom where it had been fastened around a metal bed frame that had been fastened to the floor. It appeared that the chain was long enough to let Louise move around most of the trailer, but not reach the key.

The trailer needed a good cleaning.

I looked back at Michelle and Louise. What a stark contrast. Despite being covered in dust and hiking around the woods for over an hour, Michelle still looked sharp. Louise, on the other hand, was dressed in a faded pink bath robe. Her graying blond hair had probably not seen a brush or a comb all day – if not longer. Although not filthy, her face, hands and bare feet could all use a good washing. Louise was closer to my age than Michelle's, and the years had been hard on her. Despite the chain, I noticed she didn't display any outward signs of physical abuse.

I heard Michelle ask if they had a phone. Louise shook her head.

"Carl has the phone."

I took a look at my cell and saw that I still had no signal.

"Don't worry Louise. We're going to get you out of here."

"I don't want to go anywhere," Louise replied. She took a step away from Michelle.

Michelle looked over at me. The look in her eyes was definitely asking for any advice I might have. I didn't have any, but I had a couple of questions.

"Louise, are you and Carl married?"

"Yes."

"Why does he put that chain on you when he is gone?"

"He doesn't want me to wander off."

"He doesn't want you to escape?" I asked. There's a

difference between wander off and escape in my mind.

"Escape?" She looked at me perplexed.

Just then the door opened and a giant of a man walked into the room.

"Who the hell are you?" the big guy asked, none too friendly. He stood well over six feet and was broad at both the shoulders and the hips. He reminded me of a big lumberjack.

Before Michelle could respond, I spoke.

"We got a little lost walking around out there and saw your trailer. We simply stopped by to get our bearings and call someone for a ride."

I looked back at Michelle and saw her glaring at me. This had not been a good day for her already, and then to find a woman chained to a bed by some man. She was primed to take this guy down or all the way out, and this was no situation for either, at least not yet. Her hand was already at her hip. Luckily her jacket still covered her weapon.

The big guy looked at Louise. "Are you all right, honey?"

"Sure, Carl, I was just going to get these nice folks a drink."

Carl seemed to relax a bit.

"Carl," I said, "how about if you and I go outside for a moment and talk?"

He looked at me but didn't say anything right away, so I turned back to Michelle.

"Michelle, you don't mind if Carl and I go outside and talk for a minute? You can visit some more with Louise."

Michelle didn't take her eyes off Carl. She didn't answer me either. I turned back to Carl, relieved to see his eyes were on me. I moved to the door. As I passed Carl, I reached out and touched his arm, motioning to the door with my other hand. I figured this would be the point where he either ripped my head off, and Michelle would empty her Glock into his chest, or we would just walk out. Fortunately, he followed me out.

Once outside, I walked over to his large, white F-350 pickup. He had parked near the trailer, so it surprised me that we hadn't heard it drive up.

"Carl, I appreciate you stepping outside with me. You see, my lady friend in there is quite mad at you."

"Me? I don't even know her."

"When we got here, we found Louise chained like a dog inside the trailer."

"I have to do that when I leave her alone." Carl had an exasperated look on his face. "You can ask her. She's got this medical thing, but I don't see what business it is of yours."

I raised my hands in a mock surrender. "I know, I know. But, like I said, my friend went through the roof when she saw the chain. I thought she was going to scratch your eyes out when you came in. That's why I wanted to get you outside. I'm sure you can appreciate her reaction."

Carl remained quiet for a few seconds. Finally he decided to open up.

"Life's been rough for us the last five years. It's our own fault. We used to be wild in our younger days. The stuff has come back to haunt us - Louise in particular." I could see a faint smile cross Carl's lips. "We had our own rig and traveled the country hauling furniture. Kept two hogs inside and biked around when we could, too. Actually, I had good friends in a couple different outfits."

"What happened?"

"First time I noticed anything was when we were camped out in the middle of nowhere in the Petrified Forest. I woke up one morning just as the sun was rising to find Louise missing."

"Missing?"

"There was just the two of us, and she was gone. Her bike was still there. I figured she wandered off to go to the bathroom, but I could see for hundreds of yards in all directions, there's nothing out there, and I couldn't see her. That spooked me. I started calling her name, but got no response. Then I saw movement. It was so far from our camp that I thought it must be a deer, but it was all I had to go on. I jumped on my bike and rode out. It was Louise. It was like she was sleep walking. Took me a few seconds of shaking and talking to her before she came to. Then she was scared. She said she didn't know how she got out there."

"I bet that was frightening."

"We thought it would just be an isolated incident, but then it happened again. This time she went walking down the middle of a street. Luckily, a car's horn brought her out of it, and she got out of the street before she was hit. That's when we went to see a doctor. At first they discounted it, but after a few tests they diagnosed it with some long name. It's only going to get worse. They even suggested putting her into a facility. I won't do that, at least not yet."

"That's why the chain?"

"Yes. The trances can happen at any time. At night we set the alarm on the front door. Not to let me know if anyone is breaking in. It's to let me know if she's leaving. She knows the chain is for her own good. Unfortunately, her mind is slipping, too. It's not Alzheimer's, but it makes me think of it."

"Why are you parked way out here?"

It was his turn to grin. "It's only about a mile to the main road, hardly way out anywhere. Besides, Louise and I have always preferred being away from the cities."

"Carl, do you think you could give us a ride back to civilization?"

"Sure. How'd you happen to get lost out here?"

"Long story, but we can fill you in while you drive us back to our car."

"Well, let's get your friend and get going. I'd like to get back in time to grill some steaks."

We went back into the trailer. Louise and Michelle were at the small table adjacent to the kitchen drinking cokes. Michelle looked at me when we entered. She seemed more relaxed.

"Michelle, Carl said he would drive us back to your jeep, if you're ready to leave."

"You're welcome to stay," Louise said. "We don't get many visitors out here."

"No," Michelle responded. "We need to get back to my car, but thanks, Louise."

"Louise, why don't you ride with us?" I suggested.

"Want to, Sugar?" Carl asked.

"No, I'm not dressed to go out."

"Michelle, why don't we go out and wait by Carl's truck?"

I could tell she was still not comfortable with the whole situation. Neither was I. Michelle stood up, said something softly to Louise, and then followed me outside.

"That was surreal," she said, shaking her head.

"What did Louise say to you when you were alone with her?"

"She said that Carl chains her up when she's alone for her own good. She said that she used to be an addict, her brain's damaged and that it's her own fault."

"Believe her?"

"No reason not to, I guess," she answered.

"Carl told me a similar story. Other than the chain, she doesn't show any signs of abuse."

"None that we could see," Michelle said in rebuttal.

I took out my phone and was surprised to see I had a signal. "I have a signal, how about you?"

Her phone was fancier, so I wasn't surprised when she glanced at hers and immediately made a call. She turned her back to me and walked off a couple of steps. I heard her start talking when Carl and Louise came out of the trailer. Louise had changed into a grey sweatshirt and jeans, and had combed her hair. She still looked rough. I felt sorry for her.

"You coming?" I asked her.

"Yeah, Carl said the ride will do me good."

The lab was straining on his chain, as though he was asking if he could come, too.

Carl bent over and scratched the dog under the chin. "You stay here boy and watch the trailer."

Michelle and I climbed into the back seat. She told Carl where to take us and we drove off.

"Did you reach your office?" I asked her in a voice that was only a little more than a whisper.

"Yes, someone should be out there by the time we get there."

It only took Carl a couple of minutes to navigate the dirt road and get us back on Highway 24. In less than five minutes we reached the turnoff, and it took just a few more minutes to arrive at the spot where we had parked Michelle's jeep.

"Pull over there, please." Michelle directed Carl to a spot away from where the jeep had been parked.

"Where's your car?" Carl asked looking around.

"I'll show you," Michelle replied, jumping out of the pickup.

We all followed her as she led us to an overlook spot well

away from the bridge. I knew what we were going to see, so I went along with the crowd but was more interested in looking around to see if I could find any sign of someone being here before. There was nothing obvious. I wondered where the creep or creeps had hid when we arrived. I still thought someone must have watched us arrive and had, for some reason, decided to push the jeep over after our arrival.

"Whoa! How'd that happen?" Carl exclaimed. He had spotted the jeep. Louise was still straining to see it.

Before Michelle could answer him, a sheriff's sedan rolled into the parking area. Michelle ran out and signaled the driver to park over where Carl had parked. She trotted to the cruiser as it pulled to a stop.

"Are you both cops?" Carl asked.

"She is. I'm not."

"Thought you all might be. How'd this happen?"

"I don't know. We were down there when the jeep came over."

"Did anyone get hurt?" Louise asked, joining in the conversation.

"No, just the jeep and the bridge."

"What bridge?" Louise asked.

"You can see part of it hanging straight down over there." I pointed to the far side.

"Wow!" Louise's eyebrows shot up as she stared wide-eyed at what was left of the bridge.

Michelle walked the two deputies to where her jeep had been parked. I couldn't hear her conversation, but could see she was pointing to the railroad tie that had been moved. Just then, another sheriff's Crown Vic pulled into the lot. Michelle also directed this one away from the immediate scene.

"Louise, we better leave before this whole area gets sealed off," Carl said.

He took her by the hand and they walked off.

Louise turned to me as she was walking away, "It was nice meeting you!   Come by and see us again and bring your girlfriend."

I smiled at the girlfriend remark.

"By the way, what's your name again?" she asked.

"West, Jim West."

"See you later, Jim."

Carl just nodded at me.

I waved as they left. I also jotted down the license number. I've been fooled more than once in my life.

Chapter 10

Michelle watched them drive off and then looked at me. I thought she might have wanted them to stay, so I was concerned she could be mad that I had let them go, but she simply nodded at me. I moved over closer to the group, but stopped short of them and leaned against a tall Douglas fir. I was an outsider and would just be in the way.

The group moved over to the ledge and looked down.

"Damn!" I could hear one of them shout, the rest of the conversation was too soft to hear. One of the four left the group, returned to his cruiser, and got back on the radio. Michelle walked off to the side and called someone on her phone. The remaining two returned to the vehicles and got out cones and police tape. They started marking off a large section of the lot.

I walked over to where Carl had parked, thinking maybe I could do some looking of my own. Reaching the edge of the lot, I started a slow walk around the parking area where it met the shrubs, scrub oaks, and larger trees. I looked for anything that might indicate someone had recently come or gone. It had been damp earlier in the day. Maybe I would get lucky and find some tracks. Not on the hard dirt of the parking area, but on the softer soil adjacent to it.

A fire truck with its loud engine and an Emergency Services vehicle pulled into the lot. Not too many more would fit in here, I thought, and continued my own search. Nobody seemed to pay any attention to me. A couple of times I had to stop and crouch down to get a better look at what I thought at first might be tracks. Closer review disclosed uneven soil patterns but no discernible tracks.

I had almost reached the road that entered the lot when I saw them. Initially, I thought it was just one track, but then I realized there were two, one almost on top of the other. The tracks definitely looked recent. They were larger than bicycle tire tracks, but not as big as I thought motorcycle tracks would be. I made sure I stayed clear of them, so I wouldn't affect the immediate area. They weren't hard to follow if I kept within six to eight feet from them.

The tracks led up the slight incline between trees, underbrush and large rocks. In just a few seconds, I was twenty yards into the woods and up against a steep part of the hill. It didn't seem likely that a person could get a bike up the hill, and while I could see the tracks approach the hillside, they seemed to just stop there. I looked around as I stood there but couldn't see anything else useful. I glanced back at the parking lot, which was a little below me now. The trees and vegetation gave me some camouflage, but I wouldn't have felt very safe doing a covert surveillance from this point.

I decided to quit playing cop and report my discovery to Michelle. Her forensic people could do a better job than I in figuring all this out. I walked back out of the bushes and toward the ever growing crowd of first responders. I could see Michelle standing by the ledge pointing downward, likely toward her jeep, and talking to an older looking man in civilian clothes.

"Hey you, stop right there."

I turned to my left and saw a uniformed deputy approaching me. He had his right hand up, open palm towards me, signaling me to stay where I was. I did so and waited for him to get close.

"I'm with Lt. Prado, she can vouch for me."

"What are you doing out here?"

"I came out here with Lt. Prado," I answered.

"Are you a cop?" he asked, then added, "Or, a fed?"

"No, but if you could tell Lt. Prado that I need to talk to her, I'd appreciate it."

He hesitated for a few seconds. "Okay, but I need you to stay back, away from all the activity."

"Sure," I answered. I didn't have the heart to tell him I had already been in the area that was now secured, and my footprints were going to be among the ones they found.

To his credit, he went directly to Michelle and spoke to her. He pointed to me and Michelle gave me the "It will be one minute" sign; at least that's what I thought she meant. However, reading women and their hand gestures has never been my strong suit. It was a good five minutes before she walked over to me.

"What's up?" she asked.

"I found some tracks that I believe are worth checking out. They may belong to whoever pushed your car over the ledge."

"Let's see."

I walked her over and showed her the tracks. "I followed them up to where they seem to stop. I didn't get too close. The tracks appear to have been made after the rain this morning. Your experts can probably tell us more."

Michelle turned and shouted at a deputy who stood in the middle of the lot. He was the same one who told me to stay back and had probably been assigned the ignoble task of guarding the lot.

"Steve, tell Ollie to come here."

Steve shouted something to the group that was concentrated in the area where the car went over the ledge. A short, square looking person broke away from the group and walked toward us. Ollie turned out to be a woman, maybe five foot two or three. Her uniform shirt was taut at the shoulders and, when she bent her arms, at the biceps.

"Ollie, can you take a look at those tracks," Michelle pointed to them, "and let me know what you make of them? If you think it's worthwhile, we'll have forensics take a look when they get here, too."

"Sure, Lieutenant," Ollie responded and walked over to the tracks.

Michelle touched my arm and took a few steps away from Ollie and the tracks. I followed her.

"That girl is sharp. I've worked with her on a couple of occasions the last three years. I've encouraged her to finish her degree and to get into forensics or even on the medical examiner's team. She has a great eye for detail and can put the dots together better than anyone else I've known."

"Is she going to follow your advice?"

"I don't know. She says she likes it in the field and doesn't want to get stuck in a desk job. I've explained to her not all those people stay in the lab. We'll see."

"She's a weight lifter?"

"Yes, an avid one. She can out lift a lot of the guys."

I watched Ollie as she slowly moved away from us, bent over, studying the tracks and the ground around them.

"Weight lifting is becoming more and more popular with women," I said, my mind not really being on the conversation.

"She said that it's her best way to meet men. She thinks

she's not very attractive."

Ollie disappeared in the underbrush.

"What?" I asked.

"Obviously she caught your eye."

"No, I'm sorry. My mind was on the person, or persons, who pushed your car over."

"What were you thinking?"

"The jeep was parked and locked. Although the ground slightly declines all the way to the ledge, the person had to move the log, get into your jeep somehow, disengage the brake, and get it out of park. Then, they would have to push the car hard enough to have it roll over the ledge. All that takes time and is not as easy as it sounds."

"I know. We've already discussed that. In a day or two we'll have most the answers regarding how it was done. I want to know who did it. I don't care how it was done or even why. I just want to get my hands on who did it."

"I don't blame you," I said. However, my concern was on the why question. My comment on the difficulty of doing it was just my mind's convoluted way of getting at the real question troubling me all day. Why go through all the trouble of pushing the jeep over the ledge?

"Do you want me to have someone run you back into the Springs?"

"Not now. I'm just as curious about all this as you are. If you're still here in a couple of hours, I'll take you up on it."

"I'm sorry to have messed up your day," Michelle said.

"You didn't, I'm just sorry about your jeep."

"Lieutenant!" Ollie reappeared, still about fifteen yards away from the edge of the parking lot.

"Yes, Ollie?"

"Can you come here for a moment? I've something you might like to see."

"Sure," she responded to Ollie, and then looked at me, "let's see what she found."

Ollie gave me a not so subtle once over as we approached and then looked at Michelle, her eyes asking the obvious question.

"Ollie, this is Jim West. Although he's retired now, he used to be in law enforcement and is with me."

Ollie just nodded at me, and I nodded back.

"Over here Lieutenant, stay clear of the tracks."

I was surprised that she cautioned us, since she took us away from the spot where I had assumed the tracks had stopped. I looked down but didn't see anything that resembled tracks.

"There's a thick patch of bushes back there where someone parked the motorcycle. It could've been a dirt bike. He then -"

"He?" Michelle asked.

"Yes ma'am. Although I could be wrong, the tracks look like they came from one person, a man most likely."

"Okay, go on."

"Right over here, Lieutenant. Come up here behind that large boulder."

We joined Ollie about ten feet behind a large rock that stood nearly four feet high and possibly eight feet wide.

"Your person positioned himself behind this rock. If you're thinking this is the person responsible for your jeep, you can see he had an excellent view of the lot below us. He could see you as you pulled in and parked. From down there, it would be very hard to see him."

She was right. There were a series of trees and tall bushes that interfered with our vision as we looked down onto the parking lot, but they did not block it. From where Michelle had parked the jeep, the trees and all the foliage would have provided him perfect camouflage. Even if we knew where to look, it would have been very hard to see him.

I wanted to ask Ollie how she knew the man positioned himself behind the rock, since I couldn't see anything from where I stood, but didn't. It fit my theory, and I figured further forensic evaluation would either verify her claim or not.

"I'm impressed, Ollie," I said.

She smiled at me, "It's just a knack I have, can't explain it."

"Ollie, I want you to get with Steve and seal off this whole area. Everything out here needs to be gone over with a fine tooth comb. It may be related to the double murder in town."

We walked back down to the parking area.

"Were you really impressed?" Michelle asked.

"Absolutely! I was up there earlier, and while I didn't get too close, to me it looked as if the tracks just came to a dead end. She's good."

My comments made Michelle smile.

An unmarked van pulled into the lot. Three men in civilian attire came out.

"With you all?" I asked.

"Yes, the crime scene experts. They have a lot of high tech stuff in that van. Once they give us the okay, we're going to back up the fire truck and extend the ladder out across the gap. They say it'll reach."

I had my doubts, but I imagined they knew the length of their ladder better than I did.

"We also contacted the park service to see if they could help us throw together a temporary bridge, but they referred us to Ft

Carson. They claimed they've seen the army put a bridge up in minutes."

"Minutes?" I asked

"Yeah, they have some they can just unroll. Hammer in supports on both sides and you have a temporary bridge. They're on the way out, too."

"Think the bridge will be up by nightfall?"

"That's the goal," she said.

"Well, it should be interesting to watch."

"Yeah, once they get to the point of going across and building the bridge, I'll be back to watch it with you. Now, though, I better get back to the scene."

"Go ahead."

Michelle took about three steps and stopped.

"Do you think we made a mistake letting Carl drive away?" she asked.

"I don't know, hope not. You should have social services check on them tomorrow."

"I was already thinking about that." She moved off, back to the crowd.

"I hope not," I repeated to myself. I didn't even like to think about if we were wrong. There were too many real life stories of abductions where the victim was not killed, but kept as a personal sex slave for years. I knew the odds were against that in this case, and Louise had ample time to say something to us. However, after years of captivity, if that were the case, her mind could have snapped. Maybe she only thought she was married to him.

I forced myself to quit worrying about it. By tomorrow we should be able to get a more definitive answer.

My phone showed a couple antenna bars so I dialed Claire

to get an update on Perry. She answered on the second ring and sounded like she was in a good mood.

"Hi Jim, how are you today?"

Caller ID I guessed. "Fine, Claire. How's Perry?"

"He's doing really well. He's got a lot of his strength back and is eating like a bear again. At least he has the appetite of one. What's that Perry?" He must have been in the room with her. "Perry says the hospital doesn't feed him enough. He wants you to bring him a hamburger the next time you come."

"Tell him I'll sneak one in for him."

We talked for a few more minutes. Claire didn't express any of the anger that she had vented earlier and we hung up friends again.

Another sheriff's vehicle pulled into the lot. This one was specifically marked as the Sheriff's car. A tall man, sixtyish, with a full head of gray hair climbed out of the driver's seat. I was impressed – no driver. Michelle and a man in plain clothes walked up to him. I couldn't hear the conversation, but arms were pointing here and there as I imagined Michelle and the man with her were explaining what had happened and what was being planned.

The three walked over to the spot where the jeep went over. Both Michelle and the man held the Sheriff's arms as he leaned out and peered down. He shook his head as he walked back to safer ground.

Michelle pointed at me, and the Sheriff looked at me and nodded. I nodded back and gestured a wave with my hand without lifting my arm much above my waist. He turned his back to me and leaned in close to Michelle. I imagined he was worried I could read lips or something, since there was no way I could hear anything from where I stood. I saw Michelle nod a couple of times and then take a furtive glance back at me. I hoped she would not get into trouble for involving me in this.

An army truck drove into the lot and ten soldiers clambered out of the truck. A number of the deputies and the other emergency personnel walked over to them. I watched as a lot of hand shaking, back slapping, and even some high fiving took place. They reminded me of old acquaintances at a reunion. The deputy, who appeared to be in charge of the scene, led the troops around, described what had happened, and what needed to be done. There seemed to be a lot of people trampling around the crime scene, but the key areas were still cordoned off, so I figured they knew what they were doing.

When the soldiers looked down at Michelle's jeep, I could hear a number of exclamations. Four of them walked over to talk to Michelle. The light from the late afternoon sun seemed to make her face glow as she smiled, and, I imagined, reassured the soldiers that she was okay.

For the next forty five minutes, the team of firemen and soldiers totally impressed me as they crossed the gap on the fire truck's ladder, and connected the two sides with a rope and wooden slat walking bridge. The bridge swayed as individuals crossed it, but it did its job.

While the bridge was being built, Ollie brought one of the crime scene investigators over to where I had discovered the tracks. After studying the area, they placed small flags in the ground and took photos. Everyone worked hard to get as much done as possible before dark. Large lights had been brought in, but I knew working in the dark would be much harder.

"You ready to head back?"

Michelle had walked up beside me while I watched Ollie and her partner work.

"I guess so. How about you?"

"Yeah, the Sheriff wanted me to be back for a meeting at six."

"Cutting it close," I said, as I glanced at my watch.

Just then a Crown Vic pulled up next to us, and a voice inside shouted, "We need to go."

Michelle climbed into the front seat, and I got into the back. She introduced me to the driver, Alan Smith, who simply looked at me in the rear view mirror and nodded. I nodded back. Nodding must be the preferred form of greeting in this area. Better than hugging, I had to give them that.

I remained silent on the drive back, while Alan and Michelle talked constantly. First they discussed what Michelle was going to do about getting a new car, then moved on to what it was like to see the jeep appear as it rolled over the edge above us, and finally, to why someone would do such a thing. By the time we arrived at my hotel, they hadn't resolved either issue.

Michelle said she would call me after her meeting and I said fine. I stood there at the entrance to the hotel and watched them drive away. Suddenly, I felt something. Nothing obvious, but the hairs on the back of my neck started dancing. I sensed someone was watching me. I looked around, stretching my arms and shoulders back like I was yawning, while trying to stay as calm as possible. I didn't see anything.

I went into the hotel lobby and walked over to a large window. I still couldn't see anything. Getting paranoid? It could be, considering all that had happened in the last couple of days. But over the years I had learned not to ignore these unexplained sensations. Once I had tried to explain them and had found it almost impossible to do so. The best example I could give was to compare how I felt to the scene in one of those animal documentaries where the gazelle suddenly freezes with its nose in the air. It seems to know the lion is out there, even though he can't see it. Except I don't have a nose that can smell the lion's scent – at least not yet.

I walked around inside the lobby and saw nothing suspicious. In fact, other than two couples checking in and an elderly lady waiting for the elevator, the lobby appeared empty. Five people sat in the adjacent bar, but none of them were positioned to observe people coming and going from the hotel.

I went to the desk to ask if Claire had ever checked in. To my surprise, as the clerk checked the computer, Claire walked in through the front door with Doris.

"Claire, good to see you," I said. "And you too, Doris. How's Perry doing?"

"He's doing well enough to insist I sleep in a hotel room tonight. I'd rather be there with him, but he wouldn't hear it. Doris was nice enough to ride along with me to show me how to get here. Of course, I had to bribe her with a Giuseppe's pizza dinner."

"Best pizza in the world," Doris said.

"Have you been discharged from the hospital?" I asked Doris.

"No, not 'til tomorrow, but sneaking out is easy," Doris said and then turned to Claire. "I'll need to be back by nine."

"I know, you already told me that twice. We'll be back on time, even if we have to get the pizza to go, but we should have time."

Claire proceeded to check in, and I escorted Doris over to the leather couches in the center of the lobby.

"You want to come with us?" she asked.

"No, I already have plans for tonight, but thanks for the offer."

"The pizza is really good there."

"I know. I used to eat pizza at Giuseppe's when it was at its old location," I said.

"That was a long time ago. Where was it? Just off Fillmore, wasn't it?"

"I don't remember. You're right, though, it was a long time ago."

Claire walked up and collected Doris. She also asked me to join them, but didn't seem to care when I declined. They left the hotel with Claire saying that she didn't need to put her stuff into the room until later. I wondered if she planned to spend the night at the hospital.

Despite Michelle's comment that she would call me after her meeting with the sheriff, she never did. I had dinner at the hotel and watched television until I fell asleep.

Chapter 11

At some point just before dawn, my peaceful sleep turned into an anxiety filled, toss and turning one. I awoke in the pre-dawn darkness with my mind churning over the last few days' events. I felt like I was a student again and had realized in my sleep that I might not have answered the questions correctly on a major exam. Not that I didn't know the answers, rather I had misread the questions. The type of questions I never liked: "Which one of the following is the least likely to be the correct answer, and why?"

I couldn't tell if the murders had caused my mind to go into overtime while I was trying to sleep, or if it was the situation with Carl and Louise. I lay there trying to figure it all out but made little progress. There was still too much I didn't know. I wanted to call Michelle, but she would be asleep.

Sleep continued to elude me, so I got up and made myself a cup of coffee. The room came with one of those new, individual cup coffee machines and one package of coffee. Nice, if you only wanted one cup. I wanted a whole pot. Ten minutes later, I was driving back to the Schafli Donut Shop I'd been to before.

Three cups of coffee, two cinnamon cake donuts and a thorough scouring of the Denver Post's sports section later, my phone rang. Caller ID identified Michelle as the caller.

"I didn't wake you up, did I?" she asked.

"No, I've been up."

"Just realized I forgot to call you last night."

"That's okay, is everything all right?" I asked.

"Yes, but I need you to come by the office this morning. Things are starting to move fast, and I need your help on a few things."

"No problem, what time would you like me to come by?"

"The sooner, the better, Jim. Say eight or eight-thirty?"

"I should be able to get there by eight. Any update on your jeep?"

"No, but they should get it out today."

A deputy escorted me into Michelle's office at three minutes after eight. She sat there by herself wearing a blue blazer, white blouse and dress blue jeans; her red hair pulled tight into a pony tail. She stood up when I entered. Her eyes still mesmerized me, and it took an effort not to lose myself in them again.

"Come in and sit down, Jim. I've got a lot to tell you, and you can, hopefully, help us out on a few things."

"I'll certainly do what I can."

There was a knock on the door and the same deputy who sat in on my earlier interview with Michelle walked in with three cups of coffee. Once he passed them out, he took the chair in the corner and pulled out his notebook.

"Jim, we received some interesting info from the FBI. The man killed in the hotel, the guy we called Grazzard, found with the female victim you knew, well, he's connected with organized crime elements in Chicago."

"You mean like the mob?"

"That's right. His real name was Serge Branovich. We identified him through his fingerprints. Grazzard is an alias he's used before. Justice apparently has evidence that indicates Grazzard, or Branovich, is a mob enforcer, although the FBI has not yet offered us anything solid on his specific activities."

"That's obviously what got them so excited when he popped up here murdered. Do they know what he was doing in the Springs?" I asked.

"No, and they can only guess what he had to do with Mrs. Ball." I didn't say anything, so she continued. "Again, this is only speculation, but there are several state – that's New Mexico, not Colorado – construction contracts that have gone to a large national road company that the FBI suspects has ties to organized crime. Through her marriage, Mrs. Ball had a lot of contacts in the state government. It's the only link anyone has been able to come up with so far."

"It's a plausible theory, but does it get us any closer to who the killer might be?"

"No," Michelle said. "Take a look at these photos."

She passed two pictures that looked like they had been extracted from security cameras. I could tell one was from the parking lot at the Colorado Brewing Company and one looked like it was from a hotel's system. Neither one was very good, although the one from the hotel at least wasn't taken outside in the dark.

"Could this have been the other man you saw at the restaurant?"

"It's certainly possible. You don't have anything better than these?"

"We're still working at it. We think his name may be Leroy Fox."

"That doesn't sound like anybody's real name."

"It was the name used to reserve the table that night. The receptionist said someone called in earlier in the day and reserved a table using that name. Later when he showed up, he identified himself as Leroy Fox. He arrived a few minutes before the other two came and joined him."

"The receptionist should be able to identify him as well as I could."

"We're getting a statement from her, too. However, she saw so many people that night and all nights, it's hard for her to be sure."

"Makes sense. Any idea who this Leroy Fox is?"

"Not yet. No one local we can find. We're working DMV records right now, but so far nothing fits with the general description we have. Hotel checks were negative. We did find a record of a Leroy Fox flying into Denver the same day you saw him. In the morning, so he could've driven down here in plenty of time. Fox flew in from Oklahoma City on Southwest. We're trying to get video from TSA, but I'm not optimistic."

"How about as they pass through the gate at check-in?"

"We're hoping that will work, but anyone with half a brain knows that a hat, especially a cowboy hat, can block most of what those cameras catch as you go through. The pros never look up at the camera and smile for us."

"Think he's the guy?"

"We doubt it, Jim. Without knowing who he is, we don't have a motive. Preliminary reports strongly indicate all three of the victims were shot with the same gun. If Fox is the guy who flew in, then that puts him elsewhere when the first hit went down. At this point, we see Fox as a person of interest, nothing more. The FBI believes he may be dead, too, and we just haven't found the body yet."

"Could all this be a rival gang hit?"

"It's one theory, but I don't like it. Garibaldi didn't have anything to do with organized crime."

"Could he have stumbled into something?" I asked.

"Sure," she said. "It's possible he learned something by accident and put himself in danger. Poor guy, if he did, he probably didn't know it."

"What can I do for you?"

"We need you to describe the guy to us so we can work up a facsimile," she said.

"Okay, but I didn't put the guy's face to memory. I mean, at the time, he was irrelevant to me, so it won't be perfect."

"That's okay. We'll take what we can get. First, though, I want you to take a look at someone. Will you follow me?"

I did. She walked me down the hall and then down the stairs. Her note taking, assistant stayed behind. We rounded a corner and stopped just outside the one way glass window of an interview room. Inside sat a man alone.

"Do you recognize him?" Michelle asked.

For a second the faintly familiar face appeared to be the second man at the table with Lynda. Then I realized that was just the power of suggestion. The man sitting in there, staring blankly at the window, was Lynda's husband. He was not the second man at the table.

"It's her husband, Ball. Why do you have him in there?"

"We learned that he came up here the day his wife was shot. He didn't tell his office or anyone else as far as we can determine. He checked into the Marriott alone."

"What's his story? Is he a suspect?"

"He claims he came up here believing his wife was having an affair. However, he says that he never laid eyes on her here in the city. He claims he wasn't sure how he would even find her here, but was set on making the effort."

"Believe him?"

"Not entirely, but we can't place him at the scene, and he claims he was in New Mexico when Garibaldi was killed."

"Do you think Garibaldi was working for him?"

"Possibly, although he denies it. Claims he did talk to some P. I. up here on the phone a couple of days ago about his wife coming up here, but decided not to use him. Doesn't remember who the guy was he talked to."

"Why would he deny it, if it was true?" I asked.

"Not sure, but none of this makes sense," she said.

"Has he visited his wife?"

"She died yesterday, thought I told you?"

"No. At least I don't remember if you did, but a lot happened yesterday. Are you all going to hold him?"

"Don't think we can. Hell, the DA thinks this New Mexico connection puts you more on the hot seat than it does him."

I couldn't tell if she was kidding or not.

"What a can of worms," I said.

"You can say that again. Every time something seems to fit, it falls apart. Her husband being here really got us excited at first."

"Could still be him," I said without much conviction. "But, my money is still on the guy who pushed your car over the ledge."

"What? That was just some punks having a good time at my expense. Let's go get the description of Fox done."

She walked off, and I followed her. I disagreed with her inclination to blame a group of anonymous punks for her Jeep taking the dive. I had my own theory, but I still hadn't figured out why the guy I blamed would take the risk. Until I had that piece of the puzzle, none of this would make sense.

Even though it didn't seem like that many years, the process to build a likeness of someone had been completely computerized since my days. Back then we used various cards that depicted different shaped noses, eyebrows, lips, etc. The technology had certainly evolved even if people's memories, like mine at this time, hadn't. I remembered the guy had short dark hair and that he wasn't wearing glasses, but I couldn't remember on which side his hair was parted, the length or width of his sideburns, color of his eyes, thickness of his lips, what his chin looked like, etc., etc…

"Not much help," I confessed, when I was done.

"No, this will be good," responded the deputy compiling my inputs into the computer. He had used a software program called Faces, or something like that. "May be a bit generic, but it's a lot better to show a possible witness a picture like this than nothing at all. We'll compare this with the one we got from the receptionist, blend them together a little and, in just a few seconds, show you a final product."

I looked up at Michelle who was standing behind the deputy and watching him work.

True to his word, in less than a minute he spun the computer screen back around for me to see. I couldn't see the difference.

"The nose is a little thinner and the eyebrows a little grayer." The deputy said, as if he knew I hadn't seen the subtle changes. "I also put a slight indentation in the middle of his chin."

"Very good, I think this is a better likeness." I looked at Michelle who was smiling proudly. "Once again, I'm impressed, Lieutenant."

"You should be, in your day I bet they had to carve the images in stone."

"Just about," I said, playing along.

Her phone rang, interrupting further conversation. I saw the color start to drain out of her face as she listened.

"Yes, I will," she said to the phone, and then, "thanks Marcia, I'll let you know what we find out." She hung up her phone and slowly put it away, the whole time looking at me. "They weren't there, Jim. Social Services went out to check on Carl and Louise and they were gone. The trailer, the dog, everything was gone."

"You're kidding me," I said, knowing she wasn't.

Chapter 12

When I left Michelle, I drove straight out Highway 24 in search of any evidence I might find regarding Carl and Louise. I hadn't had to stay at the sheriff's office very long after I finished the description. Neither Michelle nor I had much interest in the murders at that point. In fact, Michelle had spoken first.

"We need to find those two."

"Let's take a drive out there. Maybe they went to the wrong spot," I said.

"No, it was the right one. I can't leave right now; I've got another damn meeting to get to."

"Do you mind if I go?"

"No, by all means, go out there and let me know what you discover."

"Will this investigation keep you tied up today?" I asked, referring to the murder case.

"No. I've just been helping out. You're my only real involvement in the case."

"Me?"

She smiled as she answered. "Don't sound so disappointed."

I wasn't sure where she was going with that comment, so I went with a safe answer. "I wasn't."

She scurried off to her meeting, and I left.

Now, on the road, I had a few minutes to focus. Michelle

had run the tags on Carl's pickup. Carl's last name was Pike. The truck was registered in his name only. The address listed on the vehicle registration was a residence in Fairplay. It appeared bogus since a widow by the name of Wynona Nelson lived there. She claimed to have never heard of Carl or Louise. She said she had purchased the place a year earlier from a single woman whose last name was Barone. Michelle had had no luck in tracking Barone down, although she had discovered that her first name was Anne.

I turned my Mustang onto the narrow dirt road. Rain started to fall. By the time I arrived at the empty spot that was home to Carl and Louise yesterday, the dusty, dirt road had turned into a messy, muddy one. I got out of the car, pulling on my windbreaker. The air had become chilly, and the rain didn't appear to want to let up.

The grass was still packed down where the trailer's wheels had been. I could see the tracks they made when the pickup pulled the trailer away. I walked around in the rain. First, I stayed close to where the trailer had been. Then, I slowly moved out in ever widening circles. I proceeded to get myself thoroughly soaked and cold, but I failed to find one scrap of evidence that anyone had been in the area. If it hadn't been for the tracks in the grass and the gift their dog had left behind for me to step in while I was walking around, I would've thought I was in the wrong location.

My drive back out of the area was rough on the Mustang. The mud on the road made the tires slip, and the potholes were hard to spot. I quickly discovered that the seemingly harmless puddles on the road could hide a pothole that might be up to six inches deep.   When I finally made it back to Highway 24, the sides of my black car were a lumpy reddish brown.

I turned left rather than back toward Colorado Springs. I was looking for any place a person could buy groceries. In less than a mile, I entered the small town of Green Mountain Falls and spotted a small grocery store that occupied most of a strip mall, which was itself half hidden behind a Wells Fargo bank building.

I knew it was a long shot and after asking a handful of employees if they remembered a person meeting Carl's description, I walked out knowing no more than when I entered. Next, I went to the only gas station in town. After filling up the Mustang's tank, I sauntered into the station to try my luck again. A young kid, maybe twenty years old, stood behind the register. He had his black hair greased back, and his white t-shirt had one sleeve folded up with what I swear was a pack of cigarettes stuffed in it. Talk about going retro, this kid belonged in the 50's or early 60's. No one else was in the store.

"Excuse me," I said, "I'm looking for a man who has been camping in his trailer near here for the past few weeks. A big guy, thinning light brown hair, needs a shave, looks like a lumberjack."

The clerk still hadn't even acknowledged my presence.

"He drives a big Ford pickup, a 350. Like I said, he's a big, heavyset guy, but not really fat."

"Why you asking?" At least he could talk.

"I'm working for a Doctor Riley, in C. Springs. He asked me to find him. It's rather important. I can't be specific, but in a nutshell, the Doc ran some tests on him last week and one came back bad. The guy was staying back in the woods in a trailer, but for some reason has gone somewhere. The doc wants to talk to him as soon as possible."

"Why doesn't he call him?"

"He's tried, of course, but either the phone isn't working or the calls are being ignored."

"Don't know him." The kid shook his head as he said this.

I stood there looking at him for a few more seconds. He returned my gaze but didn't say anything else. I had an urge to grab one of the Zippo lighters displayed on the counter and light the punk's slick hair on fire, but somehow I resisted. Instead, I just turned and walked to the door.

He surprised me when I opened the door to leave. He spoke to me again.

"Try the diner across the street. I've seen him go in there a few times."

"Thanks," I replied, now happy that I hadn't started a grease fire on top of his head.

The diner had a one story log cabin appearance to it. Inside there were about a dozen square, four person tables scattered about, each covered with a blue and white checkered, vinyl tablecloth. A bear's head adorned the wall at one end of the room, and an elk's head hung at the other. Behind the cash register, situated on the counter directly opposite the front door, I noticed a large trout mounted on a wooden plaque.

A very old man sat at a table next to one of the front windows. He held a coffee cup in his hand. He was the only customer in the place.

"Please, come in and have a seat anywhere." A woman standing behind the counter said to me. She looked to be in her mid-thirties, had brown hair and wore a blue and white apron that matched the tablecloths, but probably wasn't vinyl.

I grabbed a table close to the counter.

"Bee, you've got a customer out here," the woman called to someone who must have been in a back room.

A woman emerged through a door that gave me a brief view into the kitchen. She came over to me wearing a big smile and the same kind of apron the woman behind the counter had on.

"Howdy, Mister, do you know what you want, or would you like to see a menu?"

"Oh, I don't know. What's good today?"

"Most folks around here think our Pikes Peak Burger is about the best thing they've ever eaten."

"Then let me have one of those."

"Fries?"

"Yes and a diet coke, please."

She turned and went back into the kitchen. She looked a few years younger than the woman behind the counter, but, other than that, they look like they could've been related. Neither was very attractive, but I didn't think Carl would've come here looking to pick up women.

Bee walked back out with my diet coke.

"Bee, I'm trying to track someone down for a doctor in the Springs. The man I'm looking for is a real big guy. He's got thinning brown hair, and the couple of times the doc saw him he looked like he needed a shave. Lived in a trailer parked back here in the woods for the last couple of months with his wife. His name is Carl and his wife is Louise."

Bee turned toward the other woman. Some form of acknowledgement passed between them.

"Why does the doctor want to know where he is?" Bee asked.

"I'm not totally sure, but I know the doctor ran some tests on him and one came back bad. He tried to get in touch with Carl, but he seems to have disappeared." I paused for a moment to let my ruse sink in. "I'm just checking around the neighborhood here to see if anyone may know where they could've gone. The guy across the street suggested I should talk to you all."

"The guy's name was Carl wasn't it, Bee?" asked the woman behind the cash register.

"I think so," Bee replied. She looked back at me. "Carl has come in here a lot to eat in the last month or so. I think he had a part time job here in town. He's real chatty and nice. He brought his wife with him a few times, too. Seemed like a nice couple. What's wrong with him?"

"I don't know, the doc wouldn't tell me. He just said to try to find him, and quickly."

It was the other woman's turn to talk. "He was here this morning. He asked for two large coffees and two orders of wheat toast to go. He said he was heading out to visit family."

"Do you know where?"

"I want to say he mentioned Fairplay, but I can't be sure. He did say, though, that he would be back. He likes our apple pie."

"Did he mention a name or anything else that might help me find him?"

"Not that I can think of," Bee answered. Her partner behind the register just shook her head.

"Well, I thank you, and I'll be sure to pass it on."

"He's not contagious, is he?" Bee asked.

"No, that was one thing I was told."

Bee went back to the kitchen and a few seconds later the cashier joined her. I wouldn't have been surprised if they both weren't back there debating if I was legit or not. I discovered long ago that using a doctor as an imaginary client was more effective than most other ruses. Everyone understood medical privacy rules, so most people readily accepted my reluctance to provide any specifics to them. Similarly, a lot of people felt they were helping the person I was looking for by providing information they may not have otherwise shared.

The old man by the window had fallen asleep in his chair. I could hear his soft snoring as it interrupted the silence in the room.

I tried calling Michelle, but her phone went directly to voice mail. I left a brief message. I remembered she had said that the vehicle registration mentioned Fairplay. It made sense that if Carl and Louise were constantly on the move living out of their trailer that they'd use a relative's address for vehicle registrations and other things. Michelle had said that the address hadn't panned out, but it had been recently purchased. Maybe when they tracked down the previous owner it would turn out to be a relative. I wanted Carl's story to turn out true.

"Here's your lunch," Bee said as she walked back into the dining room.

"Bee, do you know where Carl worked?"

"No, sure don't. I know a few times he ate in a hurry, because he said he had to get back to work. I got the impression it was here in town, but I never asked where."

"But you say it was part time?"

"Yeah, he said once that it wasn't full time. I was kidding him for being a workaholic because he was rushing out before dessert. I think he said something like he didn't work fulltime - that he just needed to work hard enough to put food on the table."

She walked over to the old man by the window and gently shook his shoulder. She leaned down close and talked to him. He smiled at her as he talked. I wondered if they were related.

I looked down at my lunch and immediately wondered

what I had gotten myself into. The Pikes Peak burger was a huge bacon, cheddar cheese burger smothered in sautéed onions and barbecue sauce. I knew I didn't need it, but I set aside any residual health concerns I might have had and wolfed it down. It tasted great and I understood why the locals might rave about it.

When I left the diner, I felt like I wouldn't have to eat again for at least three days, maybe four. I headed the Mustang west toward Fairplay. I hadn't yet decided to make the trip. I knew Fairplay was hours away, and a trip there would have to be an overnight endeavor. I didn't relish the idea of paying for two hotel rooms, but neither did I want to head back into Colorado Springs.

I knew the various law enforcement agencies were focused on the murder investigation. Let them have it. My priority was finding Carl and Louise. I needed to know the truth.

I had only driven a mile outside Green Mountain Falls, when I noticed a lone motorcyclist following me. Normally, I wouldn't have thought anything about it, but something nagged at me. I started paying attention to it. It stayed with me, about a half mile behind for fifteen miles. At one point I sped up by ten miles an hour and a few minutes later slowed back down to the speed limit. The motorcycle kept its distance.

I knew curiosity killed the cat, but I wanted to know who this guy was. I considered my best options to get behind him when a series of sharp bends in the road, followed by a bridge about a hundred yards long, gave me the perfect opportunity. Seeing a dirt road that peeled off to the right just past the end of the bridge, I slammed on the brakes, took the sharp turn, and then made a quick u-turn. I parked my car next to some thick underbrush and small trees.

My position would have been perfect if my only purpose was to hide. I had parked a good ten to fifteen feet below the road and the underbrush hid my car. But, I wanted to watch him go by and, if possible, to get his tag number. I jumped out of the car and scrambled up to the edge of the bridge. He made the last turn in the road and shot onto the other end of the bridge.

I crouched down, staying on the outside of the metal side railing and quickly moved to a wooden post about ten feet further in on the bridge. I realized that my cover was poor as soon as I tried to conceal myself behind it. The post stood only three feet tall and wasn't even a foot wide. The metal side railing was approximately two feet wide. If I was a poodle it might have worked. If the person on the motorcycle was anyone else it wouldn't have mattered.

The black motorcycle slowed rapidly as it passed, pebbles and dust flew and the bike spun around about thirty feet from me. Behind it, I could see a large truck silhouetted a few hundred yards down the road and coming fast.

Suddenly, the bike started back at me. I saw the flash before I saw the gun. He rushed his first shot, and something whizzed by my left ear. I instinctively backed away towards the center of the bridge, knowing at the same time I had only one place to go. I moved around on barely two feet of pavement, but it wouldn't have mattered if I was in the middle of the road. The only direction that provided any safety from the gun was down, into the fast moving water below.

I jumped as the second shot nipped at my jacket. The fall wasn't that significant, twenty feet at most, but I still hit the water hard. My feet hit the rocky bottom even harder, jarring my teeth. Any concern I had about the impact was instantly overwhelmed by two more significant factors. The power of the current immediately got all my attention. I had no control over what happened to me, and it took all my strength just to keep my head above the water. The second was the temperature of the water. It was absolutely freezing.

I struggled to get my head up for a breath of air. When I finally succeeded, I saw my shooter straddling his motorcycle and looking in my direction from the bridge. The racing water carried me away from him. I only saw him for a second while the current spun me around. I didn't see a gun; however, considering my situation, I couldn't have cared less if he was still trying to shoot me or not. I had more immediate concerns.

I slammed into something, but the current simply tumbled me over it. The river started to curve around a bend and slowed a little. I tried to stand and was able to get a foot on the bottom, but the current wouldn't let me do anything more than make contact. The next thing I knew the current accelerated to the point it had me totally at its mercy. I stopped fighting it and used all my strength to keep my face out of the water enough to breath.

Physically exhausted, I wanted to give in to the numbing, cold water and just go to sleep, when I suddenly realized my feet were dragging on the bottom. The current had pushed me into a small pocket of the river next to the bank where the current moved at a slower pace. Rather than race down the river, I slowly drifted past a nearby boulder. A warning bolt of lightning shot through my brain. Get out of the water! The warning slammed against my barely conscious mind.

I stood up, but the tug of the current wanted to pull me back. The bank was only a few steps away. It would be so much easier, though, just to lie back down. I watched a leaf float by, slowly at first as it passed me, but a few yards away it sped up as it rejoined the main current and disappeared down the river.

Get out of the water! Don't be that leaf! I took a step and then another. I made it to the bank and collapsed. I remembered crawling to a spot in the sun, but then everything went blank.

Looking back, I realize there were a number of things that let me survive that day. Most importantly, the bullets didn't hit me. Next, the fast moving river took me away from my attacker. Third, the current released me before it drowned me or the cold water killed me. Fourth, the sky had cleared and the sun baked me while I lay there unconscious and cold. Finally, my attacker didn't do anything to disable my car.

I woke up shivering and with a pounding headache. My lips hurt and my face felt funny. The sunshine had moved off my body and was now about a foot to my left. I sat up and moved my body back into the sunshine. The warmth from the sun, at this altitude, had an immediate impact. I took off my shirt; the back of it was still wet, and laid it out flat in the sun. My shoes and one sock were missing. I removed my jeans to let the sun do its thing.

For the next fifteen minutes, I studied the bruises and scratches on my body and tried to get my bearings. Surprisingly, the parts of my body I could see didn't look nearly as bad as I expected. A nasty bruise tattooed my left hip, but that was all.

I figured I couldn't have gone that far from where I parked my car. I couldn't have been in the river for more than a few minutes. At first, I felt lost, unsure which direction I'd need to take to get back to my car. But then my dummy light went on, and I realized I simply needed to go against the current of the river. I still had my car keys, my wallet and my now defunct cell phone.

My clothes were a little damp when I put them back on, but they were warm. While I gingerly followed the bank of the river back to the bridge and then my car, I thought about my attacker. Dressed from head to toe in black, including a black helmet with the visor shut, I couldn't be sure if the person was male or female. Michelle would have criticized me for stereotyping, but I couldn't help but think my attacker was a male.

The way he handled the motorcycle and the fluidity in his handling and firing the gun swayed my thinking into believing it was a male. Plus, a germ of an idea was rapidly growing into a theory.

All along, the incident with Michelle's jeep had bothered me. I accompanied Michelle that day as an observer. I didn't take anything that happened personally, readily accepting the idea that Michelle – or the police, in general - were being targeted. No one could have expected or known that I would be there that day.

Today, however, someone had specifically targeted me. I couldn't rationalize it away as a random act of road rage or something that ballooned into an act of violence. The guy shot at me in a premeditated attempt to kill me. He didn't want to talk to me. He could've just driven by, but he didn't.

For it to make any sense at all, it had to be connected to the past few days. I must have seen something or witnessed something that I wasn't supposed to, and only one thing came immediately to mind: the second man at the table talking with Lynda Ball. The one named Leroy Fox.

I not only saw him up close, I talked to him. I could identify him and specifically link him with Ball and the other man. The restaurant staff might be able to, but they see lots of faces and could more effectively be cross examined by a defense attorney, if needed.

If he was there watching as Michelle and I drove up, it made sense that pushing the jeep over the ledge was actually targeted at me and not her. His reaction to suddenly seeing me with the police could have rushed him into the act. He likely jumped to the logical, but in this case incorrect, conclusion that I was associated with the police and already working with Michelle to locate him.

If he got rid of me, it would be much easier to build an alibi claiming to be somewhere else. Following that same logic, if he was indeed a professional assassin, killing me would just be another Colorado kill. No big deal.

But if that was the case, why hadn't he tried to find me after I had jumped into the river to see if he completed the job this time? The truck may have spooked him into leaving, or another car may have come by. The more I thought about it, a quick departure may have been the wise decision. No one had apparently called the police to report my being shot at or going over the bridge. If someone had, they hadn't taken it seriously. As far as I could tell, no one had come looking for me.

The Mustang appeared to have been undisturbed since I left it. I rummaged through the trunk of my car and grabbed my golf shoes. Better than nothing, my feet were cold and the one without a sock felt a little raw.

The air had developed a chill to it. I turned the heat to high after I jumped into my car and started the engine. A few minutes later, I was back on the road heading east to Colorado Springs. I needed to talk to Michelle and fill her in on what had happened. However, with my cell phone soaked and useless, our conversation would just have to wait.

I wondered what Fox would do next. If I were him I'd get out of town. In fact, I'd have already gone. That was the weak link in my theory. Why would he still hang around? Did he have more to do here? Was there another target? If he was just trying to keep a low profile and hiding out somewhere, he wasn't doing a very good job of it. I couldn't believe he stayed just for me.

The other thing that puzzled me was where had he first seen me today and when had he started following me? For that matter, how did he know what I was driving? I didn't see him before lunch. He certainly wasn't tailing me when I went out to where Carl and Louise had been. I only saw him after I left the diner and got out on the open highway. Both the bike and the driver were nondescript, but I was sure he wasn't back there for long before I spotted him.

If he picked me up in Green Mountain Falls, what was he doing there? The town didn't offer much of a reason to visit. I drove back through the small town on my way to Colorado Springs, and didn't notice a single hotel. I guessed one may sit further back in the woods, but I didn't even see a sign for a hotel.

Without any answers and before I reached the El Paso County Sheriff's Office, I detoured into a shopping mall and headed into the closest store that carried men's clothing. I needed shoes, socks, jeans and another shirt. The clothes I had on were going into the trash. I found a restroom and changed into the new clothes.

Chapter 13

Michelle was still at work and listened intently as I related my day's events. She started to sidetrack me when I mentioned that Carl and Louise may have gone to Fairplay. I cut her off and told her we could come back to that. She remained silent for the rest of my story. I told her my theory that the shooter was Leroy Fox. When I finished, she contacted Bob and asked him to come into her office.

"I wondered how your face got so sunburned," Michelle said as we waited.

"My lips feel like they're seriously chapped, too."

She pulled a small mirror out of her desk drawer and passed it over. I studied my face for the first time since the incident. I looked like I had spent the afternoon skiing in the sun without any suntan lotion or lip balm.

Bob entered as I passed the mirror back to Michelle. She introduced him to me as Detective Bob Ashworth. He looked several years older than Michelle. He wore his brown hair cropped short, almost in the old crew cut fashion. I'd describe him as thin, but skinny might be the better word. I instinctively pegged him as a very picky eater. Although he didn't have on glasses, I could see the distinct creases on the sides of his head where he had worn them for years.

Michelle instructed me to recite my story to Bob, starting at the point where I first noticed being followed. I did. It didn't take long.

"Are you serious?" Bob asked when I finished.

"Of course," I replied to his stupid question. Obviously, Michelle hadn't co-opted Bob into the Jim West fan club.

"Bob," Michelle added, "I think we can believe Jim."

"Okay, okay, sorry to doubt your story West. Explain to me why you think this guy was Fox, and why he would have any interest in you."

I went over my reasoning again, this time in more detail.

"You know," Bob said when I finished, "we're not even sure Fox is his real name."

"I understand that. My guess is that it isn't. But that just supports my theory. If Fox is just a pseudonym, and if he did kill Lynda Ball and the other guy, then I might just be the best witness you have putting him here in Colorado Springs and face to face with the two victims."

"That's true," Bob conceded, "but we don't even know if he's the killer."

"I know. But if he isn't, then the incident today makes absolutely no sense at all."

"Have you got other enemies?"

"None that want me dead, I hope." I actually could think of a few, but I didn't want to cloud my argument.

"Additionally, we have the discrepancy between Fox's arrival and the shooting of Garibaldi. As far as we know, Fox wasn't even in Colorado that day."

"You know, Bob, that argument is weak. There are a hundred explanations for it."

He didn't argue. "Okay, Jim, let's suppose it was Fox, or whatever his real name might be. Where does that leave us? You don't know where we can find him, do you? "

"No. As far as I can figure, the attack on me today only

serves to further implicate Fox with two murders. I thought that might be significant."

"It is, Jim," Michelle jumped back into the conversation.

"Hell, Michelle, Fox was already a person of interest in this investigation. I'm not sure this helps us any at all." He turned his attention back to me. "You didn't, by any chance, collect the shell casings from the incident did you?"

The question stung me. I could easily rationalize why I hadn't done so, but I simply didn't think of it at the time. I should have.

"No."

"You should've. It might've made your whole story more credible."

"Hey, come on, Bob," Michelle stepped in again, "we've got no reason to believe Jim's not telling us the truth."

"Okay, okay. Excuse me West, it's been a hectic couple of days. I believe you, and I suggest the two of you head out at first light tomorrow to find those shell casings."

"We will," responded Michelle without conferring with me.

"I know," Bob said to both of us, "you think I'm skeptical. But, I still have to pass this on to the sheriff and to the FBI. How do you think they'll receive this?"

"Hey, I don't really care what they think about it. It's what happened, and my theory is just that – a theory. All in all, it's possibly one more piece of the puzzle. Keep it low key and pass it on to them as just that – that's my advice." I knew he didn't need to hear my advice, but I'd been in his shoes many times before, and I thought it was good advice.

I could see a trace of a smile try to form on Michelle's lips. Simultaneously, Bob opened and shut his mouth. I figured he wanted to say something but decided not to. Instead, he mumbled something to Michelle about staying in touch and left.

"Thanks, Jim. Bob's been under a lot of stress. There's a whole lot of pressure coming down from somewhere, and we don't know why. Bob's bearing the brunt of it. I understand the PD and even the FBI are being squeezed to get some results."

"No explanation why?"

"Not to our level. Bob doesn't even think the sheriff knows what's driving the interest. We do know the sheriff received a call from someone in the governor's office and from the FBI's agent in charge in Denver. The DA and the police chief are getting the same pressure. If they know what's driving it, they aren't saying."

"It makes sense," I said. "You've got a state politician's wife and an organized crime guy murdered. You said Garibaldi comes from a wealthy family. That adds icing to the cake. Any possibility Garibaldi was assisting the Feds? Or maybe Lynda Ball?"

"Not to my knowledge." Michelle responded. "You know, I have someone over at the Bureau I might be able to talk to, off the record, of course. Maybe she can fill me in."

"It's late," I said. "May I buy you dinner?"

"I'd love it, but I want to follow up on a few things. Can I have a rain check?"

"Sure." I could see her mind was working on something other than me.

"Do I need an escort out?"

"I'll walk you out, Jim."

"What's the status on your Jeep?" I asked as we walked down the hall.

"They got it out, but it's toast. I guess the good news is that I get a new car."

She didn't sound all that excited.

Chapter 14

Outside the sky had darkened; the mountains blocking the last rays of the setting sun. The temperature had fallen another five to ten degrees. I contemplated heading back to the hotel for a heavier coat, but decided to return to the mall and pick up a new cell phone. If I had been back in Clovis, I'd likely hold off getting a new one for a while. I've never really cared for cell phones or pagers.

The clerk at the aptly named Phone Store tried to talk me into one of the newer phones that did everything but the laundry, but I held my ground. Ultimately, I walked off with what the sales rep described as last year's, last year model. It didn't cost me a penny.

"Well, I think you can still text with it, but I don't know if that model will let you get on the internet," he had said it as a disclaimer.

"Perfect," I responded. I could count the number of times I had texted on one hand. In his defense, maybe he thought I had a lot of friends.

Seeing the food court in the mall made me hungry, but the choices there didn't make me want to stay. I returned to my car and headed back out to the Colorado Mountain Brewery. There were a few things I wanted to follow up on.

A waiting line extended to just outside the door, so I squeezed through and found an empty seat at the bar. I could wait until things slowed down. Besides, they still offered four beers on tap that I hadn't tasted.

Because of the crowd, two young ladies were handling the receptionist duties. I recognized one of the two from earlier in the week. They stayed busy taking down names and funneling people to tables as they became available. After about thirty minutes, and well into my second beer, the line disappeared.

I made it a point to wait until the receptionist I remembered seeing on my prior visit was alone at the front counter. I didn't have to wait long.

She greeted me as I approached.

"Sorry, it's been so busy tonight, sir."

"Oh, that's all right. It's comfortable at the bar." I was surprised that she had noticed me. I didn't check in when I arrived. "Can I get a table in Tasha's section?"

"Sure, but you may have to wait a while longer."

"That's okay. I'll just be at the bar. My name is Jim, Jim West, if you need it for your list."

She wrote something down on her clipboard.

"May I ask you a question?" I asked.

"Sure."

"I was here the other night and talked to a couple of your customers. Later, the police needed my assistance in getting a description of one of the men. They told me they also talked to a receptionist that worked here. Was that you?"

A sudden look of apprehension crossed her face.

"Please, I'm not here to cause you any problems. You don't have to talk to me if you don't want to. We can also talk later, elsewhere if that would be better," I said.

She looked around and leaned toward me. When she spoke, I had to lean in to hear her.

"Wait here a second." She said and walked off in a hurry.

I smiled to myself. When she leaned towards me and spoke in that whispering conspiratorial manner, I didn't expect her to simply say wait here.

She returned in no time at all, Tasha in tow. They stopped a few yards from me when Tasha had a clear view of me. They spoke briefly together. I smiled and nodded at Tasha, and she did the same back to me. The receptionist let go of Tasha and returned to me. Tasha disappeared into another room.

Rather than return directly to her small counter, she moved to the side of the room and motioned me over.

"I just wanted to make sure Tasha recognized you," she said, still whispering. "I've been afraid ever since the police talked to me. I told them I'd help them with a description, but I won't testify in a murder trial. No way. I live by myself. I don't want to get involved."

"I understand."

"Steve worked their table that night, and he outright told the police he doesn't remember anything about them."

"Do you think he does?"

"Sure. I mean he has to remember a little about them. They were here the night before the police talked to us. Steve had to remember something about them, it wasn't even twenty four hours, but he won't talk."

"Did anyone else see or notice anything?"

"No. At least nobody has said anything to me." She said, her voice getting back to normal.

"Thanks. By the way, what's your name?"

"Holly."

"That's a pretty name."

"Thanks. Did you talk to the police, too?" she asked.

"Yes."

"Aren't you afraid?"

"A little, of course, but I'm also a very curious guy. Did you notice if any of the three seemed nervous or worried about anything that night?"

"No, I didn't, but Steve could answer that question better than me – if he wanted to."

"Is he here tonight?"

"No, come to think of it he hasn't been here since that night?"

I could see some dread working its way back into her imagination.

"I wouldn't worry about him. I'm sure he's fine. It's only been a couple of days."

A family walked into the restaurant, and Holly instinctively motioned to her partner to take care of them.

"Do you know Steve's address?" I asked.

"No."

"That's okay, it's not that important."

Another couple entered the restaurant.

"I'd better get back to work," Holly said and walked off to greet the new arrivals.

I went back to the bar but ordered a diet coke rather than another beer. The two I had were great, but I still had things to do tonight.

Another fifteen minutes passed before Holly motioned to me that I had a table. I followed her out to the side patio to the same table I occupied earlier in the week. Due to the coolness of the evening, the restaurant had turned on their portable gas heaters. One loomed nearby spouting its heat out across four tables. The warmth felt good.

"Nice to see you again, Jim." I was pleased she remembered

my name. "Thanks for requesting my section."

"You know I couldn't come here and sit anywhere else."

Her smile widened with my comment. "You look like you've gotten some sun since the other night. It's easy to burn at this altitude."

"I know," I said.

"What can I get you tonight?"

"Just the chili tonight, Tasha; I ate too much the other night."

"To drink?"

"Just water, I've already had a couple beers at the bar."

She left to get my water. She didn't seem to be aware of my conversation with Holly, despite Holly grabbing her earlier to verify who I was. I wondered if Holly hadn't given her an explanation.

I looked over at the table where Lynda Ball and the two men had sat. A coupled huddled close together now occupied the table. The way they sat, their backs faced me, made them less of a distraction.

I did my best to recreate the vision from earlier in the week of the three people - two of whom were now dead. I remembered Lynda sitting there, glancing now and then at me and jotting down something on her tablet. I focused harder. They hadn't appeared to be arguing, but at times they did appear to be engrossed in conversations with a lot of hand gestures and nodding or shaking of their heads. Not angry gestures, I remembered them more as emphatic ones, like they were all in agreement about something. I easily recreated Lynda's face in my mind, but could do nothing with the two men's. Of course, at that time I wasn't interested in them, just her.

Tasha brought me the water and chili at the same time.

"Tasha, are you aware that two customers who sat right over there at that table, the night I was here, were murdered later that same night?"

"Yes, can you believe that?"

"Did the police talk to you about the incident?"

"Not personally. They talked to us as a group and asked if any of us remembered anything about the three. I told them I didn't notice them at all. Is that why you were talking to Holly? I didn't think you were a cop?"

"I'm not, but that's what I was talking to Holly about," I said.

"Did they talk to you, too?" she asked.

"Yes. By coincidence I knew the woman. That's why I'm personally interested in knowing a little more about what happened."

"A former girlfriend?" Tasha asked. For whatever reason, I got the impression her youthful mind wanted to romanticize the relationship.

"I wouldn't go that far." I replied in a manner that I hoped left doubts in her mind.

"I thought I saw the two of you sneaking peeks at each other. She was kind of attractive, for an older woman. What was her name?"

"Lynda Ball. She was also from New Mexico."

"What was she doing up here?"

"I don't know. That's part of the puzzle I'm trying to figure out. Do you know who waited on them that night?"

"Yeah, Steve did."

"Did the police talk to him?"

"No. They tried to, but he said he couldn't remember a thing about them."

"Is he here tonight?" I had asked Holly the same questions and didn't expect different answers from Tasha.

"No. He hasn't returned to work since that night."

"Has anyone checked on him?"

"Oh, he's fine. He gets a little melodramatic."

"What do you mean?"

"He's a little strange."

"Do you think he would talk to me?"

Tasha paused for a minute before answering me. For the first time, she looked at me as though she had a serious side to her. Her natural smile faded out.

"I don't know?" she finally answered. Then, as if she came to a decision, "He probably wouldn't want to if I called and asked him, but if I took you to him he would."

"You know him well?"

"Every now and then we hang out. I've given him a ride to and from work on a few occasions, and he's done the same for me. Nothing serious, he's just a friend."

"Can we go see him tomorrow morning?" I asked.

"Best to go tonight, I get off in twenty minutes."

"Won't it be a little late?"

"Steve will be awake," she replied. "I'll see if I can take off a few minutes early. When you finish your chili, I should be ready." She turned and walked back into the restaurant.

The chili was as delicious as it was earlier in the week. I ate it quickly wondering all along what could have spooked Steve.

True to her word, twenty minutes later, Tasha and I departed the restaurant.

"Let's take my car," I said as we approached the Mustang.

"Oh, cool car!" Tasha remarked. "But, Jim, I want to drive. I'll be able to find his place if I'm driving. Besides I have to come back by the restaurant to get to my place."

She was insistent, so I gave in. Getting a chance to talk to Steve had a higher priority than my concern that I might be in any danger with her. She walked me to the far edge of the parking lot and we climbed into her old Suburban. My seat had a tear in it.

"Sorry about my car. It's seen better days."

I noticed a four inch crack in the windshield.

"I've been in a lot worse. How far does Steve live from here?"

"About ten minutes," she responded as we pulled onto the road and headed away from the mountains.

"Is this area still referred to as the Black Forest?"

"Yeah, at least a part of it. Steve rents a rundown house. He loves it, but I couldn't live out here by myself, too spooky."

"I don't blame you."   The clouds hid whatever moonlight there might be, and street lights were few and far between. The area was dark and very rural.

"Thanks for letting me drive, Jim. I've been with a couple of jerks who have taken me out to the middle of nowhere and then threatened to kick me out of their cars if I didn't put out."

"Unfortunately, the world is full of jerks," I said.

Actually, I was a little surprised she didn't just tell me to follow her in my car. I thought about asking her what she had done on the occasions she referred to, but decided not to.

"I don't mean to say that I think of you that way," Tasha said. "It's just I feel safer driving myself in an area like this, especially at night."

She made three turns before I realized I hadn't paid enough attention to find my own way out, and two more turns on unmarked roads convinced me that I had no idea where we were. Everything looked the same outside the car. Tall pine trees, old houses interspersed with newer ones, and the occasional field all blended together.

Suddenly she braked hard and turned onto a driveway. She stopped the car next to an old model Corolla. The house looked dark.

"Maybe he's not here," I said.

"He's here. I called him before we left," Tasha said.

"Does he know you're bringing me?"

"No. I didn't want to worry him," Tasha replied.

Tasha knocked on the door and then put her face right in front of the peep hole. I wondered if that was a habit of hers or if she simply didn't want Steve to see me. Either way, it worked, as Steve opened the door.

"Tash, my dear, good to see…." Steve stopped talking as soon as he saw me. By then, though, Tasha already had taken a step into the house and prevented him from slamming the door.

"It's okay, Steve. Jim is a friend of mine. I didn't tell you he was coming with me, because I knew you'd find some excuse to say I couldn't come."

Steve looked skeptically at me. I could see fear in his eyes. He wasn't a big guy, but I wouldn't have called him puny either. He just needed to put on some weight and exercise a little. His hair was a mix of colors. A small patch of the hair up front was a fire engine red. The rest was an ordinary brown, with the exception of a small streak above both ears that I swear looked blue. He had a small snake tattooed under his left ear. He was barefoot, wearing jeans and a black sweatshirt.

"Relax, Steve," Tasha said. "Jim knew the lady who was murdered. He just wants to ask you a few questions."

"That's right. I'm not here to cause you any problems."

"You a cop?" Steve finally spoke.

"No."

"A private eye?"

"No, Steve, not even that. It really is like Tasha said. I knew the lady you waited on the other night, the one who was later killed. The police interviewed me because she had jotted down my name on her notebook that night. It was a form of doodling that I believe she did after she noticed I was there in the restaurant. We never got a chance to speak. I'm trying to figure out what happened."

He still looked apprehensive.

"Steve, why don't you and I go make some coffee in that fancy new coffee machine you showed me last time I was here. We could all use a cup, right Jim?" Tasha asked.

"That would be nice," I replied.

She half-dragged Steve out of the room.

The room we had entered appeared to be the living room. An overhead light provided the lighting in the room. A couple of used, unlit candles sat on a crate that served as an end table at the end of a couch. The carpet on the floor looked terrible. Dried mud covered part of the carpet by the front door. A large tear in the far corner and multiple cigarette burns rounded out the rug's appearance. It might have originally been a light blue, but now it looked a dusty grey.

Rather than pictures, Steve had tacked posters from the Star Wars movies on one wall and from the X-Files television show on the other. The large window was completely covered by a dark, wool blanket that had been tacked at all four corners to the wall.

I glanced around the corner of the room into the dining room. The same carpet extended into the dining room, and other than a large red stain by the table, looked in better shape than it did in the living room. A basic square, four person wooden table, with only two chairs, made up the only furniture in the dining room. The table had no table cloth. A computer and a stack of comic books covered half of the tabletop. From what was on the computer monitor, it appeared we must have interrupted his video game.

I went back to the couch in the living room and sat down. A brown sheet had been tossed over it. I didn't have any desire to lift the sheet and check out what the couch actually looked like. Just sitting down seemed to disturb the air around the couch, and the slight scent of marihuana drifted into my nose.

"How do you like your coffee, Jim?" Tasha shouted from the kitchen.

"Just black."

A moment later, Steve came into the room carrying two cups of coffee. Tasha followed close behind him with one for herself. Steve kept the cup that looked like it may have contained more cream than coffee and gave me the other.

He sat on a large pillow that was on the floor, and Tasha slid onto the couch next to me.

"Tasha said I can trust you to keep whatever I tell you to yourself. Is that right?"

"Yes, that's right, unless you confess to the murders." I tried some humor to ease the strain, but I doubted it worked. He didn't respond, so I started my questioning.

"The other night, did you get the chance to hear any of their conversations?"

"I'm not a snoop," Steve answered.

"I'm not saying you are, but it might be important."

He looked at Tasha. She nodded at him, and he started

talking.

"They did a lot of talking about large contracts. I think they had something to do with road construction. They also talked a lot about money, lots of money."

"Did you hear any specifics?"

"Not really. I was getting the table next to them ready for a customer, and I heard one of the guys say something like 'that should be worth at least fifty million'."

"Fifty million?" Tasha asked.

"Yes, that's what got me interested. I tried listening from then on just out of curiosity. There's nothing wrong with that."

"I agree. It's only normal. Did you know which of the men said that?" I asked.

"No, my back was to them. After that I know all three talked about more ideas for other road projects. It all sounded legit to me. All three appeared to be having a good time."

"Did you hear any names mentioned?"

"No, not that I recall."

"Did you get the impression that any of them were afraid of anything?"

"No, like I said, they each had a good time."

"How did they pay?" I asked.

"Cash - and they left a good tip."

"Have you seen any of them since?"

My question surprised him.

"What?" he exclaimed. "Two of them are dead, and the third person I hope to never see again."

The spontaneity of his answer assured me he hadn't noticed the surviving member of the trio since that night.

"Steve, why wouldn't you talk to the police?"

"I didn't want to get involved. It's none of my business."

"Okay, Steve, just a couple more. Did you notice if the woman left before the two guys?"

"Yeah, I saw her on her way out. She thanked me for the service."

"Did she seem all right?" I asked.

"Yeah, just fine."

"That's all I have, Steve. Any questions for me?"

"Did you get to see the dead bodies?" he asked.

"No, nor do I have any desire to do so."

"Which one of the guys was killed?"

"If I remember right, the one who sat next to her."

"Not the guy with the wig, then?

"The what?" I asked.

"The hair piece," Steve answered.

"Why do you think he was wearing a wig?"

"Well, to me, it looked obvious. I guess I could've been wrong, but I doubt it," he said.

"Why haven't you gone back to work?"

"I was there, I waited on them. Two, maybe three of them get whacked. I'll just stay here for a couple of weeks. I don't want to get involved."

He was overreacting, but he was an odd guy anyway.

"Tasha," I asked, "do you have any questions for either of us?"

"Do you think any of us are in danger?" she asked.

"No, I don't believe so." I certainly wasn't going to tell them about the guy taking a shot at me. "But if either of you feel like you are, I recommend you go talk to the police in person."

As if on cue, a buzzer sounded in the kitchen. Steve quickly turned off the lights in the room and headed for the kitchen.

"It's just the deer again," Tasha said loud enough for Steve to hear. She looked at me and shook her head.

"What's going on?" I asked Tasha.

"Steve has motion detectors in the front and back yards. He likes to take pictures of the deer at night when they come into his yard. He actually has some good ones."

My reaction to learning something had just come into the yard more closely matched Steve's than Tasha's, who took everything in stride. I did my best to act nonchalant, but moved to peek out around the edge of the window.

"No," Steve said. I turned back to look at him as he turned off the light in the dining room. I saw that he had already turned off the kitchen light. "It's too dark out there."

In the darkness, I moved away from the window for two reasons. First, I noticed he had a set of night vision goggles in one hand. He would be able to see a lot better with those, than I could without them. The second reason was more compelling. In his other hand he carried a shotgun. I didn't feel threatened, but I had made it a habit long ago not to argue with anyone carrying a shotgun.

"Let me look," Tasha said, standing up and moving toward him.

In the dark room they both looked like vague shadows. As my eyesight adjusted to the dark, I realized a plug-in nightlight by the entrance to the kitchen provided just enough light to make out my surroundings.

"No way," Steve responded. "Not 'til I know for sure what's out there."

"Oh, you're getting carried away," Tasha remarked.

I didn't say anything. Steve moved to a position on the floor by the window. Squatting low, he peeled up the right, lower corner of the blanket and peered out into the darkness. He didn't say anything for nearly a minute.

While Steve stared out into the darkness, Tasha sidled up close to me. "Ten bucks it's only some deer."

"Couldn't it be a skunk or something else?"

"No, he moved the beams up higher off the ground the day after he installed it. The little critters kept him up all night. I think he has it set three to four feet off the ground."

"Makes sense."

"Come here, Tash," Steve finally spoke up.

She hurried over to a position close to him. He passed her the night vision goggles.

"Oh, he's a big one."

"I counted eight points. What do you see?"

"I think you're right," she said.

"Jim, you want a look?"

"Sure, why not."

It was an impressive buck. He stood barely ten yards in front of the window and had his nose to the ground searching for something to eat.

The visit by the deer had a calming effect on Steve. He seemed more accepting of my presence. He even offered me another cup of coffee.

"Would you be willing to tell the police what you told me?"

"No way, I don't trust the police."

The conversation digressed and after another five minutes I realized that, though less defensive, Steve had nothing more of substance to offer. I suggested to Tasha that we leave, and after I thanked him for his time and coffee, we left.

"He's a little strange, don't you think?" I asked Tasha as she backed the car out of the driveway.

She looked at me with a big smile. I thought she might break out in laughter.

"More than a little I would say. He's a sweet guy, but I can only take so much of him. Those blankets he covered the windows with are new. Not the blankets," she corrected herself, "but that is the first time I've seen them on the windows."

"Do you think he knows more than what he told us?" I asked.

"I doubt it. He gets carried away. You probably noticed he's big into conspiracies. That's what all the X-File stuff is about."

We had made our second turn of many that I knew we would eventually make on our way back to the restaurant, when I noticed a single headlight following us. The events of earlier in the day jumped back into my mind.

Tasha took the next intersection to the left, and the headlight behind kept with us. I didn't like it. I wished I was driving and fought the urge to say anything to Tasha. She talked more about Steve, laughing at a comment she made about him. I tried to pay enough attention to her to grunt a response or two, but the potential threat following us dominated my mind.

I knew it could be anyone on the motorcycle, but with every subsequent turn, the bike stayed with us and my paranoia increased. The darkness prevented me from getting a good look at the bike or its driver.

"Hey, Jim, what's the matter?" Tasha asked, for maybe the second or third time.

"Probably nothing, but it looks like that motorcycle has been following us for some time."

"Little bit of Steve rubbing off on you? There's only so many ways to get out of there."

I grinned. She had me there. Maybe my imagination was getting the best of me.

We turned right, onto the road that would go past the restaurant. The motorcycle didn't turn and continued, instead, directly into the city. Two people rode on the motorcycle. A big person was driving it, and a woman passenger sat tight behind the driver. The bright lights of the intersection let me get a good look at them. However, they both wore helmets, so the lights did little good.

Carl jumped to mind. He was as big, if not bigger, than the driver. But did he even have a motor cycle? And why should he be a suspect? We didn't even run into him until after the murders and the incident with the jeep. Of course there may be no connection between the person taking a shot at me today and the earlier incidents. That could explain my assailant picking me up in Green Mountain Falls. Maybe Carl only moved his trailer a mile or two.

"Does that mean you're not interested?" Tasha asked, interrupting my thoughts.

She had just pulled her car into the mostly empty parking lot and stopped next to mine.

"I'm sorry, my mind was elsewhere."

"I know. I've asked you twice if you'd like to come to my place for a drink, and you just ignored me. Doesn't do much for a girl's ego," Tasha said.

"I ..."

"Plus, you know the way that motorcycle bothered you; you're starting to frighten me. At least you could make sure I got home safely."

"I'd love to have a nightcap with you," I said, wondering why I said it.

I followed her to her apartment, rationalizing the situation I had gotten myself into. After all, I did drag her deeper into this mess. Making sure she got home safely was the decent thing to do. One quick drink and I'd be gone. No ifs, ands, or buts.

Chapter 15

She was still asleep the next morning when I woke up at six thirty and crawled silently out of bed. I found my clothes and went into the kitchen. I found a tablet next to the phone and wrote her a quick note telling her what a great night I had. I reminded her of the appointment I had mentioned the previous night, before I had given up on making excuses, and that I would call her later in the day.

I drove back to my hotel wondering why I always complicated my life. Tasha was a sweet, pretty girl, but that was also the problem. I was nearly old enough to be her father and had no time or desire to get into a relationship with her.

At the same time, I knew I was probably overreacting. If anyone had relationship issues it was me. I'd been married for twenty years. Since the divorce, I had done my best to avoid relationships and certainly couldn't be described as leading the life of a playboy. The few women who entered my life, for the most part, were closer to my age.

I pulled into the hotel's parking lot finally convincing myself to quit overanalyzing what had happened between Tasha and me. Activity buzzed in the lobby of the hotel as a long line of people waited to check out and others stood in a handful of small groups, some drinking coffee, and planning the day's events.

I edged my way through the lobby and headed down the long hallway to my room. I had inserted the key card into its slot before I realized the door opened freely with just the pressure of my card being inserted. I saw the damage on the frame as soon as the door moved inward. Somebody had broken into my room. I instinctively went into a crouch, which would have been fine if I had a weapon. Realizing this, I quickly stood up and slid my body behind the door frame, and peeked around the corner as I pushed the door the rest of the way open.

I saw no one. I quietly moved to the bathroom and pushed open the door. Empty. I looked around and saw that a number of things had been tossed on the floor. At first glance, the evidence suggested burglary. I reached for the phone, being careful to hold the receiver with just the tips of my index finger and thumb. I didn't worry about my prints on the telephone, but I didn't want to smudge any others that might exist.

Three minutes later the hotel manager and head of security arrived.

"What happened here?" The manager, a thin grey haired man in his mid-fifties to sixties asked while he leaned down to look at the damaged door frame. "Look at this, George," he instructed the security chief, who could have passed as the manager's slightly younger brother.

George also leaned in close to look at the damage. "Definitely forced," he remarked.

"Nothing appears to be missing," I said. "Everything has been rummaged through. A lot of it simply tossed on the floor, but I don't think anything is missing. All I brought with me were some clothing and my golf clubs. The clubs are in my car."

"Any idea why someone would do this?" George asked.

"Not off the top of my head." I had a few wild theories but kept them to myself.

"Think it could be connected to the reason the police came to see you yesterday morning?" the hotel manager asked.

"I hope the police explained to you that I was cleared of any and all suspicion in that matter."

"They did," both men answered in unison.

"I only reported this to you so you wouldn't think I did the damage. Plus, I thought you'd like to know."

"We do want to know, Mr. West. We don't mean anything by our questions. We're just as curious as you are. Especially, as you say, since nothing is missing," the manager said as he slowly walked around the room. He studied the window frame and then turned back to me, "Would you like a new room?"

"This room is fine, as long as you can fix the door."

"We'll get someone on it right away," the manager responded.

"Doesn't appear we need to call this into the police," George commented to his boss.

"I agree George. Mr. West, how much longer do you expect to be here at the hotel?"

"Do you mean today?"

"No. How many days…"

"A few more, I don't really know, but I hope to be heading back home soon."

They left after telling me the door would be fixed before noon. I thought the manager might offer to comp a night or two for the inconvenience, but he didn't bring up the subject.

I secured the door with the inside clasp and jumped into the shower. When I turned the water off, I heard the hotel phone ringing. On a different day, I would have let it ring, but I grabbed a towel and hurried to the phone.

"Jim, I just heard someone broke into your hotel room. Are

you okay?" Michelle asked.

"News travels fast, but yes, I'm okay."

"I understand the break-in happened last night, where were you?"

"It's a long story. We can talk about it later, but I'm okay and nothing appears to have been taken."

"I know it's early, but, if you don't mind, let's take a drive out to where you were shot at yesterday."

"Sure. What do you have for wheels?" I asked.

"I have a rental, a Dodge, but it's okay."

"Let me drive. I'll come get you," I said.

She agreed, and a half hour later, I picked her up in front of the sheriff's office.

"I received some interesting news this morning," she said as soon as I pulled away from the curb. "The FBI and the Boulder police were able to track down and speak to Leroy Fox."

"Great," I said.

"Not really. The Leroy Fox who flew into Denver is not the same Leroy Fox you saw at the restaurant. The real Leroy Fox attended his mother's birthday party with a dozen other people that night."

"So we're back to square one with our Leroy Fox?"

"That's right," Michelle said. "Other than making the reservation that night at the restaurant, we still can't find any record of a Leroy Fox being in Colorado Springs during the last few days."

"I guess that means our Leroy Fox, or whatever his real name is, could have been in town when Garibaldi was shot."

"Only because we don't know a damned thing about him. Do you still think it was Fox who took the shot at you yesterday?"

"He's still my first guess."

"You don't seem as sure now as you were yesterday," Michelle said.

"This whole thing with Carl has been nagging at me. Last night a couple on a motorcycle seemed to be following me around. When they finally passed us, the guy on the motorcycle was dressed in all black, like the guy who took the shots at me yesterday. He was huge, just like Carl, and the female passenger had some blondish hair hanging out the back of her helmet."

"Like Louise?"

"Kind of. It was dark, and I'm not sure they were actually following us, anyway."

"Us?" Michelle asked.

"I went back to the Colorado Mountain Brewery last night to see if I could dig up anything else. I talked to the receptionist the police had already talked to and ended up going over to the house of the guy who waited on the victims and our Fox guy."

"I thought he claimed not to remember anything."

"He's a bit strange and overly paranoid. But he remembered more than he claimed to the police."

"What did he tell you?"

I summarized the major elements of my conversation with Steve. She listened intently and nodded her head a few times. Her first question then, after I'd finished talking, surprised me.

"Did the receptionist take you out to his house?"

I had purposely left Tasha out of the story, focusing solely on Steve and his comments.

"No, there's a waitress there..."

"Server."

"What?" I asked.

"Server. We don't say waitress anymore."

Who doesn't? I thought.

"Okay, a server there named Tasha. She waited on me the night I was there. I asked for my same table so I could also talk to her about that night. She ended up taking me over to Steve's house."

"I wondered why you weren't in your hotel room last night."

I kept my eyes straight ahead watching the traffic, but I knew she had a "gotcha" grin aimed right at me.

"I thought the hotel management wasn't going to report the break in to the police."

"They may not have," Michelle said. "The call I know about went to homicide, not burglary. Don't forget, the PD still has you as a person of interest. I imagine they get routine calls from the hotel on you."

"Swell," I said.

"So you want to tell me about this Tasha person?"

This time I did look over at her. Her attempt at not smiling was barely successful, and the twinkle in her eyes undermined her attempt at being serious.

"Don't tell me they're having me followed, too."

"Not to my knowledge. Well, if you don't want to tell me about your night with Tasha, I guess in the interest of law enforcement, I'll just need to interview her myself."

I felt like calling her bluff. I didn't think she was serious, but I didn't want her to mess up my rapport with Tasha.

"Michelle ..."

"Oh, I'm just playing with you. If you think I need to talk to Tasha, I know you'd tell me. Sorry, but I couldn't resist. You're an easy target."

I didn't know what she meant by that, but I was happy to be

able to change the topic.

"Right on the other side of the bridge is where I pulled off yesterday." I slowed and took the turn to the right. I made the same u-turn and parked in the same spot. We climbed out of the Mustang and walked up to the end of the bridge.

"When I got to this spot, the motorcycle was just starting to cross the bridge. As I said, he'd been following me for a couple of miles. I instinctively ducked down and tried to hide behind that short post over there." I pointed at the post as I spoke.

"Not much of a hiding place."

"I know. My instincts took over. Not a good hiding spot, but if I had simply stayed here, I'd have been an easier, closer target and my escape would've been much harder. I didn't think that at the time, though, I just moved. He came to a stop right over there." I pointed to a spot about ten yards down the road.

A red pickup drove by us. Other than it, the road looked empty in both directions. We walked quickly out to the spot where the motorcycle had started back in my direction.

"He took his first shot right around here."

We both slowed and looked around unsuccessfully for a spent shell casing. I noticed a large truck coming at us from behind.

"The second shot came from somewhere around here," I said, as we moved closer to the bridge and further away from the outside lane of the road. We stood there for a few seconds searching the area with our eyes, until the truck came close enough to make it a good idea to get off the road entirely.

After it passed, we walked back out onto the road. Five more minutes of searching and avoiding traffic left us without any discovery.

"Looks like nothing is here," I said.

"Where did you jump from the bridge?" Michelle asked.

"Over here." I walked her to the spot where I had leapt into the water. "I think this is where I last saw him when I was able to glance back up at him from below."

The river underneath the bridge rushed noisily by us.

"I don't know if I could've jumped in," she said.

"Believe me, if someone is shooting at you, you could."

"Look at this!" she exclaimed and moved a couple steps away from me before leaning down and picking up something I still hadn't seen.

She turned and, in a handkerchief, gingerly held up a half crushed, shiny, small caliber shell casing.

"Eureka," she said.

"Amen to that. What caliber is it?"

"Give me a second, Jim." She walked a few yards away in the direction of the Mustang.

She popped the shell casing into a small zip lock plastic bag, and then pulled out her cell phone. She talked to someone for a few minutes.

"Can we go back and wait by your car?" She asked after she was off her phone.

"Sure," I said as I followed her back. "What was that all about?"

"I called Ollie. I knew she'd be out in this direction today. We're actually not in El Paso county, but what I need Ollie to do I think will be okay."

"What's that?"

"I want her eyes. I want you to take us to the spot where you got out of the river."

"You don't believe me?" I asked.

"I believe you. But, as you can imagine, there may be a few

others that have their doubts about you."

"I'm not surprised."

"By the way, the shell casing was for a 9mm."

"Could be important. The victims were all shot with a 9mm. However, until we find the murder weapon, there's no way to really know."

For the next ten minutes, we discussed all the possible ways the shell casing could have found its way to that spot on the road. We figured its only value at this time would be to add a tad bit of credence to my story.

Ollie pulled up barely a minute before a Teller County sheriff's vehicle pulled in beside us. Ollie had given us a heads up that we would be joined by a Deputy Troy Banion.

When he jumped out of his vehicle I leapt to the immediate conclusion that Ollie and he had met lifting weights. Other than being approximately six inches taller than her, he had the same muscle builder frame stuffed into his uniform. They shook hands like old friends and then both looked at Michelle.

"What can we do for you today, Lieutenant?" he asked.

Michelle briefly ran through my experience on the previous day, and concluded by showing them the round which she said we happened to find while we waited for them. They both looked at the round as though it was conclusive proof to my story. I doubted that the FBI, or even Bob, would accept the evidence so readily.

When she told the two of them that she wanted to find the spot along the river where I crawled out, I was surprised by Deputy Banion's quick response.

"Cool, let's do it!"

I wrote his enthusiasm down as being a result of his positive attitude and a lack of better things to do in his daily routine.

Other than the difficulty of hiking through the thick underbrush and the clambering up and down over the rough terrain, finding the spot along the river bank wasn't hard to do.

"Right here, I think. No, I'm pretty sure. I got out of the water right here. I collapsed over there. Fortunately, the sun was almost straight up and warm yesterday, much like it should be today."

"How about the three of us stay right here for a minute." We were only a few yards away. "Ollie, I need you to see if you can find any signs to corroborate Jim's story."

"Sure," she said and moved carefully to the water's edge.

"Cool," Banion whispered. "I've heard the stories about Ollie. Never had the chance to see her in action."

We didn't have to wait long.

"Were you only wearing one shoe yesterday?" Ollie asked.

"I had two on when I went into the river. Only one when I came out."

"You were here for some time. Sleeping?"

"Passed out would be a better description."

"Had to be for more than an hour."

"Can you really see all that?" Deputy Banion asked.

"Sure," Ollie answered. "Lieutenant, are you in need of protecting this, or can I show this to Troy?"

"No need to protect it. Go ahead and take a look," Michelle said to Troy.

He joined Ollie and got down on his hands and knees trying to see what she had seen.

"She's good," I said.

"Extremely."

I considered joining them, but they looked so much like a teacher and a student going through a practical exercise, I decided to let them have the scene to themselves.

"You ready to head back, Jim?" Michelle asked.

"Anytime."

"Ollie, we're going to head back."

"Okay, we'll be heading back ourselves in a few minutes."

As we hiked back to my car, I asked Michelle what she thought about the two Leroy Fox's.

"What do you mean?" she asked.

"I mean Leroy Fox isn't the most common name. I know there must be a few of them around, although we could find none living in the Springs. I find it interesting that one Leroy Fox flies into Denver the night before another Leroy Fox shows up at a restaurant in Colorado Springs."

"Why is that interesting?"

"Assuming Fox isn't the real name of the guy at the restaurant, why did he pick it?"

"I don't know. Why?"

"Maybe he was on that same plane and knew the real Leroy Fox was, too," I said.

"So, he took the name to use at the restaurant. That could make sense, but that also means he wasn't in the Springs for the first murder. They were all done with the same weapon."

"Which tends to indicate he may not be our killer," I added.

"You know, you aren't helping this investigation out with your theories," Michelle said with a grin. "First you want to point us at this guy, and then you want to give him an alibi."

"Do we know anything more about Mr. Ball?"

"He also seems to have dropped off the face of the earth. But, other than being the third vic's husband, I have a hard time seeing him as the killer."

"I'm inclined to agree with you. But, what if we stick with

the theory that he had hired Garibaldi to follow Lynda, his wife? Let's say that they had a meeting at the rest stop, where Garibaldi was supposed to brief Ball. Something went wrong..."

"Like what?"

"Say, for instance, Garibaldi had discovered something big. Something that if known by the public could do more than just ruin Ball's marriage. Like something that could damage his future in politics."

"From what I've heard about Garibaldi, I think he would've been discreet," Michelle added.

"You know that, but it's probable that Ball didn't. Murder is rarely a rational act."

"An interesting theory, but until we find Ball, or our Fox, theories are all we're going to have."

"I know," I said as we climbed into the Mustang and headed out onto the highway. "I'm also concerned that when we find Ball, we may find him dead, too."

"Don't say that, Jim. This case is already a mess. It's not even mine, but it's gotten under my skin."

"Yeah, I meant to ask you why you're spending so much time on it."

"I've been asked to spend as much time as possible helping Bob on this. Like I said, there's a lot of pressure coming down from somewhere. My other cases are sort of on autopilot. Unless something new pops up, I'll be running a lot of peripheral leads on this one."

"Am I a peripheral lead?"

She broke out in a big smile. "You're the big peripheral lead. Bob and the entire PD would like to find a way to hang this on you. However, for some reason, the FBI discounts your involvement. I think they've said something to the sheriff, too, because he's personally told Bob and me that I should stay close to you. However, he made it clear to both of us, at the same time, that he believed trying to pin this on you would be wasting time that could best be spent solving the case."

"What do you think he knows?"

"I don't know. I can't believe that he would keep anything from Bob or me. My guess is that the FBI may know more than we all do. Rather than tell us more than they would like to, they simply cautioned the sheriff not to expend resources in the wrong direction."

"Nice of them," I said half sincerely. Agencies rarely share everything, but if the FBI said enough to help take me off the hot seat, it was good enough for me. "I wish my cell phone still worked."

"What happened to it?"

"The river, yesterday."

"Oh, yeah."

"I have a couple of old FBI friends I could call, but I can't remember their phone numbers."

"Do you think they would tell you anything?"

"I don't know, but it's possible. We go way back." I didn't elaborate, but one I met when he was the LEGAT, or Legal Attaché, in Paris. The other was assigned to the FBI Headquarters in Washington D.C., in the nineties, when we became friends.

"Did you get a new cell?"

"Yes, with the same number."

"What did you get?"

"You mean type of phone?"

She nodded.

"One similar to the one I had before." I said.

"That was an antique."

"My new one might be its older cousin."

Michelle just shook her head. When we passed the turnoff to the spot where her Jeep had been pushed over the ledge, our conversation turned to cars. Michelle said she had originally wanted to replace her Jeep with another Jeep but that a number of people in the office had suggested she buy a Toyota, or more specifically a Lexus. I simply recommended she buy what she liked, not what other people recommended.

"Do you think the break in of your hotel room could be connected to the investigation?" she asked as we approached the Sheriff's offices,

"Could be, but we can only guess at this point. If it was, I don't like the implication, but the whole break in seemed unsophisticated. I'd like to give our killer more credit."

After she stepped out of my car, she leaned back in before shutting the door and asked, "Are you still thinking about Carl and Louise?"

"Yes."

"Me, too."

Chapter 16

A half hour later, I found myself back in my hotel room. The door frame and lock looked as good as new.

I kicked off my shoes and stretched out on the bed. If nothing else, I needed to clear my head and prioritize the things I had to get done in the next day or two or I would never get back home. Michelle's decision to corroborate my story about being shot at, along with the fact that my hotel room was broken into should help diminish any doubt about me. With any luck, the authorities would soon want me out of town before I became another victim for them to worry about.

My phone buzzed, interrupting my thoughts.

"Hello."

"Jim, it's me, Claire."

"Hey, Claire, is everything all right?"

"Yes. Perry's feeling a lot better. He says he's ready to go home, but the doctor wants him to stay here a few more days."

"Can't blame the doctor. Perry had a heart attack."

"I know. I'm on the doctor's side, too. I just wanted to call and thank you for asking Doris to keep an eye on us."

I almost said that I didn't, but instead simply muttered, "She's an interesting lady."

"I'm not sure I'd use those words, but she's funny, nice and knows everything about everybody."

"I thought she was going to be released yesterday or the day before."

"She said she had a small relapse."

"I think she simply likes it there."

"That's what one of the nurses said, too," Claire replied.

"Is there anything I can do for you or Perry today?"

"No. Steve and Mike have been in and out a lot the last two days and are taking good care of us."

"That's nice."

"They seem to be irritated with you, Jim. Did you do something to irritate them?"

"No. Everything happened so fast the day of Perry's heart attack. I simply never got around to calling them. I imagine that's what it's about." I hadn't been in touch with them since either, but I didn't want to get into that.

We talked for a few minutes more before hanging up. Perry's improvement took a lot off my shoulders.

I looked at my basic, out of date phone. "Some people don't like old dogs either," I silently said to it.

In response, the phone buzzed and vibrated in my hand. My first response was to toss it across the room, but I managed to hang onto it.

"They've found Ball," Michelle said cutting through any preamble.

"About time. Had he gone home?"

"No, he never left. He's dead Jim – been shot just like the others."

"You're kidding me. No, scratch that, I know you're serious. Where did they find him?"

"Near a camping recreation area west of the Air Force Academy."

"Wonder what he was doing out there?"

"Your guess is as good as mine. Want to a take a drive out

there with me?"

I responded that I would, and in fifteen minutes I was back on the road with Michelle. This time, however, she drove and we traveled in one of the sheriff's sedans.

"It's going to be a mad house out there, Jim."

"I'm surprised you invited me."

"I cleared it when I talked to the sheriff. I kind of said you were with me at the time, and asked him what I should do with you. He was with someone else at the crime scene, and I heard him mention your name to someone. He then said to bring you along."

Interesting.   "This is only going to raise the profile of the case higher."

"I think it already has. I understand all hell's broken loose."

"Press involved already?"

"I'm not sure. I just picked up some comments before I left. May be just rumors but I heard both governors are now personally involved in making sure we get this solved ASAP."

"That'll help," I said shaking my head. "So Ball was shot twice in the chest, too?"

"Don't know about that," Michelle answered. "I just know he was found dead and that he was shot."

It took a half hour before we finally rounded a sharp bend on a narrow dirt road and saw the dozen or so vehicles of all shapes and sizes parked in a mass on an adjacent field. Nearby I saw a small horde of investigators. Seven crowded around what I figured was the location of the body. The remaining fifteen to twenty had fanned to search the surrounding area. Three individuals, who looked like they were with the press, were huddled together on the road about twenty yards away from the crime scene. A uniformed deputy, who had been standing with them, rushed toward our car. Once he identified Michelle, he directed us to park near the other cars.

"I'll stay here," I offered as the car came to a stop.

"Okay. Once I know what's going on, I'll be back."

When she left, I climbed out of the car and leaned against the hood. I had a good angle to watch all the activity. The body still lay lifeless on the short grasses that covered the ground. As people shuffled about around it, I got a couple of glances at the body. I could see right away the victim had been shot with something significantly more powerful than a 9 mm handgun.

I only had brief glimpses of Ball, but the red, jagged portion of the skull I did see shouted out shotgun.

A person I assumed to be the medical examiner led the team as it meticulously studied and photographed the victim. Periodically, they collected items of evidence. I heard the sounds of their voices, but I couldn't quite make out their conversation. I saw Bob among the men standing next to the body. He said something and pointed down. The medical examiner looked up at him and raised an open palmed hand at Bob. I got the feeling he didn't need Bob's advice.

Michelle had walked over to one of the men, who, in turn, had broken away from the others. The two stood close to each other engrossed in a serious conversation. I could see surprise in Michelle's expression.

Another official looking sedan pulled into the make shift parking lot, and two men in suits jumped out. FBI, I imagined. The nearest man eyeballed me as he got out of his car. He nodded and I returned the nod. I was getting pretty good at this nodding thing.

Just beyond the two new guys, I saw one member from the press group snap some photos of the new arrivals. I wondered if they had already taken one of me.

A cloud covered the sun and the air immediately became cool. We were in the heart of the foothills. While the immediate surroundings were flat, steep hills climbed close by on all sides of us. I thought I could see snow pockets in some of the nearby peaks. A road sign about a mile back had said we were at seven thousand feet.

"Wait 'til you hear this," Michelle said as she returned.

"What?"

"He wasn't shot with a 9mm --"

"I didn't think so. I can see him from here."

"The murder weapon is most likely a shotgun, 12 gauge."

"That would do it," I said.

"But listen to this," she said. "They found a 9mm next to Ball. The new theory is that Ball may have killed everyone."

"Except himself."

"I know that. I mean the new thinking is that his wife had been fooling around on him. He came up here determined to kill her and her boyfriend."

"How about Garibaldi?" I asked.

"If he was going to kill the other two, then he had to kill Garibaldi to cover his tracks."

"A long shot, but I've heard worse scenarios."

"The only fly in the ointment is this killing," Michelle said.

"Had the 9mm found next to Ball been fired recently?"

"Yes, but no one knows at whom, or whether he hit what he was shooting at. They did do preliminary testing for residue on Ball's hands, and it appears he had recently fired a weapon."

"And the assumption is that he fired the 9mm?" I asked.

"Yes. I know it's only theory at this point, but it makes sense."

"How did they learn about the body?"

"Two men, setting up a picnic area for a family reunion later today, about a half mile further down the road, heard the shots. They didn't think much of it, but they were bored and decided to drive back this way to see what was going on. They drove by the body and went on about another half mile before turning around. They saw the body on their way back."

"A grisly discovery."

"It will certainly liven up conversation at the reunion," Michelle said.

"West," a new voice called me from the side.

I turned and saw a man I hadn't met before.

"West, I'm Justin Moore, with the FBI,"

We shook hands.

"Jim, how well did you know this Ball guy?"

"Not well at all. I attended a couple functions he also attended."

"Functions?"

"One was a charity gala I got roped into, about eight months back. That's the one where I sat at the same table as his wife, Lynda. It was a big table, but we talked a little. That's why I recognized her the other night. They had everyone spread out. He was at a different table. The extent of my conversation with him was to say hello when she introduced us after the meal."

"And the other?"

"A thing at the University. Some kind of alumni and faculty event. I do some part time lectures and teaching around the state for the University of New Mexico. That was over a year ago and the three of us chatted while we waited in line for drinks. There were no introductions, but that's why we recognized each other later."

"No idea why he was up here or where he was staying while he was here?" Moore asked.

"None at all, haven't seen or talked to either of them since the charity event I mentioned."

"You sure there's nothing you can add to help us out with all this?"

"Sorry," I said and shook my head.

"Where were you this morning?"

I had no doubt he already knew the answer to that.

"Agent Moore, I can vouch for his whereabouts this morning," Michelle said.

Moore looked slowly from Michelle to me. "Lieutenant Prado, I'm sure you can."

He started to turn to walk away, but stopped and looked back at me again. "Little old for her, don't you think?" he said softly and walked off to the crowd around the dead body.

Maybe in the movies this would be where the character would take a swing at the wise guy, but I figured Moore was just establishing the pecking order and being a jerk in the process. If he wanted a reaction from me, which I didn't really think he did, he was picking on the wrong guy.

Michelle, on the other hand, hadn't developed such thick skin and had already taken a step into her charge mode before I grabbed her arm. At first I thought she might rip my hand off, but then common sense prevailed, and she let Moore walk off unmolested.

"Jackass," she mumbled.

"Let him go."

"I should file a complaint."

"I think his comments were more directed at me. He wanted me to know who was in charge."

"Well, it still pissed me off."

She was about to say something else when Bob started walking our way. He stopped a few feet away and signaled for Michelle to follow him. He led her about half way back to the body where they stopped and talked. Bob purposefully kept his voice low so I couldn't hear what he was saying. After a few minutes she came back to me.

"What was that all about?"

"A couple of things, but first, Bob wants you to identify the body for us."

"Me, you all had him downtown just the other day."

"I know. We're sure it's him, but it's always good to have someone other than us make the ID."

"Let's go," I said.

She walked me over to the dead person on the ground, and despite the fact that one third of his face wasn't actually there anymore, I recognized him as Ball. Once I made the ID, Bob motioned to Michelle to take me back away from the crime scene. No thanks, no nothing, just a quick motion of his head. I don't know why, but that irritated me more than Moore's comments had.

As we walked back to the car, two more county vehicles pulled into the makeshift parking lot. One was another van for the forensic team.

"They found a hotel key from the Edgewood Inn, in Manitou, in one of his pockets. Bob wants me to check it out."

I saw Ollie off in the field searching an area as Michelle maneuvered the vehicle back onto the road.

During the trip back, Michelle summarized her conversation with Bob. Although he didn't have an explanation for Ball's death, Bob believed that Ball was the killer we had been looking for. The 9mm resting on the ground next to his extended right arm provided all the evidence he needed.

I told Michelle I didn't think it was that simple and she agreed.

"Another thing he said might interest you," she said.

"What's that?"

"It was Moore's request that I bring you to the scene. He wanted to see you. He used the rationale that you could identify the body, but Bob said he had wanted to see you face to face for a couple of days."

"I hope he was impressed."

"You know," I could see a grin trying to work its way back onto Michelle's face. "Maybe the Feds have had you followed. That comment about being too young for you might have referred to that teenage receptionist you spent the night with last night."

"It wasn't the receptionist and she wasn't a teenager," I said. Michelle was not going to let me live that down.

As we were getting back on the main road, a television van from one of the local networks raced by us toward the crime scene.

Chapter 17

The Edgewood Inn turned out to be of little value. We met two Manitou Springs police officers at the hotel who introduced us to the manager, a white haired man in a leg cast and crutches. I figured he was a little older than me, but when he said he broke his leg in a skate boarding accident I had second thoughts.

Ball had registered under the name of Bell, which explained why the police hotel checks hadn't located him. He paid cash and had spent two nights at the hotel. He had not used the hotel room phone to make any calls, and, as far as anyone could remember, had no visitors. He had not checked out, but he had only registered for the two nights. No one had any idea if Ball had been in the area before his arrival at the hotel, or if he had plans to stay longer.

To ensure Ball was in fact Bell, or vice versa, Michelle shared a copy of a photo she had gotten from somewhere with the hotel staff. The consensus of "I think so" from various members of the hotel staff was good enough for us. A careful search of his room produced nothing but an open shaving kit, an empty suitcase, and a few items of clothing - items that could have belonged to anyone. Forensics would have to do more. The room was sealed, and we left the hotel in the good hands of the Manitou Springs PD.

"So, what do you think?" Michelle asked me while we sat at a small table on the narrow sidewalk, waiting for our sandwiches. We had only driven a few blocks from the hotel when, stopped by a red light, the diner caught her eye, and she suggested we have a late lunch. I'd always been a fan of eating so we stopped.

"About Ball?"

"Yes."

"I don't think he's our murderer. He may have gotten messed up with something illegal, or maybe his wife did, and he had only recently learned about it. I do think he's in the middle of this whole thing, but not as our killer."

"Why?"

"Nothing substantive, unfortunately. It's just my gut feeling on this whole thing. Whoever's done the shooting, even this one, has done this before. It reeks of a professional hit. The alleged link with the mob along with the FBI's interest in what should be a local homicide investigation make me think that there's no way Ball is our guy."

"Unfortunately, I think Bob is going to push Ball as the killer. It clears three homicides off the backlist and takes a lot of heat off him. We know Ball was in Santa Fe the evening of the day Garibaldi was killed, but that doesn't mean he couldn't have done the shooting and gone back south. He was in his office during most of the day his wife was killed, but again, he could have left early and driven back up. It's not so far that it would make it impossible."

"Maybe."

"The investigations will continue, and, of course, Ball's killing will have to be thoroughly looked into, but I can see a lot of people taking the easy way out on this one."

"You're probably right, and I guess it doesn't really matter. I think whoever is behind Ball's death was also behind the others.   Further investigation into the other killings is still necessary to solve the mystery behind Ball's death.   If blaming Ball for the first three lowers the pressure everyone is under, then it may just be a positive."

We ate our lunch under a hot, Colorado sun.   Our conversation drifted between the investigation and people we saw walking by. I enjoyed the lunch and Michelle's company. Her eyes were still bewitching.

Once back in the car we drove in silence to my hotel. She pulled the vehicle adjacent to the front entrance, and I was about to get out when a thought that had been nagging me somewhere in my subconscious for the last couple of days came to surface.

"What else did you find out about the man who was killed with Lynda Ball, in the hotel?"

"Not much at all, the FBI files on him are fairly vague. They have him linked with organized crime but not many specifics. State records indicated a couple of local arrests for assault, but only one conviction that resulted in time already served."

"I thought someone had told me the FBI believed he was an enforcer."

"That's what we were told at first, but the files released to us don't go into that."

"I wonder how much more the feds have that they haven't released?"

"They did say more would be forthcoming," Michelle added.

"Could mean they have a whole bunch and need to screen the files first."

"Well, Grazzard, or whatever his real name is, is dead and he wasn't from here. As far as I see it, unless someone comes up with a link to someone here – other than Ball – I don't expect much from any additional FBI files they do give us."

"You're probably right," I said.

She drove off, and, for the third time that day, I went back to my hotel room. I decided it was time to find out how friendly some old friends might still be.

Rather than going to my room, I headed to a dark corner in the bar and made use of my new cell phone. My first call, however, had to go to my neighbors. After making sure Chubbs was doing just fine, I asked Kaiden, the oldest daughter to retrieve a couple phone numbers from a journal I kept next to my phone in the den. She said she knew exactly what I was referring to, which made me suspicious of how much time she was spending in my house while I was gone. I also told her that I would be gone an extra couple of days. She took that in stride.

My next call went to Debra Devoreaux, a former colleague of mine in OSI. A smart and talented agent, she had spent the five years since her retirement researching organized crime in the United States for a book that she was going to get around to writing someday.

The call surprised her since we hadn't talked in years. After a few minutes of catching up, I got around to the purpose of my call.

"Deb, how thorough has your research into the Mob gotten?"

"It's to the point where I now get calls from the FBI for info. Unfortunately, it's gotten so expansive it intimidates me. I don't know how I can ever get my hands around it enough to write a book."

"Writer's block?"

"That's putting it mildly."

"Would your files have anything on a Frank Grazzard, also known as Serge Branovich, from the Chicago area?"

"Why's that Jim?"

"He was shot and killed here in Colorado Springs...."

"I thought you had settled in New Mexico?"

"I did and I still live there. It's just that I came up here to play some golf and wound up in the middle of a homicide investigation."

"Why should I be surprised?"

"It's a homicide in which the FBI has a great deal of interest."

"You think he's connected to certain elements of organized crime?" Debra asked.

"The FBI has let on that much, but their interest seems to be much more than it should be despite the connection."

"Does this have to do with that politician and his wife being killed?"

"News travels fast. Yes it does," I answered.

"Tell me what you know about Grazzard, and I'll see what I can find about him."

We talked a little more before hanging up. She promised to call me back in a few hours.

I dialed FBI headquarters for my next call. The call was pleasant enough but turned up nothing specific. My contact did tell me that the murders of Grazzard and the Balls had garnered some serious interest at high levels in the Bureau. However, he was out of the loop on this one and didn't want to speculate. The fact that he didn't meant whatever was going on was indeed important in the eyes of the FBI.

I left the darkness of the bar and entered the bright foyer. My eyes had just started to adjust when I heard my name being called by someone sitting on a couch next to the entrance. The sun shone in through the large glass expanse which made up the main entrance to the hotel. The bright light behind the man made it even harder for my eyes to focus on him clearly.

He was dressed in a suit, and I could see his hands clearly. He didn't look like a threat. I approached him as he stood.

"What can I do for you?"

"Just some unofficial advice, West. I'm with the FBI, but I'm not here officially. No creds, no names."

"Except mine," I said.

"Well everyone knows you."

That almost sounded like a threat.

"Okay." I said.

"You've gotten yourself into the middle of something that can be very dangerous for you. We want you to go home now. Just grab your stuff and go home today."

"I'd love to but I've been asked to stay."

"Check again, if you want, and then go home."

"I will."

"Thanks Mr. West. It really is in your best interest, and, if it's important to you – it's in our best interest, too."

He turned and walked away.

I had no interest in following him. He had worn dark sunglasses the whole time. He looked in good shape and had no distinguishable blemishes or other special identifiable features. He could have been a poster boy for the FBI.

So, I had been cautioned away. Was it for my own safety or for the best interest of their investigation?

For some odd reason, I had mixed emotions. I felt relieved that I could now leave, but I never have liked someone telling me to go home. As a compromise to my ego, I decided to clear my departure right away but not leave until tomorrow.

I returned to my room and considered packing, but realized that it would take less than five minutes to do so. Packing could wait until tomorrow. I dialed Claire to let Perry and her know I would be leaving. The call went directly into voice mail. I left a brief message and then repeated the same process with her room phone at the hotel.

I fought the urge to drive out to the Colorado Mountain Brewery to tell Tasha goodbye. That would be awkward. I'd be better off sending her some flowers with a note that said something came up and I had to return to New Mexico. My lack of confidence in handling these rare situations since my divorce demoralized me. Luckily, I had my ex to blame for my predicament.

A return call from Debra interrupted my brief dive into self-pity. It had only been an hour, but she had obviously done some digging.

"Jim, I don't have anything specific about your friend Grazzard; however, I think something serious is going on."

"What do you mean?"

"Bear with me here. What I have is simply a germ of an idea, but I think it may have legs."

"Okay."

"I may be wrong and I need, we need to be careful in what we say on the phone."

"Okay." Did she mean her phone was tapped? "Are you worried about my end or your end?"

"Oh, no, I'm sure our phones are okay, but we may be touching on areas that are best covered on secure lines."

I felt like saying either tell me or don't, but quit beating around the bush. Instead I mumbled another, "Okay."

"There's nothing much yet on Grazzard's death on the net.

But I imagine there will be soon. His real name is Branovich. His death makes the third hit on an alleged member within the organization in the last two weeks. Looks like somebody is cleaning house."

"Interesting."

"There's more and this is the sensitive part, so keep this to yourself. There's been significant FBI interest in each of the homicide investigations. The same assistant deputy director is working all three, and there has been congressional interest in all this."

"That's interesting," I said.

"About a month ago, I learned, unofficially that is, that the FBI was getting close to bringing down a major corruption ring. I haven't heard anything since. I didn't even pay attention to the two prior murders. Now, though, looking at these three killings, the involvement of the Balls, and the fact that the Bureau has gone code red over all this, it appears to me that someone inside the Mob learned about the Justice Department investigation and took steps to plug the leaks."

"That could certainly torpedo the Bureau's efforts and would certainly explain their interest in the homicides."

"Not only their interest," Debra said, "but also their sensitivity over this whole matter. They're not use to leaks affecting their investigations."

"May not be from them, especially if Congress has been kept briefed."

"While that's obvious to you and me, unless the leak is identified, you know both Congress and the press will blame Justice and, more specifically, the FBI."

"I know. I bet the Bureau is jumping through hoops right now."

"I'm glad I retired," Debra said.

"Me, too."

"Jim, I'll keep digging on Grazzard, I mean Branovich."

"Appreciate it. And thanks for the call. I think you're right on with your theory."

I hung up and flopped down on the bed. Debra's hypothesis fit the facts that we had. If so, it made sense that they didn't want me messing around. The FBI could keep local prosecutors and police focused on the homicides, but it traditionally had more difficulty with outside independent investigators and the press. Undoubtedly, the press scared them more than I did. Still, they didn't need me digging around the edges, and I couldn't blame them. I would leave tomorrow.

The only question I had to answer for myself was whether I would spend a day tracking down Carl and Louise. For whatever reason, the urgency I had felt earlier had diminished. The chaining of Louise had shocked me. However, Louise definitely gave me the impression that she accepted it, and she appeared very comfortable around Carl. Bizarre as it seemed to me - perhaps they looked at it as a better solution than a lot of medication or the hiring of a companion.

If only they hadn't disappeared so soon.

Chapter 18

I ended up grabbing a bite to eat in the hotel's restaurant. The rest of the evening I spent in my hotel room watching television.

The vibration of my cell phone woke me up. I noticed the clock in the room said it was seven o'clock, too early for a call. Fighting the urge to ignore the phone as it danced on the night stand, I finally grabbed it.

"Jim, this is Debra. Hope I didn't wake you."

"What's up?" I asked, rather than saying what was really on my mind.

"I woke up early to do some more research on the matter we discussed. As you know, we use the terms Mafia, Mob and organized crime as generic terms to identify groups of individuals loosely or tightly connected in controlling criminal enterprises that can span cities, states and even countries. Depending on their origin, we also use the terms cartel or triads…"

"I know," I interrupted in a tone that was a little harsher than I meant.

"Sorry, it's the lecturer in me."

"That's okay."

"I dug as deeply as I could into Grazzard and the other two bad guys I mentioned yesterday. I'm pretty certain all three had close links with the branch of the Mob that has its fingers into federal and state highway construction. It's not an exact science

Jim, but I'm fairly certain there's a connection."

"It fits very well with your theory, too. I think you have something."

"Me, too. I'm tempted to call an old friend at the Bureau."

"Couldn't hurt, could it?"

"Might be touchy, but I know how to ask the questions."

"If you find out anything specific, will you give me a call?" I asked.

"Sure. I love this stuff."

After I hung up, I thought about Ball. Politics can corrupt people, or maybe it's people who corrupt politics. He was a member of the New Mexican legislature and had a role in determining how the state spent its money. If I dug deeper, I'd likely find that he had focused most of his influence toward highway construction funds.

The same question returned: Were both Balls involved? If so, why the separate travel, and why had he stayed in a different hotel. More importantly, if he was the killer, what was his motivation for killing his wife and the others? If he was involved in the corruption and she wasn't, why was she here in the Springs?

Bob's theory that he had hired Garibaldi to follow his wife, and then killed Garibaldi to keep his discovery silent seemed a stretch. Could Ball be that cold blooded? Bob theorized that after killing Garibaldi, Ball drove back to New Mexico. He returned the following afternoon to find his wife and her "lover" and killed them both. Possible, if he was that cold blooded. The police interviewed him after Lynda's murder. Rather than go home, he stayed in the area and tried to kill another person, unknown. This time it backfired, and he was killed.

I still didn't like it. I could see its attractiveness to Bob, but I didn't like it. The murder investigation intrigued me. I had to admit that. However, I had officially been warned off, and if the locals would also give me the green light today, as I expected them to do, by nightfall I would be back in my own bed.

I packed my stuff, loaded my car and checked out of the hotel. I started to drive to the sheriff's offices but realized that it was Sunday. Someone would be there, but more than likely Michelle was at home. I decided to wait an hour or so before I called her, so I headed out to find the Schafli's Donuts I had been to earlier in the week.

Sitting there sipping very hot coffee and munching on a couple of cinnamon donuts, my thoughts moved from the murder to Carl and Louise. Fairplay was a very small town, but driving there and spending a couple of hours to locate them, before heading south, would result in an extremely long day.

"Domestic situations always suck," I said to myself, repeating an axiom I had heard dozens of times, years ago. An old, grisly veteran agent I had worked with early in my military career would invariably say that phrase every time our office had a domestic abuse case thrown our way.

He would usually follow the statement with the same question, "Did I ever tell you the time both husband and wife beat each other to bloody pulps?"

We would quickly answer him by saying that he had, many times. Both husband and wife drank too much, quarreled too much, and got violent too many times. But they stayed together. It wasn't even that interesting.

What fascinated me about the old agent was his ability to follow up our response by saying, "Well, how about this one?"

He would then go into a totally different case each time. Why he invariably used the same example in his opening question always baffled me. I even asked him once why he always asked us about the same case when he had so many other ones he could ask about. He simply said he didn't know.

No matter what type of crime, if it involved family member on family member he referred to it as a "domestic situation."

If we got to the alleged crime quickly enough there might be physical evidence we could use to help us prove or disprove the allegation. However, if the allegation involved incidents that had happened in the past and the physical evidence was just not there, the case usually turned into the proverbial can of worms.

Carl had chained Louise - not normal, but not acceptable? My dad once told me that when he was a toddler and wanted to play outdoors, his mother would put him on a leash in the backyard, so he wouldn't wonder off while she was in the house doing chores.

And yet, I had also heard the horrible stories about women who had been kidnapped and kept for years.

Maybe I should just leave Carl and Louise to the authorities, too. Who was I to solve all the problems in the world?

My phone buzzed in my pocket.

"Jim," Michelle said, "the sheriff just called me and said to send you home. I told him I would pass the message to you, but that I didn't think I could make you go home. He told me to make my best effort. Just yesterday they wanted you close by. I don't know what's going on."

"Not a problem, Michelle. An FBI guy came by yesterday and told me to go home. I think someone up high doesn't want me messing around."

"But you aren't messing around. I mean, when you get right

down to it we aren't doing anything. None of us are doing anything but responding to one murder scene after another. I don't know what business it is of the FBI's anyway."

"Don't get yourself worked up, Michelle. I should go home."

There was a long pause at the other end of the line. "This pisses me off," she finally said.

"I can always come back."

"I guess that's true." Another pause, "Can I buy you a going away, thank you for your help lunch before you go? I'm treating Ollie to lunch as a thank you, and I know she would love for you to be there, too."

I told her I'd be happy to have lunch with her, and we arranged for her to pick me up at the hotel just before noon. That would give me just enough time to swing by the hospital and check on Perry.

At the hospital I found Perry, Claire and Doris playing dominoes together in Perry's room. Since Perry was still hooked up to monitors, a mobile cart served as a playing surface. Both Doris and Claire sat in chairs next to the bed, on opposite sides of the cart. I could hear their laughter before I arrived at his room.

They must have been playing for a while because they seemed pleased with my interruption. I stayed and visited for about an hour. Perry's condition had improved and he believed he would be released in another day or two. Doris' eyes didn't appear as sharp as they had on the previous occasions I'd seen her, but I kept my thoughts to myself.

I told them I would be leaving for Clovis later in the day. They wished me a safe trip, but I sensed that they had little interest if I stayed or left. Maybe I wasn't completely out of Claire's doghouse.

Michelle called while I waited for her in the hotel's lobby. She had been delayed and asked if I would drive myself to the restaurant. She thought Ollie might already be there, but she hadn't been able to reach her on her phone to tell her she'd be late. She started to apologize for the inconvenience, but I cut her off.

The restaurant turned out to be easy to find. I had driven by it just about every day I'd been in Colorado. It was on Highway 24 close to the turn off Michelle and I had taken when we were following up on the anonymous report on the gun. The last turn Michelle's poor Jeep would ever make. The restaurant sat about two hundred yards from the main road and shared a building with the Rocky Top RV and Camping Rentals.

I almost didn't recognize Ollie in the restaurant. She was sitting by herself next to a front window wearing a black sweatshirt with the hood up. She was reading the Sunday paper.

I walked over to her, but a young, bouncy blond server carrying a cup of coffee beat me to the table. Ollie looked up and thanked the waitress. Only then did she see me.

"Mr. West, good to see you."

"It's Jim, not Mr. West, and it's good to see you, too."

"I'm supposed to be having lunch with Lieutenant Prado, but she hasn't shown up. Would you like to join me?"

"Love to," I said, as I scooted into the booth opposite her. "Actually, Michelle asked me to come to lunch, too. She's been delayed but should be here soon. She wanted me to keep you company until she arrives."

"If I'd known you were coming, I would've worn something nicer."

"You look fine," I said.

"Sunday, when I can get it off, is my day of rest. No weights, no cleaning, no yard work."

"As it should be," I chimed in.

"I like to read and take long walks, weather permitting."

"Play golf?"

"No, never tried it. Been a cart girl, carrying the beer around in a couple of tournaments, but that's about the extent of my time on a golf course."

Her left hand went up to her hood and, after a moment's hesitation, pushed the hood back onto her shoulders.

"Sorry about my hair."

I didn't know what she meant. Her hair looked fine.

"I have a small cabin about three miles from here. I often walk in for breakfast or lunch when I'm off. I walked today," she said.

I sensed she said this as an explanation for her hair or her overall appearance.

"You own your own place?" I asked.

"Yes. An actual log cabin, I purchased it last year, about this time."

"Neat."

"The original owners went through a divorce and were happy to get rid of it. The housing market had been in the dumps and neither of them wanted the place anyway. My good luck to hear about it first."

"Live there by yourself?"

"My mother lives with me."

"Is it in a town?"

"No, it's in a small development of about twenty scattered homes just off 24, a mile before Green Mountain Falls. Most people there commute to C. Springs for work."

I had a cup of coffee as we sat there and talked. Michelle, it appeared, was going to be really late.

Ollie and I hadn't spent any time alone before this, and, although there was no reason for it to have, it surprised me to find Ollie such an interesting person and a very good conversationalist. She also had a dry sense of humor that I really liked.

While we discussed whether we should order or wait longer for Michelle, I noticed a man walk by my Mustang, stop and do a double take. I hadn't been watching him, although I was aware of his presence as he walked through the restaurant parking lot. When he stopped and stared at my car, he got my full attention. I could see him quite well.

"Ollie, that's the guy."

"What guy?"

I realized she had not been involved in the early stages of the investigation.

"That certainly looks like the second guy at the table with Lynda Ball. The one everyone is now trying to locate."

As we talked about him, the man did a smooth about face. He didn't display any panic. He simply turned around and left. He never looked back to see if anyone was watching him.

I stood up. Ollie did the same.

"Are you sure?" she asked.

"Pretty sure. He stopped when he saw my car. I saw him look down at my tags and then he left." I repeated what I was thinking. "He was coming in here, but he left when he saw my car."

"Does he know your car?"

I moved toward the entrance as she asked the question. She followed. Our server came quickly around the counter, and I motioned to her we'd be right back.

"What are you doing?" Ollie asked as we reached the door. This time she had a hand on my arm.

"I want to get a license tag number and a look at where he's going."

We both walked out into the bright sunshine and, in unison, grabbed for our sunglasses. The sound of a motorcycle revved up from the side of the building. I instinctively stepped back behind the open door as the motorcycle raced out of the parking lot. The guy now had on a helmet and wore a partially zipped black leather jacket. The motorcycle took a sharp right at the edge of the lot and disappeared behind the trees. He was heading away from Highway 24 on the same road we had taken to get to the restaurant.

"Damn," I said.

"What?"

"I couldn't see the license number."

"Colorado tag, D435G," Ollie said.

I didn't question her. I jotted the number down on the paper napkin I had brought from the table. I tore the napkin in half and jotted the number down again. I gave Ollie the second copy.

"Where does that road go?" I asked.

"Nowhere. It goes back into the woods a mile or so and stops. There are a few cabins back there and a lot of places to camp just off the road. The place next door has an area out back and on the side of the building where RV's and campers can stay for a fee. They have showers and sell necessities. But back there, it's open land. It's part of a state park, so a lot of people make use of it."

"Good place for someone to stay if they didn't want to be found."

"Certainly would be," Ollie agreed. "Do you think that might be the guy who tried to kill you?"

"Yes."

"Jim, I want you to wait here for Michelle. I'll take a quick spin down that road just to see if I can get an idea where he may have gone."

"Hold on, you shouldn't be doing that by yourself."

"You can't go. He knows your car anyway."

"Ollie, you walked here."

"I know someone here who will loan me his truck."

"Let's wait for Michelle, or at least get some backup."

"I won't do anything stupid." She patted her hip, "I'm not defenseless. I'll just drive down that road, get to the end and come back. Anyone who sees me won't think anything of it." She ran back into the restaurant.

I walked out to my car. I didn't like Ollie's idea. After a few seconds, I returned to the restaurant. I didn't see her anywhere inside, so I went back to our table to wait. I started to dial Michelle's number when I saw Ollie and a tall skinny guy wearing an apron, his hair in a hairnet, walk out to an old, beaten up pickup truck that was parked on the side lot.

Ollie jumped into the truck and drove off. The man turned and sauntered back into the restaurant.

I finished dialing Michelle and finally reached her.

"Hey, Jim, you at the restaurant?" she asked before I could say anything.

"Yes, but we've got a situation here." I went on to explain what had just happened and my reservations about Ollie taking off on her own.

"She's a smart one. I don't think she'll do anything stupid."

I didn't feel any better.

"Anyway, Jim, I'm only a mile or two out. I'll call her and ask her to come back and wait for me."

"Thanks," I said.

I flagged down our server and asked for the bill. I explained that we had to run for a few minutes and should be right back. She mumbled something like, "No sweat." I realized then that I was sweating.

I walked outside and stood by my car. If I had Ollie's number, I'd have called her. The hairs on the back of my neck were doing the cha-cha. I waited a very long five minutes before I saw Michelle turn off Highway 24. At that same moment, I saw a pickup with an attached camper on its bed come out of the woods.

Carl? The thought raced through my mind as the pickup passed in front of me and drove past Michelle, who approached from the highway. I stared at the pickup, my mind racing with thoughts, before I realized the driver was staring back at me. It wasn't Carl. Not unless he had shrunk. Plus, this guy didn't look anything like Carl. The pickup wasn't even the right color and Carl had a large trailer that he towed. This one was much smaller.

Michelle pulled in to park in a space two cars down from me. I walked over to her.

"Ollie's fine," she said as she climbed out of her jeep. "Sorry about my being late. The press is all over the sheriff and the DA. There's going to be a big briefing this afternoon and everyone involved was called in this morning for a meeting. I couldn't get away."

My focus was back on the pickup. It had turned onto Highway 24 and headed away from Colorado Springs. Nothing felt right.

"Can you call Ollie again?"

"I just called her, not five minutes ago. Weren't you listening?"

"I heard you. Try her again."

She looked at me dubiously, but she took her phone out of the side pocket of her purse and dialed Ollie's number. As she did, I noticed she had gotten dressed up today. An odd realization for me, I thought, since my mind had been so focused elsewhere. I wondered what the occasion was.

"No answer. That's strange," she said almost to herself.

"Might mean nothing," I said, "but why don't we drive down there?"

"Oh, I'm sure she's okay. The signal is spotty out here."

"I'll drive."

"Okay, you win, but I'll drive."

I walked quickly to her car.

"You sure it was the same guy?" Michelle asked as we drove off.

"Pretty sure. He looked the same as I remembered him. I wouldn't have even noticed him if he hadn't done a double take when he passed my car."

"Did he get a look at Ollie?"

"I don't think so."

"That's good."

As soon as we entered the woods, the road turned from pavement to dirt and narrowed. The trees and thick underbrush made it hard to see more than a few yards into the woods. I described to Michelle the pickup Ollie had borrowed. We hadn't gone far when I spotted a cleared area about twenty five yards off the road that had been used recently as a campsite. I looked hard but didn't see anyone there.

We spotted another empty campsite, then another. Each area included a large metal trash can and a concrete picnic table. I thought of the pickup truck that I saw leave the area. It would be possible to maneuver a trailer into one of the campsites, but it would take a skilled driver.

"How far have we come?" I asked.

"I don't know. I didn't look at the odometer when we left the restaurant. Sorry."

"It doesn't matter. I'm not even sure why I asked." I would have checked, but there was no reason to put any blame on her. I certainly could have asked her to check when we left the restaurant.

We came over a rise and the area surrounding the road cleared into a large field. Two camper trailers had been pulled a few yards off the road and were parked close together. An old Suburban was parked next to them. I didn't see anyone. Michelle slowed the car as we looked. I shook my head and we drove off. A motorcycle could have been hidden behind the trailers, but not the old pickup Ollie had driven.

Michelle had taken her phone out of her purse and once again dialed Ollie's number.

"No answer," he said. Her face took on the same apprehensive look that I already wore.

After another hundred yards we were back in the thick forest and the road became bumpier and crooked.

"Looks like we must be coming to the end of the road," I said.

The road turned sharply to the left and we climbed a short steep hill. At the top, the road turned back to the right and after about fifty yards ended in what I would describe as a cul-de-sac if it was situated in Clovis. We saw the pickup Ollie had driven.

Michelle hit the brakes, and we stopped hard. The front right tire dropped into a pothole as we did. In different circumstances I would have ribbed her about her driving skills. In different circumstances she would have likely apologized for the jarring stop. But we both sat still and quietly took in the scene.

The open driver's door of the pickup screamed out at me and a bad memory flashed back. Years ago, I raced to an informant's house to warn her that she may have been compromised. We couldn't reach her by phone. I had pulled into her driveway and stepped out of the car before I saw the front door to her house wide open. Like now, I had rationalized there could be a million reasons why the door might be open. Yet, I knew better then, just like I knew better now. I found our informant with her throat sliced open. Her blood was still flowing out of her when I found her. She died before an ambulance arrived.

"Stay here!" Michelle ordered as she jumped out of the car. She approached the pickup, her issued Glock held tight in both hands and pointed in front of her. I felt like the proverbial character in a movie who is told to "stay here", only to not do so. I compromised by getting out of the car but standing by it.

I looked quickly around but couldn't see anything of interest. Michelle, approaching the pickup didn't have a better view of the surroundings than I did. However, as she made her way around the front of the truck, that changed.

"Jim! Come here quick, it's Ollie!"

I saw her disappear on the other side of the pickup. I ran to her. Ollie was sprawled in an unnatural position on the ground. There was a pool of blood around her head and left shoulder. Michelle was already there checking vitals.

I fought to take my eyes off her and studied the area on this side of the truck. I still didn't see anything.

"I've got a pulse!" Michelle shouted, and then more quietly, "I mean I think I do. Damn, girl, hang in there!"

I grabbed my phone out of my pocket and dialed 911.

"Michelle, here," I held out my phone to her. "I dialed 911, but you can better tell them where we are."

She grabbed my phone from me. I could see blood on her hand. As Michelle started talking on the phone, I bent over and studied Ollie as delicately as I could.

I couldn't find a pulse at first, but then I felt it. Faint, but at least she was still alive. Ollie had two obvious wounds. The least significant appeared to be a bullet wound to her left shoulder. It looked nasty but had missed all vital areas. The one that scared me was the one to the head. The top right corner of her forehead looked like it was missing, or maybe the bullet simply crushed that part of her head into her brain.

The flow of blood out of her wounds into the large pool that partially surrounded her head seemed slow. I hoped that implied shock or some other defense reaction by the body.

"Hang in there, kid," I whispered into her ear. "We're getting you to a hospital. You just hang in there."

I looked up at Michelle. She had taken a few paces away, my phone still plastered to her ear. I ran back to the car and retrieved a first aid kit in the trunk. By the time I had it opened next to Ollie, Michelle leaned down to help.

"They said to cover the wounds with something clean and to keep pressure on the one on the shoulder."

"The shoulder is the easy one," I replied. Michelle and I made a good team. In less than a minute, we had the sweatshirt cut open and her shoulder wrapped as tightly as we dared. The head had us both scared. We gently pressed a clean gauze pad against the wound and wrapped her head to hold the gauze bandage in place.

"God," Michelle said, "I don't know if the ambulance will get here in time."

"Take her in your car back to the restaurant. That can save her a few minutes. You can't miss the ambulance, even if they beat you to the restaurant."

Michelle didn't argue. We gently picked Ollie up and placed her on the back seat. We used the middle seat belt to hold her in place.

"Aren't you getting in?" Michelle shouted, as she jumped in.

"No, I'll stay here with the pickup and the crime scene."

Michelle drove off, and I stood there in the growing silence. She disappeared around the first bend in the dirt road, but I could hear the distant sound of her engine for another thirty seconds. Then everything was quiet, almost eerie.

I walked back to where we found Ollie. Her police Glock was still lying on the ground next to where her body had been. I squatted down and studied it. I don't really like guns. I never had. Sure, I'd handled a lot of them and spent my entire twenty years in the military assigned one. First it was a big .38 revolver, then a more compact one, then a .45 semiautomatic pistol, and finally a 9mm. They were all effective and each one was an improvement over the previous one.

I had grown up in a family that owned a lot of guns. I even joined a teenage shooting club that did fixed target shoots and skeet competition. In the military, I routinely fired expert at my quarterly qualifications with OSI. It's nothing to brag about, most agents routinely qualified as expert.

While I never joined the National Rifle Association, I have

always been a staunch advocate of the second amendment. I can even appreciate why some people collect guns. The danger is rarely with the gun – it's almost always with the person.

My dislike of guns is purely a personal thing. There's a great responsibility that any person who carries a weapon has to shoulder. When I was younger, I took this responsibility for granted. Over time I realized that I shouldn't. Finally, by the time I left the service, I realized I had come too close to shooting an innocent person on more than one occasion. I had also almost gotten myself shot once or twice by another agent because of something stupid I had done during the heat of an operation.

By the time I retired from the service, turning in my weapon was a relief. Since then, I have tried to focus my life on enjoying the simple things. It hadn't always worked and like Michelle had said, dead bodies seemed to pop up around me. Maybe that was fate, but it wasn't my desire. I don't carry a weapon anymore because in the life I want, I wouldn't have a need for one. I didn't hang up a sign announcing "private dick for hire," because I never wanted to. However, as I have painfully learned, fate writes its own script.

It did so again, right then and there, as I stared at Ollie's pistol. In the distance I could hear it, the faint sound of a motorcycle engine starting up. I could understand his trying to kill me. I had stuck my head right into his face and made myself a problem. Ten minutes ago, I would have been happy to go home, to stay away from this guy, and let the police do their thing.

But I liked Ollie. I considered her a sweet kid and, perhaps more importantly, a friend. She wore civilian clothes when they had encountered each other. He didn't know she was a cop and shouldn't have shot her – probably killed her.

I reached down and picked up the pistol. It didn't smell as though it had been fired recently. I checked and found the magazine fully loaded. I tucked the weapon under my belt and went to the pickup. I found another loaded magazine in Ollie's large bag purse and slipped it into my pocket.

I looked around again and tried to see where the sound of the motorcycle engine was coming from. It suddenly stopped, but I thought I had a fix on its direction. I inspected the pickup truck for bullet holes or any other damage that might appear recent. I saw nothing. There was nothing remarkable on the ground around the truck. I expanded my search of the area to the rest of the dirt road. I didn't worry about ruining any footprints as the ground was extremely hard and dry. The immediate perimeter of the area looked just as bare.

Two wide areas, on opposite sides of the cul-de-sac, had been mowed and leveled to serve as campsites. Each had the same cement picnic table and trash can that I had seen at the other campsites along the dirt road. One area looked like it hadn't been used in a while. Even the trash can was empty. I inspected the area but didn't see anything interesting.

I walked over to the other campsite. Someone had recently used the site. I found the trash can partially full and a paper towel positioned on top of the trash looked as though it still had a couple of wet spots. I spotted an area on top of the soil, about ten feet to the right of the picnic table, where oil had apparently leaked from a vehicle. I estimated the spot to be about six inches wide. The oil was still wet. A lone Frito chip perched on the bench of the table closest to me.

He or they couldn't have been gone long, I thought. A bird or squirrel wouldn't let that chip last too long. My mind drifted to the pickup truck with the attached camper that I watched leave the area as Michelle had driven in. The driver definitely wasn't the man I had seen earlier, but someone else could have been concealed elsewhere in the truck or camper.

I reached for my phone to call Michelle. For a second I checked all my pockets, but then I realized I had given my phone to Michelle to talk to the 911 operator. She hadn't given it back. I wanted to tell her that she needed to get someone to check out the pickup I had seen. Something about the pickup gnawed at my mind.

Closing my eyes for a minute, I tried to concentrate on what I had seen. The side of the camper displayed a leopard or a cheetah as a logo. A dent scarred the driver's side rear corner of the pickup. Then it jumped out at me like a flare in the darkness. On the back of the camper, to the right of the door, I had seen a reinforced bike hitch. No motorcycle or bike hung on it, so it didn't mean anything to me at the time.

As if on cue, the distant sound of a small gas engine broke the silence. I walked over to a well-worn hiking path that ran off the dirt road. The path was almost as wide as a sidewalk and disappeared in the forest about fifty yards away. I walked a few yards down the path, staying on its left edge.

"Ollie, I could sure use you now," I said to myself. I got down on my hands and knees and scrutinized the path. A soft cool breeze blew by, interrupting the otherwise calm air. Suddenly I saw them - the tracks of a tire. Once I knew where to look the track line seemed to jump out at me. I had no way to be certain how long ago a set of wheels had rolled over this part of the path, but I had a pretty good idea.

I stood up. The sound of the small engine had again stopped. The engine appeared to be used intermittently.

Driving the bike on this path would be easy, it was fairly flat. Down further, though, I wondered if it became much harder to maneuver on. He might only be using the engine in short hops where he could ride. Another thought crept to mind, what if he only used the engine to help him push the bike over steep areas where it was too hard to push it.

Another sound broke the silence. This one grew over time. A car approached. I walked back to the spot where we found Ollie and then moved around the pickup, so I had a clear view of the approaching car. I didn't have to wait long.

A sheriff's sedan pulled into view with its lights flashing. The driver had to have seen me, but I waved and smiled anyway. I've dealt with nervous lawmen in the past. A young deputy jumped out of the car, his gun in hand. Fortunately, he kept it aimed at the ground.

"Are you Jim West?"

"Yes, I am. Do you know if they got Ollie to an ambulance?" I didn't expect much of an answer, but I wanted to reinforce the fact that we were on the same team.

"I don't know. I passed Lt. Prado just where the road turned to dirt. She told me you would be down here. I'm here to guard the crime scene." He looked at the pickup truck. I could see he was trying to piece together what had happened.

"Over here, I'll show you where we found Ollie."

"Yeah, I see the blood," the deputy said when he approached the spot.

"I know you need to seal off the area, but before you do can you call Lieutenant Prado for me. I need to give her a message."

He looked at me dubiously.

"What's your connection with all this?" he asked.

"I'm just a friend. I was with Michelle when we found Ollie. I stayed here to preserve the scene until someone official could come and relieve me."

He studied me for a second longer before he dialed his phone. He must have gone through a central dispatch, because I heard him ask someone to patch him through to Michelle. Once he had her, he handed me the phone.

"Jim," she sounded breathless. "The ambulance is taking her out of my car right now. A helicopter is approaching to take her to the hospital."

"She'll make it. She's a tough one."

"I don't know. There's blood all over the back seat."

"There was blood all over her when we put her there. The doc's can do miracles nowadays."

"I know, I know. I just feel so awful."

"Me, too. Michelle, I have a suggestion for you." I paused for a second, but she didn't say anything. "When you were pulling onto the road to the restaurant a pickup with an attached camper was pulling out. Did you see it?"

"If I did, I don't remember it."

I described the vehicle to her.

"I still don't remember it," she said.

"That's okay, but I suggest you have someone check it out. I have a feeling it may be worthwhile to find out who's driving it and what all is inside it."

"You think he's the guy?"

"Not the guy I saw before, but someone had been camping out here next to the spot where Ollie was shot. There's a hitch for a motorcycle on the back of the camper and one wasn't there."

"Hardly damaging information."

"I know, but someone has a motorcycle out here moving away from this spot right now."

"You mean back in the hills?"

"Yes."

"That doesn't make sense. You can't get a bike through those hills unless you're on a trail."

"There is a trail here. I have a nagging suspicion the camper and the shooter are connected somehow. Can you get someone to try to check it out?"

She said she would, and I again described the pickup and camper. I told her it headed away from Colorado Springs and gave her the time I last saw it.

After I hung up, something about the motorcycle that my assailant had driven that day came to mind. I hadn't thought much of it then, but the motorcycle hadn't been a big, powerful one. I knew they made motorcycles that could be used both on road as well as off road. I wondered if that was, in fact, what he was driving out there right now.

The deputy had already sealed off the entrance to the cul-de-sac and had started to mark a large perimeter around Ollie's borrowed pickup and the spot where we found her. I returned his phone.

"If you have a way back, you can go," he said. "I assume Lieutenant Prado knows how to reach you."

A sarcastic response tried to slip past my lips. It couldn't be hard to see there was no other transportation in the area.

"I'll stay out of your way. I need to head out into the woods for a few minutes anyway." I figured he would take that as meaning I had to go to the bathroom and not worry about me for a while – if at all.

I left him guarding his little piece of the earth, and I walked away down the same path I believed the man with the motorcycle had taken. As soon as the trees hid me from the deputy, I started jogging. I'm not fast and I don't particularly like to run, but I can jog for a long time.

I had already done the calculations in my head. He had left at least twenty minutes ahead of me, but no more than forty. That could be a lot of territory to make up. I also realized the more time he could ride his bike on the trail, the harder, if not impossible, it would be to catch him. However, I had also figured that there would be lengthy patches where riding a motorcycle might not be possible, and in those areas where he had to push the bike, I would make up time. Finally, he might only be going to a fixed spot to hide out for a day or two. Somewhere in my brain the realization came to me that this guy had to be extremely familiar with the area we were in.

The reality of my situation didn't escape me. I fully realized that the odds were that I would never catch up with him. Two and a half hours, and I would turn around. That would get me back to the crime scene by six or six thirty. My return trip would likely be slower. It would still be light enough to see my way. Once on the road, if no one was there anymore, I could walk it in the dark. Worst case - today would be a day of exercise. At least that's what I thought at the time.

Chapter 19

The fact that Michelle had my cell phone would keep her, her bosses and the FBI off my back until I returned. I knew not having one could also be a bad thing if something were to happen to me.

I transferred Ollie's Glock from my waistband to the right pocket of my windbreaker and carried it in my right hand. If you haven't done it before, trust me, jogging with a pistol when you're not wearing a holster can be quite uncomfortable.

After about a half mile the trail entered an area where it passed through a narrow canyon. The trail itself became uneven, the ground pockmarked with softball sized rocks and holes which appeared to be scattered strategically to trip the unwary hiker. I slowed to a fast walking pace. I couldn't see anyone driving a bike through here. The path crossed a dry streambed and then climbed a series of naturally tiered rock steps.

Above the steps, the incline became steeper but smoother. The tracks of a motorcycle had recently dug themselves into some soft soil. He must have turned on the engine to help get his bike up the hill. I imagined he still pushed it, using a low gear to have it move on its own as he guided it. That was what I had heard: his periodic use of the engine to help him maneuver the bike up steep grades.

He wouldn't have come out here just to push his bike forever. He must have had something in mind. If he really knew the area, he might know a spot where the path crossed another road, dirt or paved. If he could access a way to drive his bike out to a different highway, the police would never catch him. All the police checkpoints would be focused on Highway 24, either heading into Colorado Springs or deeper into the mountains.

The other possibility was that he had a hideout somewhere out here. There could be any number of old abandoned cabins or even a cave - somewhere he could lay low for a few days. Perhaps both, I thought, as I picked up my pace when the ground flattened.

Suddenly two large deer broke cover to my left and dashed from some shrubs into the denser forest. Tall pines towered over me and closed in nearer to the trail. They blocked the bright sunshine, and the air instantly became cooler. I ran across a couple of fallen pines that blocked my way. I easily jumped them as I went by, but I knew they would significantly slow down my quarry.

The trail continued to weave through the tall pines. The thick underbrush restricted my visibility in all directions. Two Coke cans littered the side of the trail, evidence that the trail was used by hikers. More concrete evidence popped up alongside the trail, and it came in that form. A short concrete pillar with "1 mile" etched in black paint stood on the edge of the trail.

I glanced at my watch. Twelve minutes, not bad for this terrain, I thought. Still, I picked up my pace. I didn't worry about suddenly running into him. The odds were that I'd never catch him. If I did, he'd be more surprised than I would. He had to believe that no one would think he headed into the woods. Additionally, he wouldn't have anticipated we'd find

Ollie so quickly, and that someone would be after him on the trail shortly thereafter. Surprise would be on my side – unless he saw me coming from a distance, and in these thick, hilly woods seeing me from a distance was highly unlikely.

I jogged another quarter mile until the trail zigzagged up a steep hill. I looked for more tire tracks thinking he would use the bike's engines to help climb the hill. I didn't see any. For the first time, I started to have serious doubts that he stayed on the trail this long.

"Stay focused," I told myself. If he had already left the trail, there was nothing I could do about it. Besides, I hadn't seen any practical place he could have turned off. Hiking away from the trail would be very strenuous. Pushing a motorbike through the terrain out here would be impossible.

I'd be lying if I didn't admit that while jogging through those trees, a substantial part of me wanted him to be already gone – out of reach. I wasn't fooling myself; I knew I had no business doing what I was doing. Wasn't this one of the reasons I was happy to turn in my badge and retire?

But I'd already debated this in my mind, and I had made my decision before I picked up Ollie's gun. If it was simply a matter of locating him and pointing him out to the authorities, I would have left the gun on the ground and chosen that option. I knew then, as I stared at that pistol, what I still believed. The only chance to catch him was for me to follow him down the trail as soon as possible. I could've told the deputy and urged him to go after the killer, but he wouldn't have left the crime scene. If he even gave my theory any credence.

By the time a pursuit could've been organized, it would have been way too late. The killer would escape. He would blend into society and be free to kill another Garibaldi, another

Lynda Ball, and another Ollie. And that was it really, wasn't it? He crossed a line shooting Ollie. She had been with me moments before. We had just been sitting there talking and laughing together. She was a good kid, in her mid-twenties. I liked her. Hell, I could've been her father.

I shouldn't have let her drive off alone. I'd have to live with that guilt. She was the cop, but I had years of experience on her. I let her go down that road by herself, while I simply sat there and twiddled my fingers. He shouldn't have shot her. Now, I owed it to Ollie not to let him kill again.

The trail started to follow a steep, rocky slope down the side of a hill and I had to slow to a careful walk. The pines spread out, and for the first time in a while, I could see for a distance out in front of me. I paused and studied the trail in the distance as it appeared and disappeared a dozen times before it disappeared completely behind a far off hill.

A short but bright flash in the distance caught my eyes. I stared hard at the spot but couldn't see anything. His bike reflecting the sun? Could be, I thought, maybe a mile ahead, maybe less.

As the trail flattened out at the base of the hill, the terrain around me opened up even more. I was in a field with no cover to hide me from searching eyes. Tall hills on both sides of me shot up into the sky. A shorter one in front of me appeared as a wall that would surely block my further progress in less than a mile. I could only hope that he hadn't stopped and was now watching the trail behind him. I picked up my pace. The tree line stood about three hundred yards ahead of me, but my fatigue limited my acceleration from the slow jog to one that was simply a little faster.

Eventually, the trees at the far end closed around me and I

slowed my pace to preserve energy. The cover of the thick underbrush and pines sent a calming shadow over me. I considered the silence of the forest, interrupted only by the occasional bird, almost eerie. If he started up the motorcycle again, I had no doubt that I would hear it.

The trail took a sharp right and started a seemingly non-ending weave of twists and turns, up and down, but mostly up as it traversed some of the roughest terrain I'd seen since beginning my chase. This would be almost impossible with a motorcycle. I looked at my watch and saw that twenty-five minutes had passed.

I slowed to a walk. I didn't have the strength or desire to run up the hillside. Thinking that this might have been the spot where I saw the flash of sunlight reflecting off his bike, I looked backwards. However, with all the turns the trail had, I couldn't be sure which direction to look.

Following the trail remained easy, but it wouldn't be easy to do so in the dark. I had time, I told myself, but if I didn't find him in the next hour, I needed to turn around. That would cut off a little time that I had originally planned for my pursuit; however, now that I was out here, my fear of getting lost had grown.

As I continued on, the trees and underbrush became thicker. Another small concrete pillar jutted up from the ground. The words "two miles," etched in black, had been written on both sides of the pillar. I kept moving. The uneven ground slanted from left to right indicating I was on the side of a hill. When it flattened out, I started jogging again. I still couldn't see more than thirty to fifty yards in any direction.

I crossed a creek bed that had a couple of inches of frigid water in it. Early run off from the mountains, I guessed. I managed to jump from rock to slippery rock without getting wet. The trail continued up a gradual slope and then leveled off, the trees and shrubs suddenly disappearing. I found myself staring out into a vast valley. I could see ranch houses and a road in the distance. A fence stopped any further progress, and a final small cement pillar said end of trail. A sign on the fence read, "Private property, stay out!"

What I did not see was another human being. I didn't see or hear a motorcycle. I sat down on a large boulder, admiring the view and getting my strength back. I had sweated through my shirt. In the cool air and bright sunshine, I could see the steam escaping from inside my jacket.

"This guy is smart," I mumbled to myself. I had no doubt if he came this far, he knew a way to get past the fence and down to the road. From there, he could simply disappear again. I'd be lying if I claimed that part of me wasn't happy that he had gotten away.

I sat there for about fifteen minutes until the distant sound of thunder reminded me I'd better start back. I looked at the sky but didn't see anything ominous. Of course, storms frequently came in from the west, and my view to the west was blocked by the towering hills.

I began my return trek at a more relaxed pace. If I got wet, I got wet - a fitting finish for a bad day.

Chapter 20

Less than a minute after I started my return, I found myself back in the dense forest. My eyes had to adjust to the change in lighting. Traveling slower and in the opposite direction, I decided to make a special effort to study the area along the return trail just in case I could find any evidence that indicated the killer turned off early. Not likely, I thought, but I had nothing else to do.

A hawk screeched somewhere above me. As it did so, the birds around me became quiet. The terrain started its downward slope and I could hear the gurgling of the water in the stream I had crossed earlier.

I stopped at the water's edge to select my safest way across. Eight feet wide and barely a foot deep at its deepest, the creek didn't pose much of a barrier. However, the last rock I had used crossing it was a good three feet from my shoreline, and its small top barely broke the surface. It had been easy to use coming from the opposite direction as it sat there only about a foot and a half from a larger rock. An even further rock had made my first crossing a simple matter of a few easy steps from the far shore and then a leap to the shoreline on which I presently stood. Now my first step would consist of a leap to a very small target.

Not wanting to get wet, I decided to look for an easier crossing. As narrow as the creek was, I didn't think it would be hard to find one. I had only taken a few steps to my left, my attention focused on the creek, when the sound of a nearby motorcycle engine roared to life.

I instinctively leapt for cover behind a small scraggily bush. At the same time I willed my heart back out of my throat and back into its normal place. I took some deep breaths in an effort to get my heartbeat back down below redline and decided to check later to see if I had ruined my underwear.

The motor sounded as though it had to be right on top of me, but I couldn't see it. I slowly stood up, Ollie's pistol in hand. I moved to a more secure position behind a pine tree. The engine sound didn't appear to be moving. It had to be to my left, not too far past the nearby bend in the creek.

I moved in its direction, hugging the tree line until it ran into the rocky face of a small ledge that had diverted the creek. I couldn't move further along this side of the creek without getting into the water. I took a tentative step onto a log that partially traversed the creek. The motorcycle had to be across the creek and couldn't be more than a few yards away, but the dense brush continued to hide it.

I took a second short step on the log looking for a dry way across, while at the same time keeping one eye on where I believed the motorcycle to be. Suddenly the sound erupted into a different pitch, and, simultaneously, the bike with its rider appeared out of the trees and turned into the stream. For a split second the vision seemed surreal. The bike came right at me, maybe ten yards away, with water spraying away from the front tire in outward arc. I stared at the biker, dressed in all black, but his helmet's visor blocked my view of his face.

Without hesitation I crouched and aimed. My right foot automatically went backwards to give me more stability. With one foot on the slippery log, and the other on the rocky streambed, just the opposite happened. I staggered backwards and across the creek in an effort not to fall.

He didn't fare much better. Upon seeing me, his first reaction was to try to bring the motorcycle to a stop. His bike started to slide out from under him, his front tire moving to his left and rear out to his right. I had no doubt he could have easily corrected the slide, even in the shallow water, but his focus had to be affected by the gun in my hand.

His right hand disappeared inside his partially zipped jacket, and reappeared just as fast. As soon as I saw the pistol, I pulled the trigger. They never let you practice shooting a pistol while you're slipping and sliding across a shallow creek. If they had, making expert marksman wouldn't have been so easy. As the gun roared in my hand, I saw fabric fly off my target's left shoulder.

My shot did little more than distract him for a second. He let go of the motorcycle in his own effort to stabilize himself. The bike flattened out and, in what seemed like slow motion, sprayed a wave of water in the air toward me. I took advantage of the minimal cover the wave provided to scramble out of the creek, rolling as I did behind what little cover I could find. He fired, and a rock exploded as I rolled over on it. My stomach felt like it was punched by a heavyweight wearing gloves covered with red hot needles. I kept rolling and fired back at him in a purely defensive reaction.

I would have loved to have had a direct hit, but I had no time to stop and aim. At a minimum, I needed to keep him off balance. This guy was a pro. Only the surprise and slippery footing had kept him from killing me, and, for that matter, prevented my killing him.

I rolled to a stop behind a pine that was just wide enough to cover me and aimed again at him. I watched as he scrambled out of the water back in the direction he had come. I steadied myself and fired at his moving target. The trunk of a thin Aspen tree spewed wood fiber out in all directions. It would have been a good hit. I saw his form pass directly behind the tree as my bullet hit it. The top four feet of the small tree toppled over to the right.

He disappeared behind the small rise and thick underbrush. I sprinted twenty yards deeper into the woods and crouched in a spot where the underbrush appeared especially heavy. I had no desire for him to know my position and maneuver back to surprise me. Better if we were both hunting for each other on equal footing.

I could just make out the motorcycle in the water. I didn't want him to get back to the bike and drive off, but I also didn't think he would try. Going back to the bike would expose him and give me a good shot. He would want to get rid of me first, and he would know he had the advantage out here. He knew the area, and I didn't.

The ground to my right climbed upward about seven feet before leveling. It blocked my view of where he had come from, and where he returned for cover. He must have a campsite or something over there, but I didn't think he went back there to wait me out.

I sprinted another twenty yards further into the woods before pausing behind a large pine tree. No shots, so he hadn't yet gotten to a position where he could look down and watch for me. A solid line of thick bushes allowed me to safely crawl a few yards up the slope. I stopped there to listen and look, but I neither heard nor saw anything. A burst of thunder broke the silence. The wind hadn't picked up, but my guess was that the storm couldn't be too far away.

I took a moment to check out my stomach. My shirt was tattooed with small holes and small rings of blood. I pulled my shirt up and counted a dozen spots where rock fragments had ripped through my skin. A few still protruded from me. I brushed off and pulled out any shards of rock I could find. Two of the nastier wounds felt like small pieces of the rock were imbedded in me; however, none of the wounds appeared to be serious.

Where was he? I had expected him to react quickly in an effort to catch me off guard. He couldn't know whether I was alone or not, or if at this moment I was calling in reinforcements. He had to believe time was on my side.

Another long rumble of thunder vibrated through the hills. The sunshine that had brightened the treetops and the few spots where it penetrated to the ground disappeared. From my vantage point, I couldn't tell if the sun had simply slipped behind the hills or if the storm clouds had gotten close enough to block the sun. Either way, the darkening made the ominous situation a little worse.

For a long three minutes, I remained as still as I could and watched movement in the forest. I even looked up in the trees, but I didn't see anything. The wind had picked up, and the treetops started swaying.

I wondered if any of the deputies back at the crime scene had heard the gun shots. Reinforcements could, in fact, be heading my way right now. Even if they were, I doubted anyone would arrive in the next thirty minutes, and due to the approaching storm it would likely be longer than that. Lightning crashed to the ground somewhere in the distance, and the resulting thunder echoed through the valleys and trees around me.

A waist high mound of rock, half hidden by the surrounding bushes, tempted me to move back toward the creek and to where he may be waiting for me. I knew it might be fatal to expose myself, but I steeled myself against an incoming round and dashed as quietly as I could to the mound of rock. Nothing happened.

"What's he up to?" I asked myself. After studying the forest on both sides of my location and behind me, I flattened myself on the ground and peered around the base of the mound. My view wasn't the best as I was surrounded by bushes.

In front of me the ground descended back to the creek. From my new vantage point I could make out the portion of the creek that had previously been blocked from my view. About twenty yards in front of me, I saw the remains of an old, maybe a century old, cabin. There wasn't much to it, and what still remained had a lot of vegetation now growing on and through it. Set off maybe ten feet from the creek, I imagined it once served as home to a gold prospector.

The creek turned toward the cabin, and then after about fifteen yards turned away, like the letter "U," with the area immediately in front of the cabin being the base of the "U." The changing direction of the current as the water flowed down the hills would give a prospector a choice spot to set up his operation.

This had to be where my target had stopped; however, I didn't see him anywhere near the cabin. I didn't have a very good angle to study the remains of the old cabin, but from what I could see, no indications of any recent human presence jumped out at me. I wondered why he had come to this location. The obvious reason was that he had stored some stuff out here, although it seemed a difficult place to pop in and out of. Of course, that may be exactly what he liked about the old place. I doubted if very many people knew about its existence.

A sound of a twig snapping behind me sent shivers up my spine. I spun my head and shoulders around, while trying to keep the rest of my body still. I saw him. He stood perfectly still, stooped over to keep a low profile. He must have stepped on the twig inadvertently and froze immediately. I could see his head move ever so slightly while his eyes searched for me.

Without a doubt, if I was still hiding behind either of the trees I had been a few moments before, I would be dead now. He had outsmarted me and had doubled-back a great deal further than I thought he would. I went back fifty yards thinking that would be sufficient, he must have gone a hundred yards from the creek before returning for the attack.

I had a clear, but long and awkward shot at him. His stooped profile didn't make it any easier, but I couldn't wait for him to stand up. At any moment he was apt to start running to a point where he had cover. There was also the likelihood if he looked hard enough, he would see me. The bushes camouflaged me but did not make me invisible. Worse still, they gave me no protection from a bullet.

Rather than roll over and try to get into a better position from which to shoot, I decided to take the riskier single handed shot. My right arm stretched out slowly, my elbow supported by my right hip. I aimed at center of mass and squeezed the trigger.

The blast of the bullet being fired and the pistol's recoil distracted me from getting a good look at the damage I'd done. I knew I hit him from his reaction. He fell backwards and I could see his body buckle in pain. However, he immediately rolled to the right. I jumped up to get another shot off and move in on him.

He surprised me by squeezing off a round at me before I could fire my second shot. The bullet creased my inner left thigh. I leapt to the other side of my rock mound and peered over the top. He was still scrambling for cover. I fired off two quick rounds just as he disappeared behind a large pine and a couple of five foot trees that looked to me like small Christmas trees. A fallen tree about half way between the twenty yards that separated us also gave him cover. At the same time, he would also have to shoot through the dead, leafless branches when firing at me.

I didn't know if either of my last two, rushed shots hit their target. I crouched down and peered around the edge of the mound. I could see the spot where he took cover, but I couldn't see him. Another bolt of lightning smashed into the forest, its bright flash of light too close for comfort. The thunder that immediately followed rattled the ground and forest around me.

The first big, cold drop of rain hit me, then a second and third followed it. Within a few seconds, heavy rain beat down on me. I zipped my light jacket, but kept focused. If he showed himself, I needed to be ready.

I crouched there until my legs and back begged me to move. I repositioned myself behind the mound, spread my legs and leaned into the mound. I didn't like having the top of my head visible as I watched for him, but he would have to expose himself if he wanted to take a shot at me. I wanted to take the first shot. I needed to keep the advantage.

The rain stopped as fast as it started, but large drops continued to fall sporadically from the tree tops above me. Thunder still shook the area and played havoc with my eardrums, but the lightning had moved off. The clouds blocked out the sunlight and it appeared darkness would fall earlier than usual. I looked at my watch. Normally there would be another hour or so of daylight, but with these clouds I wasn't so sure.

The possibility that I may have already killed my foe began to tempt me into moving. After all, how long was I going to remain leaning on this wet pile of dirt, rock and weeds? Darkness would be just as bad for him as it would be for me, I thought, or would it? What if he had a flashlight? He might have one, even a small one. He could simply lay it on something and aim it at me. It might not put out much light, but it would help him see what I was doing, and I would be blinded looking in his direction.

This guy was good. He wasn't doing anything, and I was already falling apart. To get my mind off him, I pulled Ollie's spare magazine out of my pocket and double checked it - fully loaded. I extracted the magazine in the pistol and replaced it with the full one. The Glock had a round in the chamber, so the whole process took about two seconds. Nothing like a fresh, loaded 9mm to make one feel better, I thought with a smile.

Another layer of darkness descended onto the forest around me. The wind picked up and felt cold against my wet clothing. Lightning struck barely a half mile away and once again thunder bounced back and forth off the hills around us. This time the rain brought the entire cloud down with it, and the cloud spread through the trees like fog. The rain felt like a steady spray rather than the earlier downpour. It made visibility poor, and I seriously considered rushing him. A dumb thing to do, but the storm, the growing darkness, and my desire to get this over with, waged a battle against my need to be patient.

A slight movement caught my eye. It didn't come from behind the tree but further back, off to the side, and down the slope. I had forgotten about the slope. I saw the movement again. Better this time because I focused on it. Something black was flat on the ground but moving ever so slowly to my right. He was trying to work his way around me and if he succeeded could attack me from the side. Or the bike, I wondered. Maybe he thought he could get around to the motorcycle and simply ride off. He might be in desperate need of medical attention.

He'd been smart to back away like he had. I had all but forgotten how the ground sloped downward. The terrain had shielded him for a while, but now only the scattered trees and shrubs gave him cover. He only needed about ten more yards before the terrain worked again in his favor, and he would be out of sight.

At least thirty yards now separated us, too far to be very accurate with a pistol. I needed to get closer, but I knew as soon as I started moving he would too. I had no doubt he would also start shooting. I flexed my knees a few times to limber up. I had no other choice.

I broke cover running fast toward the same trees that earlier had sheltered him, simultaneously firing six rounds in rapid succession as I did so. He rolled a number of times before breaking into a sprint toward the creek. He also managed to get a number of shots off, although his were most likely fired in an effort to distract me. I didn't see him make any effort to aim.

For my part, I worked hard to make every shot count. However, hitting a moving target, while running in rough terrain, is nearly impossible. I couldn't tell if any of my shots struck him. Rather than run directly after him, I ran back toward my mound and continued over the small ridge, jumping to the ground near the side of the old prospector's cabin.

When I landed I saw him in front of the cabin near the creek. He dove for cover behind what was left of the far wall of the cabin as I raised my arm to fire. He fired as he hit the ground out of sight and I felt the bullet rocket past my left ear. I jumped behind a boulder barely big enough to give me cover. Another bullet hit the rock as soon as I ducked.

I peeked around the edge of the rock and a shot ricocheted off it sending shards into my right ear. I repositioned myself and looked around the other side of the boulder. I couldn't see him, but he could see me – not a good thing. Now he had the advantage that I had earlier. I strained to see through the jumble of boards and vegetation.

"You're a dead man now, West!" He shouted unexpectedly. "You shouldn't have come out here. You're supposed to be on your way home."

Now that surprised me. I figured he knew who I was because I had him pegged as the nighttime visitor to my hotel room. He could've gotten my tag number as I drove off, but how did he know I had been told to go home?

"You made a mistake killing her," I replied. I didn't mind talking. I had a lot of questions.

"Who, Ball? She was just at the wrong place at the wrong time."

"No. My friend today."

"You telling me that you and that fat kid were an item? I would've guessed she swung the other way. Besides, wasn't she kind of young for you?"

The sound of his voice put him at the back corner of what was left of the cabin. I wondered if a shot would penetrate the old wood.

"You know you're toast, West. It'll be dark soon, and I have a pair of night vision goggles stored right here. You can't move now, and in another hour, you won't be able to see me when I come over there and kill you."

"Face it, Fox – or do you have a real name?"

"Fox will do."

"You're bleeding bad. You won't even make it another hour."

"A couple of flesh wounds, I've had worse."

"Well, Fox, I have to admit I'm impressed that you knew I was supposed to be heading home. Before I kill you, would you mind telling me how you knew that?"

"Sorry, West. You'll have to figure that one out on your own."

"You guys must have some pretty good connections back in D.C.," I said.

"Well, we ain't no local street gang, that's for sure. But you got it wrong."

"How so?"

"I grew up here. Hell, twenty years ago my brother and I built that trail you were just on. I used to play at this old cabin when I was a teenager. I still have a lot of friends in the area who keep me informed. Finding out about you was easy."

"I guess it would be."

"Have to give you one thing, though," he said.

"What's that?"

"You're a hard man to kill. I thought I had you the day I shot you, and you fell into the river. I went by your room later that night to make sure. You weren't there, but I didn't expect to find you. You can imagine my surprise when you showed up the next day."

"So what makes you think you can finish the job now?"

"Because you're stuck behind a little rock and it's getting dark. I have to tell you, West, I'm getting a little giddy just waiting for nightfall."

I could hear him start laughing to himself, it sounded almost like a giggle. I figured the loss of blood was causing any giddiness he felt.

"Fox, you hear me?" I shouted, but got no answer. "You're getting giddy because you're running out of blood. Surrender now and I'll get an ambulance here ASAP."

I knew there was little chance that he would ever surrender. I also doubted that he had any night vision goggles. Fully prone behind the boulder, I peered cautiously around its left side and tried to pinpoint him. I wondered if something obstructed his view of this lower left portion of the rock.

The rain started pouring, and the thick clouds did their best to extinguish the last of the late afternoon daylight. Things couldn't get any more bleak, but I had a plan.

I edged out a little further and took aim at a spot just right of where I suspected he was. I fired a shot, and then moved my aim to the left and fired another. As quickly as I could, I fired the rest of the rounds in my magazine at the flat, rock face that the cabin had been built up against long ago. It might have even served as the back wall to the cabin. I aimed at a point I thought was nearest the back corner. My idea was to flood his hiding spot with hot ricocheting lead and rock shrapnel.

I rolled back behind my rock as he began to let go a volley of rounds back at me. I thought I heard a scream coinciding with my rounds going off. Now, however, a raging howl emerged from the cabin through the sound of the pouring rain. I thought I could hear him move and run while he fired.

I ejected the spent magazine and grabbed for the half empty one in my pocket. I knew I only had seconds before he would be on top of me. Both the magazine and my hands were wet and cold. It slipped out of my hand when I tried to shove it into the pistol. I grabbed at it again and instinctively started rolling to my left, believing he would swing around to my right. The firing stopped, and I sensed he stood there just feet from me aiming down at me in smug satisfaction. Despite the odds against me, I finally popped the magazine in its place and slid the chamber forward.

My body tensed as I expected a bullet to tear into it, and I felt my hand shake as I took quick aim. I looked up through the thick dark rain but saw nothing. The mixed emotions that immediately went through my body left me numb. It took what strength I had left not to fall to the ground. I had been so sure that death had me in his hands. Somehow I had a temporary reprieve, but that only meant the ordeal wasn't over – and that was just as frightening.

Somewhere in the recesses of my mind I kept hearing, "Run! Hide!" I did neither. I stood still and slowly searched the area around me. I couldn't see him. Rain ran down my face. I wiped at my eyes and took a few steps toward the creek. Oddly, it felt good to move my legs.

A bright flash of lightning followed immediately by the pounding blast of thunder shook the area around me. It did something else, too. It illuminated a dark figure crawling through the grey water in the rising creek.

I walked slowly toward him, the pistol in my hand ready. The water level in the creek had risen by a good six inches since I had last crossed it. The current had picked up speed, and I felt the tug as I stepped into the water.

I approached him from behind. He appeared to be unaware of my presence. Although he was making slow progress in the direction of his motorcycle, now mostly submerged, I wondered if he actually thought he could escape, or if he just acted on some deep down instinct. I guess it didn't matter.

I couldn't shoot him in the back. That didn't seem right, or maybe I just didn't like the evidence it would leave behind. I took one last step to him and raised my right foot high enough to place it on his back and push him down flat into the water. He didn't have any resistance left in him. To this day I tell myself that any balance issues I had for the minute or two I stood there were caused by the swift moving current and not by him, if he struggled at all.

Another nearby flash of lightning served as sufficient motivation for me to seek whatever meager cover there might be in the remains of the old cabin. I discovered that someone had tacked a rainproof tarp to a portion of what was left of the roof. The tarp protected a small, six by eight section of the rear of the cabin. The ground below the tarp must have been slightly elevated because I could see water draining around it.

Even though I was already soaking wet, I sat down on the dry spot under the tarp. As I did so, another flash of lightning illuminated the body of a man being carried downstream by the current. I let it go. Maybe it was a good thing.

I felt the urge to toss Ollie's gun in the creek, too. I could make my way back to the car and go home. If anyone contacted me to ask what happened, I could say nothing happened, that I never found the guy. Certainly, no witnesses could pop up and dispute my story. I'm not sure why I didn't get rid of the pistol, but I didn't.

Chapter 21

As my adrenalin wore off, fatigue set in. I looked around the cabin for anything to use as a blanket. The cabin had to have a stash of supplies of some sort to draw him here before he made his escape. I could see shapes of things around me in the dim light, and I took advantage of the diminishing lightning to better identify them. Most of what I could see consisted of small shrubs and weeds that now grew from the cabin floor.

A couple of cardboard boxes sat against the few planks of wood that made up what was left of the front wall. Next to the boxes, I saw a small pile of old, and now wet, blankets. Useless, I thought. Whatever reason he had to come by this old cabin was lost to me. A thorough search in the daytime might produce something, but I would leave that to the experts.

A grinding, scraping noise in the creek in front of me caught my attention. I peered out and saw that the current had moved the motorcycle to a spot right in front of the cabin. A thought came to mind that the bike might contain a few useful things, and I ran out into the creek. Getting it out of the creek and into the cabin took a lot of effort, but I soon discovered I had hit the jackpot.

I found a dry sweatshirt, socks and a small towel in Ziploc plastic bags. I also discovered a small flashlight. Setting the flashlight aside, I undressed and used the small towel to dry myself off. The towel opened a number of small cuts and abrasions that had already scabbed over on my face. They didn't seem significant and after I blotted the towel against my face a couple of times, the bleeding appeared to be light. I checked my thigh where the bullet grazed me and decided it wasn't anything to worry about.

My light jacket had done a fair job of keeping the rain off my shirt, but my own sweat made up for the lack of outside moisture. I put on the sweatshirt and socks. I wrung out as much creek and rain water as I could from my jeans and put them on. I attacked my shoes with the small towel before putting them on.

Feeling a little better, I used the flashlight to study the contents of a wet manila envelope that I had also recovered from the motorcycle, which I noticed was a Kawasaki. Wrapped in a heavy duty rubber band, I discovered a stack of six credit cards. None had a person's name on it, so I figured they were prepaid credit cards. Using these, he could have checked into hotels, bought gas, whatever, and not left a trail – unless you knew the card number. He would be invisible going across the country. I wondered how much the cards were worth.

I also found two plastic sandwich bags, each containing a small set of personal identification documents. The driver's license in one identified the person as Samuel Black. The other listed its owner as Harold Green. The pictures on the two were the same. I wondered what name was listed on the driver's license in the wallet of the body now being swept downstream. In a separate sandwich bag, I discovered ten, fresh hundred dollar bills.

A thought came to mind that he may have kept a stash of bogus ID's buried around the cabin somewhere. I used the flashlight to again scrutinize my surroundings, but saw nothing suspicious.

The rain stopped all at once. Large drops still fell from the trees, so I remained under the tarp for a few more minutes. The rumble of thunder sounded as though the storm had moved out of the mountains and hills to the flatter land to the east. Even my surroundings lightened up as the cloud cover lifted and moved off. In doing so it allowed what was left of the remaining daylight to shine in.

The creek had turned into a small, rapidly moving river. Its edge was now barely a yard away from the front of the cabin. Small patches of fog floated by, like stragglers in a marathon race of clouds that moved east ahead of them.

I had two choices. Neither one seemed like much fun. I could stay here until daylight and be miserably cold, if not worse. My other option would be to head back, despite the approaching darkness. I didn't much like that one either, but at least I would be moving.

After a final look around satisfied me that there was no reason to stay, I worked my way around the back of the cabin and followed the creek back to the trail. Just enough daylight existed to allow me to find the trail. I knew I needed to keep the small flashlight off as long as possible to conserve the batteries.

For the second time today, I found myself jogging this path through the forest. This time though, I wasn't trying to catch someone. This time, I didn't run to avenge a fallen friend - to kill a rabid dog before it could attack someone else. This time, I simply ran to beat the darkness, and as I did so, my mind drifted to thoughts far from the events of the day. A calmness settled over me.

Chapter 22

I saw the lights long before I finished my trek back. A number of powerful flood lights that ran on generators facilitated the half dozen detectives as they scoured the two picnic areas for clues. Someone had removed the truck Ollie had driven, but the area still had the police tape stretched throughout it warning people to stay out.

Despite my approach with the flashlight on, no one noticed me. I felt tempted to go around them and continue to my car.

"Hey!" I shouted. "Who's in charge out here?"

Four or five flashlights hit me at once.

"Stay right there, mister," a male voice spoke to me from behind one of the flashlights.

I raised my hands to cover my eyes. Their flashlights carried a lot more power than mine. Despite the artificial brightness of the area, the light from the flashlights hitting my face still bothered me.

"Hey, no sudden moves!" the voice commanded.

"It's okay, I'm a good guy," I said, but remained still. "My name is Jim West. Lieutenant Prado can vouch for me. I was also a friend of Ollie."

"Then you still are, she ain't dead yet." The voice sounded softer now.

I smiled, an automatic response, upon hearing that Ollie had made it this long. My smile turned the tide of suspicion away from me. The voice said something to the others that I couldn't quite catch, before it spoke to me again.

"Stay where you are. I'll come over there."

Once the flashlights were turned away from me, I could see the man break away from the rest and approach me.

"What are you doing out here?" he asked.

"A long story," I said.

He studied my face and then the rest of me.

"What's going on?" he finally asked.

It dawned on me then. My presence there earlier in the day had somehow been lost in all the excitement. No one would have known about my involvement except Michelle, Ollie and the young deputy who showed up to take charge of the crime scene. Michelle might be concerned about me, but she had to know she had my cell phone and with all the excitement of the day might simply be waiting for me to contact her. The young deputy probably didn't give me a second thought once I disappeared.

"First, I have Ollie's issued Glock in my jacket pocket. I want to release it to you."

His hand instinctively moved to his own weapon. I raised both of mine slightly, palms facing him.

"You are welcome to get it yourself or call one of your men over. I can also simply give it to you myself," I said.

"One minute," he said. He turned his head slightly and shouted back at the group. "Steph, come over here and bring a bag." Then he looked back at me. "When she gets here, you can hand her the weapon. You can also explain to both of us how you got hold of it."

"Sure," I replied.

Steph's eyes widened when I slowly slid out the pistol and dropped it in the plastic bag. She then looked at her boss with questioning eyes.

"The other empty clip is back there a ways," I nodded my head to indicate the direction behind me. "As I said though, it's a long story. Do you mind if we sit over there?" I again motioned with my head to the picnic table in the campsite not getting any current attention by the detectives. "I believe, as you appear to, that the campsite there has little if any connection to any of the murders."

My comments caused Steph to make another curious glance at her boss. To his credit, he maintained his poker face.

"Yeah, let's move over there."

For the next twenty minutes, I briefed them on the day's events, starting with meeting Ollie for lunch. I only made a few slight changes. I told them I picked up Ollie's issued Glock to safeguard it and acknowledged that I shouldn't have. I said I went out to look for her shooter, so I could later tell Michelle where he went. I didn't expect to run into him. I told them he fired at me first, and, in self-defense, I shot and may have killed him. At that point I ran back here for help.

They asked a lot of questions, but I think they believed me. It's normal for civilians to do dumb things trying to be a hero. And, if it resulted in the death of someone who had just tried to kill a cop, they could overlook my lack of judgment. About halfway through the interview, Steph made a call to the Sheriff's office and requested that Michelle come out and get me. I told them that I just needed a ride to my car, but they ignored me.

When the interview ended, they told me to stay put until Michelle showed up. I sat there and debated whether I should tell Michelle the truth. I expected she would see right through my story, but acknowledging to anyone that I picked up the gun and headed down the trail for the sole purpose of killing Ollie's shooter might not be the smartest thing to admit. It would also be unfair to expect Michelle to be complicit with my lie.

I felt I could have walked to my car and back in the time it took Michelle to come fetch me. Irritation and cold had set in by the time I saw her car's headlights. The guy in charge met her as she entered the crime scene, and they spoke briefly before she broke away.

She grinned as she approached me.

"I understand you've had a busy day," she said.

"You've heard?"

"Oh yes. Your story was phoned in twice. The first call included a brief summary. When that was briefed up the chain, an eruption of questions and interest flew back down at Bob. He immediately called me, expecting that I would know the whole story. I told him I hadn't been in touch with you since lunchtime ---"

"By the way," I interrupted, "how's Ollie?"

"Oh, the best news, she's going to make it. She's hurt bad, but the head injury was actually a glancing blow, a serious one but ---"

"What do you mean?"

"The doc thinks she was already falling backwards from the first shot when the second shot struck her tilted head. The bullet did a lot of cosmetic damage to her forehead and cracked her skull, but the trajectory was such that the bullet never entered the brain or even the skull. The wound looked a hell of a lot more gruesome than it turned out to be, but she still has some brain swelling, so I don't mean to play it down. It's just that the doctor says she should make a full recovery in a few days."

"That's great. Do they know how her eye will be affected?"

"Not yet, but I know they're optimistic."

"Good."

"How are you doing?" she asked in a softer tone. "Your face doesn't look so hot."

"Well thanks," I said, feigning hurt feelings.

"No, not that. You know I like your face. I mean it's cut and scratched up. Your ear looks like it's bleeding, too."

"I'm fine, but I may need someone to remove a few rock fragments."

"Let's get out of here," she said. "We can stop by an emergency room and get that rugged face of yours fixed up." She wore that grin again. I liked it.

"My car's at the restaurant. I told them I could've walked to it, but they wouldn't let me go."

"Let me first get you to an emergency room. There's one a few miles down the road, next to Manitou. Then I'll bring you back."

I didn't argue. I guess I just wanted to spend some more time with her.

When we got into her car, she looked at me inquisitively and asked, "Where did you get that sweatshirt?"

I realized immediately the problem with the story I had told earlier to the detective at the crime scene. I'd forgotten I had changed shirts. My original shirt was tied around my waist. No one would have noticed or known except Michelle – and she had.

I debated what to tell her and decided to tell her the truth, or at least more of the truth. I would let her tell me how much of the story she was comfortable with.

"He was the other guy at the table with Ball and Grazzard, or whatever his name was."

Michelle looked at me quizzically for a few seconds. "Is he dead?"

"Yes."

"Are you sure?"

"Yeah."

"Good. What did happen out there?"

"I thought they told you."

She smiled, "I got the fifteen second synopsis. They made it sound like you ran into him by accident and he started shooting at you."

"So?"

"You went after him because he shot Ollie. I saw it in your eyes. I knew it when I left you there at the scene."

"I really didn't expect to catch up with him. He had his motorcycle."

"He took it with him out there? Was it a dirt bike?"

"Kind of a cross between the two would be my guess."

"How did you catch up with him?"

"He stopped, for some reason, at an old dilapidated cabin just off the trail."

"What trail?"

"There's one that runs off the dead end. I thought I lost him and had already started heading back when he came out of nowhere and almost ran me over."

"That's when you shot him?"

"More complicated than that – that's when we started shooting at each other. Enjoyed it so much, we spent the rest of the afternoon shooting at each other."

She took a longer glance at me. "Are you sure you're okay?"

"I guess that's why we're going to the emergency room."

"No, I mean inside. Are you okay with everything?"

She placed her right hand on my leg just above the knee.

"Yeah," I said and placed my hand on top of hers.

We arrived at the small hospital. Two old men and a lady with two small children sat quietly waiting to be seen in the emergency room. Michelle pointed me to a chair and went up to the reception desk. Seconds later, a nurse whisked both of us back to an examination room. Michelle excused herself to make a few phone calls. The nurse cleaned and inspected my wounds. She contemplated stitches where the bullet had grazed my thigh, but in the end I left with only a lot of bandages.

Chapter 23

"We need to go back out to where you left the body," Michelle said as we pulled away from the hospital.

"I thought we might," I said. "You have any feel for what they might want to do with me?"

"Actually, no," she replied. "My impression is that a few people are very upset that you keep popping up in this, but a number of us are on your side. And, the charges, if any, that they can throw at you are minor."

"Thanks," I said halfheartedly.

When we turned off Highway 24, I remembered the false identification documents and credit cards I had in my pocket.

"Here," I said as I handed the packet over to her.

"What is it?" she asked, only being able to glance at the top document while driving.

"I found that stuff - false ID's, credit cards, some other things, in one of the pockets on the motorcycle. I wanted to turn it over to you. I also found this sweatshirt there."

"Anything else?"

"Socks."

She laughed.

It looked like every cop in the city had turned out by the time we made it back. The flashing lights of several police sedans lit up the night.

Bob approached us as we parked. He nodded at Michelle and spoke to me.

"Do you think you could lead us out to where you last saw him?"

"Yes. It's about a two mile hike, and we'll need good flashlights."

"We got 'em." He looked over at Michelle. She had the zip lock bag open and one of the fake identification documents in her hand.

"You ready?" he asked her.

"Yes, but Bob I think we should show these to Nicholson."

Bob walked over close to her and looked at the documents. She said something to him about my finding them and their belonging to the alleged murderer. They both started walking away from me. I followed them.

They walked up to a group of three men. One I recognized from Ball's, the husband, outdoor crime scene. One of the others was the FBI agent who approached me at the hotel and told me to go home. I stayed discreetly away from all of them as they discussed the items I had earlier removed from the manila envelope and stuffed together into a larger Ziploc bag.

After about a minute the group broke apart and Michelle came back to me.

"They have some questions about how you acquired those items."

"They?"

"The FBI, and probably Bob by now. The story everyone heard earlier was that you shot him and ran back here. Doesn't leave much time to find things."

"Yeah, I figured they would ultimately want more details. Did you tell them what I told you?"

"No, I just played dumb. They'll want to hear it from you anyway."

"Let's go!" someone shouted from behind us. "West, you want to come up here and make sure we go in the right direction."

"You coming?" I asked Michelle.

"No, specifically told not to. But that's okay, you go ahead."

I nodded and started to walk away.

"Wait a second," she said. "Here," she held out my cell phone.

I joined Bob and a couple of deputies up at the front of the pack. Everyone had their flashlight on so I kept mine off.

"Straight down this trail," I said, and the trek back to the cabin began.

We hadn't gone a hundred yards when I heard a voice behind me.

"Hell, I remember this trail. I walked this a few times years ago. I knew the crew that laid it out. A couple of friends of mine did most of the work."

I looked back at the speaker - the fair haired FBI agent who had told me to head home. The hairs on the back of my neck twitched. I remembered Jack's words to me just before our final volley of shots. He said he had friends here that kept him informed.

I kept my thoughts to myself and trudged on. My feet ached and fatigue set in. I realized I hadn't eaten anything since morning.

"Here," Bob tapped my arm. He offered an energy bar.

"Thanks," I said, taking it.

"I always carry them. You were slowing down. Been a long day, hasn't it?"

"Yeah, too long."

"Amen," he said.

The hike to the cabin in the dark played a few tricks on my mind. I knew that all we had to do was to remain on the path all the way to the creek, but my mind zoned out on a few occasions only to be brought back to focus when Bob or someone else wanted to know if we were there yet. A couple of times someone asked me if we were still on the right trail. I didn't remember intersecting with any other trails so I answered with a simple yes. To be honest, in the dark, and with my mind elsewhere most of the time, we could have been miles off target, and I wouldn't have known.

Instead of paying attention to the trail, my mind debated whether I should say anything to Michelle about my suspicions concerning the FBI agent. I couldn't remember if he mentioned his name to me. I also knew I couldn't prove anything.

When I got bored of worrying about the FBI's problems, I thought about Michelle. I liked her and knew I owed her a lot. She had helped keep the wolves in the DA's and sheriff's offices off my back. I found her very attractive, especially those eyes, but after a lot of self-questioning, I hadn't thought my attraction to her was something I should pursue. After all, didn't I learn from Sarah, a newspaper reporter I had fallen for a year or so back, that chasing after younger women in the middle of their careers put both of us in a tough situation?

We finally reached the creek, still full of water but moving much slower again. No one wanted to get their feet wet, so I took the roundabout way to the rear of the cabin. Once there, everything proceeded with professional precision. Even though we were in the middle of nowhere, they judiciously taped off the area, and the crime scene investigators began their duties.

"Where the hell is the body?" someone growled.

"I saw him fall into the creek. It was moving faster than it is now. My guess is that he was swept downstream a ways."

"Great," the same voice grumbled.

"It couldn't have gone too far," Bob broke in. "Follow it down a ways and see if you can find him."

Bob had me walk him and another deputy, literally, through what had happened following my first encounter with Fox in the creek, to the point where I left him for dead. I gave him the same, almost complete version I had given Michelle. Despite the darkness, we found a number of spent shell casings.

"Looks like you guys had a war out here," Bob stated.

"It wasn't pleasant."

"Are you sure you're okay?"

"Yeah, thanks." Maybe Bob wasn't that bad of a guy.

"Hey! Down here! We found him!" Someone had obviously found the body.

Two of the crime scene investigators broke away to go to the body. Another person, whom I later learned was with the medical examiner's office, left seconds later to join them.

The FBI guy, whom I suspected was the killer's inside connection, walked by.

"Seriously, I had planned on leaving town today," I said.

He looked at me oddly, grunted something, and moved on. Good actor, I thought. If I didn't know better, I would have thought he had no idea what I was talking about.

A helicopter with a spotlight flew overhead and then moved off. I heard it land not far away.

"Reinforcements and your trip out of here, West," Bob announced. "They got our GPS fix and luckily found a place to land nearby."

"I think they landed where the trail ends. It's not far, and there is plenty of open space."

He looked at me quizzically.

"I told you, I thought I lost him. I reached the end of the trail and sat there for a while before I started back. That's when I ran into him. It's only about a quarter mile from here."

Bob sent me and a deputy to locate the helicopter and help whoever arrived in it find their way back to the crime scene. Once that had been accomplished, he sent me back to the helicopter to wait. My dismissal rescued me from a very cold night in the woods. The warmth inside the helicopter felt great, and while the seats wouldn't have won any awards for comfort, I napped until they brought the body to the helicopter for transport back to Colorado Springs.

A deputy and the rep from the medical examiner's office escorted the body on the flight back. I tagged along. They kept him and sent me back to my hotel in a taxi. Although I had checked out earlier in the day in anticipation of going home, the hotel had another room available. I took a shower and went straight to bed. I figured I'd have plenty of time tomorrow to worry about the fact that my car and my luggage were ten miles away.

I had hoped to get a sound sleep in the few hours left before dawn, but my mind wouldn't cooperate. It kept bouncing around from someone shooting at me to the FBI agent acting like he didn't know me. I could understand my mind reliving my late afternoon shootout, and while it disrupted my sleep, it didn't linger in my mind.

On the other hand, despite my efforts to ignore it, I kept seeing the FBI agent's face and his eyes looking right through me, like he had no interest in me at all. I had met a lot of people like that in the past. The type so full of themselves, that unless something happens to bring you to their level of importance, they really don't notice you. I've even seen the behavior before in FBI agents, although it's an attitude much more commonly found in politicians and at country clubs. They just don't have time for the "little people."

The behavior didn't cause my anxiety. What bothered me was my gut telling me that he didn't recognize me, that he didn't know what I meant by my remarks. That made no sense at all. I had no doubt that I correctly recognized him as the FBI agent who had told me to head home. I rationalized that he had supreme acting skills, but I couldn't shake the sensation that something didn't make sense. That dilemma kept my mind whirling despite all my attempts to sleep.

When my phone rang at eight o'clock, I felt less rested than I had the night before.

"We need you down here as soon as possible, Jim," Michelle said after we said our hellos.

"I'm sure you do," I said, not trying to hide the fatigue in my voice. "But my car is still out at the restaurant. By the way, you still owe me lunch."

"I can't come by right now, but I'll have someone at your hotel in fifteen minutes if you can be ready?"

"You do know that my luggage is still in my car?"

"No one will care if you look shabby. Everyone else does today."

"Okay, I'll be ready."

I didn't mind my clothes being dirty or wrinkled as much I was uncomfortable with their smell. Mud, creek water and sweat don't combine that well. I put the borrowed sweatshirt on and threw my shirt along with both pair of socks in the trash.

Chapter 24

"Good morning, Jim."

I turned my head and saw Claire crossing toward me from one of the other hallways that lead into the hotel's lobby.

"I thought you were going home yesterday?" Claire said it more as a question than a statement.

"Good morning. How's Perry doing?"

"A lot better. The doctor said in a few more days he can come home."

I caught a look of disapproval as Claire gave my appearance a maternal once over.

"It's a long story, Claire. I did mean to leave yesterday. My clean clothes are in my car, which right now is parked about ten miles from here."

"I wasn't going to say anything, but I don't understand why you haven't played any golf with Steve or Mike. They said they couldn't reach you and that you haven't called them. What kind of mess have you gotten yourself into? Perry even asked me last night what you were up to."

"Well, it's all over now, Claire, and once I can get to my car and get into some new clothes, I'll stop by the hospital. I promise."

"I guess I could give you a ride to your car. I don't have to be at the hospital at any specific time."

"Thanks, Claire, I do appreciate the offer, but I think this is my ride coming now." I pointed at a sheriff's vehicle pulling up to the hotel's front entrance. "I'll see you later today."

We walked out through the hotel's doors together, and while I proceeded to the sedan, I heard Claire click her tongue disapprovingly behind me.

At the sheriff's office the deputy deposited me in an empty interview room, where I sat alone for a long twenty minutes. I should have asked for a cup of coffee, but I had assumed that I would be seen right away. Irritation had started to set in when Bob and Michelle arrived together. Michelle had an extra cup of coffee in her hands.

"For me, I hope."

"Sorry, our meeting went over. I suspected that no one had offered you coffee. Black, right?" she asked as she handed me the coffee.

"Right, thanks," I said.

For the better part of an hour the two of them interviewed me. First, they had me rehash everything that had happened from the time I left the spot where Ollie had been shot until I later returned there. They didn't appear interested in trying to get me to admit to anything that might be incriminating. Rather, they focused on conversations I had with Ollie's shooter, whom they had identified as Corby Myers, and on the actual flow of events. I only strayed from the truth in two minor areas.

I didn't admit to having already started down the stream, gun in hand and ready to kill, when I ran into Myers. I left it as a surprise encounter that I couldn't avoid. Secondly, I stayed with my story that after being shot he had fallen face down into the creek, and I assumed he was dead. I didn't see any value in mentioning our last few moments together.

After they covered yesterday's events, they had a list of

questions about my earlier movements and conversations that ranged all the way back to the discovery of Garibaldi's body. When they finally finished, I asked if they would answer a few of my questions. Bob nodded.

"First, how's Ollie?"

"Better, but still not out of the woods. It's the brain swelling issue that still has the doctors worried."

I nodded. "How did you get Myers' ID so quickly?"

"A lucky coincidence," Bob answered. "An FBI agent who was with us last night recognized him."

"You know, I said that Myers' claimed to have friends here that kept him informed."

"We heard you," Bob said. "I think he'll be in the hot seat for a while."

I wanted to ask for the FBI guy's name, but decided not to.

"Why more questions about Garibaldi?"

"We know Myers wasn't in Colorado the day Garibaldi was shot."

"What? That doesn't make sense."

"We know. He actually did fly in on the same flight with the real Leroy Fox."

"A mystery within a mystery," I said.

"We need to have you take a look at the body. It's merely a formality now," Bob said.

"Okay."

"I'll take him, Bob," Michelle said as we stood. "We're due over there right now."

"Yeah, get going," he said.

I reached out to shake his hand and, for a moment, thought I would have to settle for another nod. However, just before I pulled my hand back, he reached out and shook it.

"Perfect timing," Michelle said, barely loud enough for me to hear her, as we came to a stop in front of the morgue.

I looked at her. Her eyes stared out the window, and her lips shaped into a big grin. I followed her eyes and saw Tasha, Holly and Steve being escorted by a uniformed deputy down the sidewalk toward the morgue. I looked back at Michelle.

"I suppose they needed further confirmation on Myers being at the restaurant that night." She did her best to hide her smirk.

"You're loving this, aren't you?" I asked.

She didn't say anything, but I knew her woman's intuition sensed I was uncomfortable.

"Don't you all have a photograph you could show them?"

"Actually we don't. Not a good one anyway. A few partials but it seems like nobody, including the feds, have any pictures of this guy. There's some gossip he was really bad though."

She climbed out of the car, "Sid," she called out to the approaching deputy. "We'll go in with you."

I had remained seated in the car.

"Come on," Michelle said.

I climbed out and we approached the group.

"Jim!" Tasha said and came over and gave me a hug.

I returned the squeeze. "How are you doing?"

"Isn't this great? I've never done this before, it's kind of creepy."

"I guess they told you what they want you all to do?"

"Yes," Tasha answered.

"How's Steve handling it?" I whispered.

"Terrified," she laughed back at me.

Michelle and Sid had been discussing something while we talked and now suggested we all go in. They escorted us to a small waiting room and informed us we would be taken in one at a time.

Michelle took me in first. A sheet covered Myers' body. I had no trouble recognizing him as the man I saw at the restaurant with Lynda Ball and then again as the man I shot yesterday. I told them that I could not say for sure whether I saw him at any other point since my arrival in Colorado Springs.

"What happened to his eye?" I asked the man in a white lab gown standing there with us. His eyelids were shut but significant discoloration surrounded Myers' right eye, and it appeared to me like the eyeball might not be there anymore.

"A large rock shard shattered the eyeball and got lodged deep in there. Most likely a fragment discharged by a bullet that struck a nearby rock. A nasty wound, but it's not what killed him."

"How did he die?"

"Drowned."

"Not bullet wounds?"

He looked at me inquisitively and then at Michelle. I didn't take my eyes off Myers' face.

"He had two bullet wounds and had probably lost a lot of blood before dying. Might be why he passed out in the water. The bullet wounds were serious, but they wouldn't have been fatal if he'd received treatment soon enough."

Out of morbid curiosity I wanted to ask where I had hit him, but I didn't.

Michelle took me back to the waiting room and took a thoroughly cowed Steve in next.

"What was it like?" Tasha asked.

"Not much fun, but I guess it has to be done."

"What happened to your face?"

"Scratched it on some rocks. Tasha, why did they drag you down here? I can see Steve and Holly being needed, but why did they bother you?"

"Oh, it's no bother. Lieutenant Prado asked me on the phone to come as a way to get Steve to cooperate. They picked Holly up first, then me, and then we all went and grabbed Steve."

"Steve will probably be mad at me for telling Lieutenant Prado about my conversation with him," I said, not really caring either way.

"No, he won't. By the way, are you and Lieutenant Prado, you know, together?"

"No," I said with a chuckle. "Why do you ask?"

"Just some vibes," she said as she reached out and squeezed my hand.

Michelle came back in with Steve and asked Holly to go with her. She looked at Tasha and me. I couldn't read her expression, if there was one. When they left the room, I looked back at Tasha. She raised her eyebrows with a look that said see what I mean.

I started to think I was more comfortable yesterday staring down Myers.

"That was awesome!" shouted Steve suddenly.

We both looked at him.

"I never saw a dead guy before. Did you see his eye?" Steve loudly asked me.

"Yeah."

"I bet the cops tortured him before they killed him. He probably knew something he shouldn't have. It's always about the money."

I had no idea what had gotten into Steve's mind.

"Oh, Steve, calm down," Tasha instructed. "You're letting your imagination carry you away"

Steve grinned at her. "Wait until it's your turn."

"I told them I don't want to see him."

"You're crazy. It's like that TV show, you know which one?"

"I do, Steve, but I don't think they need my help on this one."

Steve rambled on, but I tuned him out.

Holly returned pale and quiet. Even Steve realized that she might not be receptive to his enthusiasm.

Sid offered to drive them back, and they all agreed.

"Come by the restaurant again," Tasha said to me as they left.

"Sure you don't want to go with them?" Michelle asked me.

"Come on, cut me some slack. She's a good person, and what happened just happened."

"I'm sorry, but you know you made it into a bigger thing than you needed to. You're an easy target."

"I know. I screwed up a lot of my life." I don't know why I said it and regretted saying it as soon as I did.

"Oh, come on," Michelle said and grabbed my hand. "We need to check back in at the office, but then let's go see Ollie."

"Good idea."

The short drive back to the sheriff's office saved me from explaining myself to Michelle.

"What did you mean about screwing up most of your life?" she had asked as soon as we left the parking lot.

"Nothing," I answered, obviously evading an explanation. "I think seeing that body really shook up poor Holly."

Michelle glanced over at me and smiled at my subtle attempt

at changing the topic.

"Yes, it did, poor girl."

We drove the rest of the way in silence.

I never did get to visit Ollie that day.   Two FBI agents transported me to their offices in Colorado Springs minutes after my arrival at the sheriff's offices.   For the next six hours, Special Agents Marcie Dix and Justin Moore grilled me like I was public enemy number one.   Moore had the same sneer on his face that he had when I met him at Mr. Ball's crime scene a few days before.   Twice I got so pissed off, I told them I wouldn't say another word without a lawyer present.   Both times they reminded me that they hadn't advised me of my rights and that I didn't need a lawyer because they weren't interested in charging me with anything.

I didn't know what they were after, and that disconcerted me. Their explanation to me hadn't helped.

"We want to know everything you know. We want to know when you knew it and how you learned it. We want to know what you know about the "Ghost" and what your relationship is to him."

"I have no idea what you are talking about? We've gone over everything I know and what I've done since I arrived in the Springs," I said.

"And we still think you're hiding something from us," they would say, and we would start again.

I stuck to the truth, always the easiest thing to remember – except for my real motive for picking up Ollie's pistol and my holding Myers under water until I was sure he was dead. I felt comfortable that they had no suspicions regarding how he drowned, but, in my gut, I felt like they didn't believe my explanation for picking up Ollie's pistol.

"If that's so, why did you go looking for the second magazine?" Special Agent Dix asked.

Good question, I thought. "I don't know. I guess I figured there might be another one around and felt like it needed to be kept together with the pistol."

In fairness, they did let me take a couple of breaks and even brought in donuts on one occasion, but their treatment of me never qualified as cordial. I got the distinct feeling that they believed I was more involved in this whole mess than I was. At one point, I felt like they might even believe that I was this Ghost character they kept alluding to.

Toward the end of this uncomfortable experience, they throttled back on the pressure they had put me under. They summarized back to me pertinent elements of my past few days, much like a briefer might do at the end of a long briefing in an effort to capture the main points. I knew it all sounded bizarre, but I couldn't do much more than nod as they rehashed it.

Finally, they both left the room for a few minutes. Only Special Agent Dix returned.

"West," she said, "I don't know if any of us in this office believe your story. I'm sure the events happened more or less like you have explained them, but there's more to it, isn't there?"

"No."

She shook her head slowly and grinned slightly. Before she could go on, a knock at the door interrupted us. A face I hadn't seen before appeared and Dix left the room again. She was only gone a few seconds before she came back into the room.

"Jim," she started off in a more pleasant tone. Playing the "good cop" now I wondered? "I want to thank you for being patient with us and our, shall I say, extreme focus on your activities the last few days. Do you have any idea about the scope of this matter?"

"From my viewpoint the scope looks huge," I replied.

"I'm sorry. It must, but I don't mean what's happened to you." She realized how this must have sounded and quickly corrected herself. "I didn't mean that the way it sounded. I know you've been through a lot, and that today hasn't evolved exactly how you would have liked it to."

"That's an understatement," I said.

"Let me just say that what you've stumbled into this week is related to a much larger nationwide investigation that has gotten a little out of control. As if that wasn't enough, this latest character, Myers, has turned out to be a real mystery for us. There is almost no record of him for the past seven years."

"What do you mean?"

"I mean at that point he seems to have just disappeared from the system."

"System?" I asked.

"You know – no job, no police reports, no IRS filings, no press stories, no internet life, no phones, utility records, and so on."

"And, I guess he didn't just become a homeless person?"

"Obviously not. The stash of false ID's and credit cards were first class. We traced the activities of the credit cards he had on him. They show he had recently travelled to Boston under the name of Bruce Thompkins."

"And, no such person exists, right?" I asked.

"Correct. I mean there are probably thousands of Bruce Thompkins out there, but we know this one was a fake."

"I thought he was using the name Leroy Fox here?"

"As far as we know he only used that once, at the restaurant. They paid their bill at the restaurant with cash."

"Was he staying here under the Thompkins alias, or did he just go by his real name here?"

"We don't know, but we can't find any record of him using either name here in the past six months."

"I provided information about a man driving out of the same general camping area where Ollie was shot. Do you know if anything came from that?" I had forgotten to ask Michelle about that earlier.

"We're not sure about that one. By chance, he did turn out to be a person of interest to us, but nothing suspicious was found in the vehicle, except for a shotgun that the county is running some comparisons on."

Dix didn't elaborate, and I let it pass. I could follow up with Michelle.

"Who or what is this Ghost you referred to?" I asked. I figured I was pressing my luck by continuing to ask Dix questions, but thought I'd keep asking until she said enough.

"My guess is that it's just one of those 'urban legends' that runs through the intelligence community now and then. You know – the ultimate, unknown assassin that everyone is frightened of. We'd never heard of him out here until last night. Headquarters got excited when we sent in Myers' profile. Pieces of what we sent in matched the tidbits the intelligence and international law enforcement communities have on some big shot assassin known only as the Ghost. Nothing that would be valid in court, but enough to get the analysts excited enough to wet their pants."

"I got the impression you thought I might be your Ghost character."

"Special Agent Moore and I figured that if this Ghost really exists, then why couldn't it be you as well as Myers?"

I felt like being sarcastic and asking if my profile excited the analysts as much as Myers had. His lifestyle had been nothing at all like mine.

"How did he get the tag Ghost?" I asked.

"Came from Interpol, but I think they may have picked it up from the French. Over a six month period, about five years ago, four mafia big shots were bumped off. At first they thought it was part of a bigger war, but they finally decided one boss was surgically reshaping his playing field. One lone assassin was allegedly responsible for the deaths. The French failed in their attempts to identify the assassin. A year later two assassinations took place in Italy in a three week period. For reasons we don't yet know, the Europeans felt like it was the same shooter. This time he took out a politician and another mafia type. When the Italians and now Interpol asked France for everything they had in their investigations, they apparently labeled the entire file the 'Ghost.' The label stuck."

"If the murders took place in Europe why do they think this Myers guy was involved?" I asked.

"You got me. We've had a few mob related murders in the last few months. Maybe someone is trying to connect the dots," she said.

"Well, as I said, I have no idea who the guy was or wasn't. I just know that he obviously didn't like my being able to identify him as the guy with Lynda Ball and that other guy."

"I can understand his position. If you hadn't known Ball, and if you hadn't been brought into this matter early on as a suspect, he probably would never have been interested in you. You know the locals would have had no clue that he was at the restaurant that night. Your presence there and past association with Lynda Ball turned out to be the critical anomaly in all this."

I felt like giving the locals the benefit of the doubt and saying that they may have figured it out later, but instead I simply nodded.

"I imagine this Myers character will be the focus of some serious interest over the next few weeks," I said.

"Some major interest. If he turns out to be this really bad dude, you can count yourself lucky to still be walking around."

"I consider myself lucky, no matter who he turns out to be."

Dix just grinned at my comment and again went through the false apologies for giving me such a hard time.

As we left the interview room, I asked Dix about a ride to my car. She had me wait a second and went into another office. She returned a minute later and said someone from the sheriff's office was on the way over to pick me up. She claimed they had more resources and would likely be able to take me out to my car.

Chapter 25

Five minutes after I plopped into a soft chair in the building's lobby, Michelle walked in. I thanked her for coming as quickly as she had. The people entering and leaving the building were starting to look at me as if I were some vagrant who had drifted in out of the sun. I definitely needed to get into some clean clothes.

Fortunately, Michelle drove me straight out to my car. She had a couple of follow up questions for me from Bob, but nothing serious. Most of our conversation in her car before she dropped me off concerned the rumor now running rampant through the sheriff's office and city police that Myers might have been a big time international hit man – her words, not mine.

I acknowledged that the FBI agents who interviewed me alluded to something like that, but that I wasn't able to provide them any new information that might help them in their investigation of Myers.

"I did tell them I was certain that Myers shot Lynda Ball and Ollie because he told me he had. By the way, what's the latest on her?"

"She's stable, but they still have her in intensive care. I guess we just have to wait and see what damage has been done to her vision. The doctors believe that they got to the swelling in the brain early enough to forestall any long term damage, but only time will tell. She still hasn't been able to have visitors, but

I believe tomorrow they'll let us see her."

"Let's hope she makes a full recovery," I said.

"Amen," she said.

"The FBI said you all were able to stop that pickup truck with the camper that I mentioned to you yesterday." I said, while thinking that it seemed longer ago than just one day. "They said the driver was a person of interest, but they didn't elaborate."

"Yeah, that's an interesting thing, too. All we found in the camper was a shotgun. That got everyone a little excited because, as you know, Ball -- the husband -- was murdered with a shotgun. The lab is analyzing it, but you know it's tough with shotguns."

"I know."

"We drew a blank on the driver, but the feds had something on him. Apparently the driver has some connection with organized crime. No warrants on him, but, like I said, he got the FBI excited."

"How about that."

"Jim, do you know why the FBI would be so interested in this guy? Because, they sure aren't sharing with us."

"Only a theory, but I believe the FBI had an ongoing nationwide investigation that recently fell apart. I think they are trying to salvage what they have, and they are trying to figure out what went wrong. Myers and now this other character may simply be more pieces to their puzzle."

"Yeah, that's what we think, too."

"Any luck with the pistol Myers had on him?" I asked.

"Myers didn't have one on him when they found him. They didn't discover his pistol until later last night. It was the weapon used on Ollie."

"Did they find any other weapons out there?"

"No. The consensus theory is that Myers murdered Lynda Ball and Grazzard and simply left the murder weapon with Ball's husband when he killed him, perhaps with the shotgun we now have. There's no agreement yet on Garibaldi's murder. Oh -- and there is a consensus on the theory that Myers is the guy who shot at you out on the highway earlier this week, but since you're okay and Myers is dead as a result of the second confrontation, I don't think anyone is going to spend time looking any further into that first incident."

That made me grin. "I can't say as I blame them. I thought Bob was ready to hang the first three murders on Ball?"

"He was. You know, we said that wouldn't fly. He jumped at it because it was convenient."

"Now he's got another dead body to pin them on."

"Yeah. Convenient, too."

"Well, he may have it right this time. So, what's next?" I asked as we came to a stop next to my car. "Once I've had a chance to change clothes and freshen up, do you want to do dinner?"

"I'd love to, but I've already got other plans for tonight. Give me a call tomorrow morning some time. Maybe we can do lunch."

"Okay," I said and walked over to my car.

She waited until I had started my engine before she waved and drove off.

A dull light of realization broke through the cobwebs in the back of my mind. Ever since I saw her earlier in the week at the Garibaldi crime scene, Michelle had captured my imagination. I knew from that first day that she didn't have a husband, and for some silly reason in my mind this meant she was unattached.

We had a good rapport with each other, and I had no doubt that she liked me, as I liked her. I had assumed, therefore, that she was available, despite the fact that she had never indicated she was. This was the second time I had asked her out to dinner, and she had said she had other plans. Additionally, I remembered I tried to call her one evening and she didn't answer. It made sense that she already had a serious relationship with someone.

I drove back to the hotel, showered and changed. Claire didn't answer the phone in her room, so I decided to head to the hospital to visit Perry. The late afternoon rush hour made the drive a very slow one.

At the hospital I discovered they had moved Perry to another unit, but by now I had become pretty good at getting around in its maze. It took only a few extra minutes to find his new room.

Doris and Claire were both there. My arrival interrupted Claire dealing cards to the other two.

"Hey, Jim, come on in," Perry said.

They all appeared to be in a good mood.

"How are you doing, Perry?" I asked after saying hello to everyone.

"A little tired, but good. I'm ready to head home."

I felt like saying me too.

"Jim, why don't you join us? We could use a fourth," Claire asked.

I spent the rest of the evening with them playing hearts and talking. The card game had a very relaxing effect on me. I needed to get the events of the past week out of my mind, even if just for a short while. However, Doris did make one comment that definitely got my attention.

"I can't believe the news I heard on TV about Corby Myers," she had said.

I looked at her and realized that she had directed her comment to me. What could she have heard already, and why had she addressed her remarks at me?

"Did you know this Myers guy, Doris?" I asked.

"Oh, yes. My last year of teaching, he was in my class. A precocious young boy, he never gave me any trouble. He was bright and very creative. He and one of the Gold boys were inseparable. I always found that curious because," she hesitated, "oh I can't remember his first name, but this one Gold boy was a little slow witted, if you know what I mean."

I looked at her, not really knowing what she meant.

"I shouldn't say it that way," she continued. "It's just that I was impressed with Myers' wit and charm, and this Gold boy, well, he just seemed dull to me. I know that's not nice to say, but that's just how I remember him. Of course," she laughed at herself, "they were only in eighth grade at the time. I guess people do change."

At eight o'clock, the card game broke up, and I headed back to the hotel. I wanted to phone Michelle to ask a question but decided to hold off until the morning. An idea, admittedly a long shot, had entered my mind.

Chapter 26

"A lot of things are falling into place," Michelle said. Just after waking, I had called her. "That's good. What all have you got?"

"First, remember those motorcycle tracks we found out where my jeep was shoved over the cliff?"

"Yes," I answered.

"Well, the tire tread on the motorcycle Myers had matches them. Can you believe he did it?"

"If you mean pushed your jeep, then yes I can. To be honest, Michelle, for a while now I've wondered if it was his surprise at seeing me there with you and recognizing me from the night at the restaurant that caused him to do something irrational."

"So, does that mean you owe me a new car?" she asked.

"No way."

"We also discovered that Myers had camped out the last few nights at that spot where Ollie was shot. Nothing much was discovered there but once we knew who he was we were able to find out a lot more about him. You know, one of the FBI Special Agents knew him as a kid."

"Yes, I had heard that." I started to ask a question, but she continued.

"Anyway, Myers' parents own some property by Cripple Creek. There's a cabin out there that Myers has used a lot. His parents claimed they didn't know much about what he did for a living. Just that he travelled a lot and was only here for a few weeks at a time. And, listen to this. He paid off their mortgage a few months ago."

"Good son."

"Well, they certainly think so. But getting back to what I was going to say, the FBI and some deputies with the county out there searched the cabin and guess what they found?"

"I've no idea."

"More bogus credit cards and passports in two different names," she said.

"Did the passports reflect any travel?"

"No. Both looked brand new and ready to use."

"Sounds like our boy Myers was definitely well connected," I said.

"You can say that again. They also found a bunch of different weapons."

"That may not mean much, unless they come up with a something interesting on them."

"I know," Michelle said, "but they seized them all to check them out."

"Guess this is keeping you all busy."

"Actually, the pressure seems to have disappeared. The sheriff came down a few minutes ago and was patting everyone on the back for a job well done. There are loose ends to tie down and the lab people will certainly be busy for a while, but I sense I'll be completely cut loose from this thing now."

"Do you think I'm finally off the hot seat?" I asked.

"Yeah. Don't take this wrong, Jim, but starting last night and definitely into this morning I think the DA and the FBI have started looking at you as a distraction, not a person of interest."

"Well, I guess that's good to hear."

"Don't worry," she continued, "once they get all this put

together, they'll realize that you're stumbling upon Garibaldi and subsequent involvement in this was pretty much essential to its final, successful solution."

"I'm not sure I follow you, Michelle."

"It's like I told you from the beginning. It's fate."

I didn't want to go there again. "Michelle," I said changing the subject. "Was the FBI guy who knew Myers – was his name Gold by any chance?"

"Yes, how'd you know?"

"Just something I'd heard. Want to do lunch or something today?"

"Today's going to be bad, Jim. I have a ton of paperwork to get caught up with and one of the detectives in the office just had a baby. I'm going over to the hospital during my lunch hour with a couple of others to see her and the baby."

I realized she didn't say anything about after work. It didn't matter. I needed to get out of Colorado Springs.

"I plan on heading back to Clovis later today. Can you do me a favor Michelle and make sure no one cares that I do?"

"Like I said, I think you're free to go. But, I'll get the word out that you're leaving and see if anyone says anything."

"Thanks. You can always reach me on my cell."

"I know. Don't be surprised if I call someday."

That made me smile. I hung up without mentioning my concern that Gold may be the person Myers had referred to when he said he had local friends who kept him informed. The FBI didn't appreciate inside leaks. I had my own contacts inside the FBI with whom I could share my concerns.

I checked out of the hotel and swung by the hospital on my way out of town. Perry still looked tired but claimed he felt fine.

"I'm ready to go home, Jim," he had said. "It's just that these damn docs won't let me leave."

We chatted for a while, and I left. I didn't see Claire or Doris. I would have liked to have had a chance to see Doris again, but she was asleep. I wanted to confirm that Gold had been Myers' boyhood friend. I didn't have any real doubt that was the name she had mentioned. After all, Gold is an easy name to remember.

I got back into my Mustang and drove out of the parking lot and onto I-25. I headed it south toward Clovis and tried to put the last week out of my mind. If I'd been more attentive, I would have seen the large, white SUV that pulled out behind me and followed me onto the Interstate.

Chapter 27

Athousand trucks slowed the flow of traffic from Colorado Springs to Pueblo. Once I reached Pueblo's southern suburbs, the congestion inexplicably disappeared. From Pueblo to Trinidad only light traffic peppered the road; however, I still didn't notice the SUV until I stopped for gas just north of the city.

While I pumped gas into my car, the driver of a white SUV on the Interstate hit the brakes as though he wanted to pull into the gas station, but then suddenly sped on. At the time, it simply seemed like an indecisive driver. The highways are full of them. A few minutes later, however, while I drove south, I noticed a white SUV parked by the side of an old abandoned building. As I passed it, it pulled out onto the Interstate.

The hairs on the back of my neck started to tingle. The SUV kept its distance behind me. Maybe my imagination was playing games with me. What was the old saying? "You're not paranoid if someone is really following you."

Well, I definitely could see the SUV in my rear view mirror.

He made his move at the highest point on Raton Pass. I had watched him keep his distance for miles. When he started closing in, he did it fast. Though nowhere near as treacherous as many other mountain passes, the highway through Raton has a fairly steep grade when you start the descent. I had just touched my brakes for the first time, as gravity accelerated my car downward, when he moved the SUV into the passing lane.

I wanted to believe he was simply in a hurry, but I couldn't control the rush of adrenalin that surged through my body, and my grip on the steering wheel tightened. He pulled alongside of me, decelerating enough not to shoot by. I looked over and saw Gold staring back at me. A sadistic smile filled his face, and he made his move.

There is an axiom in physics that mass times speed equals momentum – or something like that. It's probably the only thing that saved my life that day. I instinctively accelerated to get away from him, but he did the same. Simultaneously, Gold nosed his SUV ahead of my Mustang and swerved the big vehicle into my lane determined to either run or knock my Mustang off the road and down the steep side of the mountain with me in it.

I crushed the Mustang's brake pedal to the floor.

Miraculously, the rear of his massive vehicle only grazed the front left headlight section of my car. The SUV shot ahead of me. I fought hard to keep my Mustang from skidding out of control, a reaction to my own braking action more so than the slight impact with his vehicle. The Mustang has a low center of gravity and a wide wheel base. It gave me the traction and control I needed. Within seconds, I had it down to forty five and driving straight.

While I struggled with my car, I kept one eye on my attacker. I watched as his brake lights came on, and the rear of the SUV swung to the right. He over-steered in an attempt to keep the big vehicle on the road, but he had chosen the wrong spot on the road to make his move on me. The road took a sweeping left turn in front of him. Easy to manage at the right speed and with a car behaving well, but Gold had already lost most of his control over the SUV.

The vehicle flipped, bounced through the air and tumbled down the steep incline. It seemed to move in slow motion. I forced myself to take my eyes off the SUV and focused them back on the road, barely in time to save myself from driving straight off the road as it now turned to my left.

I pulled the Mustang off onto the shoulder as the road began to wind back to the right. Climbing out of my car, I saw that the SUV had rolled down to a spot about a hundred yards below me. Somehow the vehicle ended upright on its wheels.

Despite the steep slope, I managed to sidestep my way down to the vehicle. It looked like a hundred trolls had attacked it with their hammers. The windows were shattered and for the most part were missing. The back driver's side tire looked like the only undamaged item on the whole vehicle. The front driver side tire, the one closest to me as I approached the SUV, was flat and shot out at a funny angle. The front of the entire engine compartment looked crushed in by nearly a foot. The hood had opened but had settled about six inches above what was left of the front of the car.

I could see Gold. To my amazement his eyes stared out at me. As I approached the SUV, I saw them twitch and follow me. He was still alive. I grabbed his door and tried to open it. No luck. The bent frame had jammed it shut.

Gold slightly tilted his head to me and tried to say something. I couldn't understand him. Blood mixed with saliva drooled out of the side of his mouth.

"Hang in there, Gold. We'll get someone here to get you out." I ran around the SUV and tried the door. It wouldn't open either. I contemplated trying to pull him out through a window, but I didn't have good leverage, and it looked like part of the engine had been pushed back onto his legs. The dash and steering wheel pressed against his waist. The air bags had collapsed all around him.

"Is he alive?" a man shouted from the road above.

"Yes, but he looks bad. Call 911!"

"I already have," he replied and then disappeared from sight.

"Hang in there, man," I said again to the person who had just tried to run me off the road. The situation had backfired so seriously on him that strangely I felt no animosity.

He coughed and briefly gagged. "West," his voice sounded like a whispered wheeze.

I looked at him, not sure if I actually heard him say something. His eyes were turned toward me. I realized he had trouble turning his head.

"Did Myers tell you about me?" he asked in a voice so soft I had to lean in the window to hear him.

"He just said he had friends that kept him informed. He didn't mention any names."

Gold closed his eyes and mumbled something. It sounded like he said, "Idiot." I didn't know if he was referring to Myers, me or himself.

I stepped back from the vehicle and looked up toward the road. Two young men had begun a descent in my direction. They identified themselves as third year medical students. They reported that an ambulance was on its way, but until it arrived they thought they might be able to help.

I told them he was all theirs and stepped away from the window. They went through the same motions I did earlier and finally realized that until someone could cut him out of the vehicle, there was little anyone could do. I thought Gold's chances of surviving were slim.

The popping and crackling sounds that had come from the

engine when I had first arrived had now stopped. I had considered the danger of a fire but had discounted it. That happens in movies at a much higher rate than in real life.

The sound of sirens finally informed us help would soon arrive. I needed to call someone before I talked to the responding police, so I left Gold with the two med students and climbed up to the highway. A state trooper pulled in behind a red Mercedes that had stopped to watch. I walked the other way and dialed Michelle.

"Hey, I thought you were heading home today," she said before I could even say hello.

"I am, or at least I'm trying to."

"What do you mean?"

"You know the FBI agent Gold?" I asked.

"Yes, I know Special Agent Gold. Why? What's up?"

"He just tried to run me off the road."

"What?" she asked.

"He tried to run me off the road. Only he went off and is in very bad shape right now. I didn't know who else to call…"

"Wait a second, Jim," Michelle interrupted. "It can't be Gold…"

Now it was my turn to interrupt. "Unless he has a twin, it's him."

The phone remained silent for a second. I thought I could hear Michelle asking someone close by a question. The impact of my own comment began to sink in.

"Jim, where are you?"

"On I-25, at Raton Pass, down by the New Mexico state line. I think I'm still in Colorado."

"It can't be Special Agent Gold. I just saw him an hour ago. But Jim," she paused.

"What?"

"Jim, I can't confirm this, but I've been told Gold has a brother who's about a year younger than him. He's supposed to look just like Special Agent Gold."

"Are you sure the guy you saw up there wasn't the younger brother?" I asked. I didn't doubt that I could have mistaken one for the other, but the Gold brother dying in the car below me had just referred to Myers. This Gold brother had been troubled sufficiently by what Myers may have told me that he tried to take me out. If he wasn't the FBI agent, then what was his relationship with Myers, and how could he keep Myers informed, or even know about me?

"Yeah, we're sure, but I'll double check right now and get back with you."

"Okay, good. I'm not going to say anything to the state troopers down here until I hear back from you."

"Good idea. I'll call you back in a few minutes," she said and disconnected.

I walked back and watched the rescue efforts. By now, a number of civilian and official cars had parked alongside the road. I decided to keep a low profile and not talk to anyone until I heard back from Michelle. I saw two troopers walking among the people trying to get statements. The two young men, who could have pointed me out to the troopers, were still down by the SUV.

Becoming impatient, I had my phone out of my pocket to redial Michelle's number when it buzzed in my hand.

"Michelle, what do you have?"

"Not much, except it's not Special Agent Gold. They aren't saying anything else at the moment over there, but I think we hit a nerve."

By over there, I thought she meant the FBI.

"What do you mean, hit a nerve?"

"I mean they aren't telling us anything, but I've gotten three phone calls from them asking follow up questions to the initial info that I passed to them through the sheriff. What?" I sensed her hand going over the mouthpiece while she talked to someone else. "Jim, I can't talk right now." The line went dead.

A sheriff's vehicle drove past me slowly. It had passed the crowded gaggle of official and unofficial vehicles and pulled in diagonally, immediately in front my Mustang. A gap of fifty yards separated my car from the rest of the cars that had stopped to help or simply view the action. Someone didn't want me to leave.

I sighed and began my long stroll to my car. Might as well get this over with, I thought.

Two deputies got out of the sheriff's sedan and walked around my car. After their inspection, the tall thin deputy stayed next to the Mustang and the other started toward the crowd of people. At about mid-point in the gap, we passed each other. He stopped as I walked by.

"Hey, are you Jim West?" he asked. He looked like he had a permanent scowl on his face. His grey hair was complemented by a grey five o'clock shadow that covered the lower half of his face. He looked as tired as I felt.

"Yes," I replied.

"Mr. West, I need you to come with me."

Part of me wanted to get belligerent. I just wanted to get home, but I knew I had to play out this hand. All I could hope was for this to be the end of it.

"Sure," I said and followed him back to his sedan.

The taller deputy rushed to open the back door of the

sheriff's car as we approached. I sat down but left one leg out so the door couldn't be closed. I made eye contact with the older deputy. I figured he was in charge.

"Leave it open," he said to the other deputy.

They both moved to my car and leaned against it. I put my head back against the back of the seat and closed my eyes. Fatigue seemed to overwhelm me.

"Hey, West," one of the deputies said.

I looked out as a highway patrol trooper approached.

"He just wants to know about the traffic accident, nothing more. Just tell him what happened – nothing else. Comprende?"

I didn't respond yes, but I did understand. The deputies had been sent here to detain me and to make sure I didn't say anything about Gold to anybody.

I thought the trooper might be irritated with the deputy's comments, but if he was he didn't show it. For the next twenty minutes the trooper took notes and drew diagrams on his forms. I didn't tell him that Gold tried to run me off the road, or that I even knew the SUV's driver. I simply said that he drove recklessly close to me when he passed and that he had lost control of his vehicle at the bend in the road.

My input confirmed information he had already received from a couple other witnesses. They had seen the SUV lose control and flip off the highway, but hadn't noticed what had happened in the few seconds before that.

The trooper left satisfied. A minute later, the older deputy leaned in close to me.

"How'd you get the white paint on the front of your car?" he grinned as he said this. He didn't expect a response. He had listened to my interview with the trooper and wanted me to know he knew something that I hadn't told the trooper. He returned to lean against my Mustang next to his partner. I realized that the taller deputy's body covered most of the white paint. The older deputy's body now covered the rest of it. The trooper, unaware of the contact, had never inspected my car.

I wondered if the omission could come back and bite me somehow. The sound of an approaching helicopter interrupted my thoughts. It landed nearby, and an emergency medical team raced out of it and disappeared down the slope. I would have liked to have watched the action taking place below but couldn't from the back seat of the car.

After another twenty minutes of sitting in silence, I heard the sound of a second helicopter. I looked out the back window and saw a Colorado National Guard helicopter fly over slowly and then move to a position about a half mile up the highway, where it landed. Traffic had already been diverted into just one lane. Northbound and southbound traffic had to take turns using the one lane. Still, it surprised me that the two helicopters could find places to land along this stretch of the pass.

Two highway patrol vehicles raced to meet the helicopter. In another minute, they returned with their passengers. The first car shot past me and pulled up next to the gaggle of vehicles closer to the accident scene. I saw three men jump out and rush down the slope and out of sight. The person in the lead, if I didn't know better, was the same person who was already down the ravine in the SUV – Gold.

I hadn't noticed that the second vehicle had parked next to us until I heard her voice.

"Jim, you okay?" Michelle asked.

I looked up at her. It struck me as funny how those big green eyes fascinated me as much today as the first time I had met her.

I nodded as I stood up. "How about you?"

"Yeah."

I looked at Special Agent Justin Moore, FBI, standing next to her. I didn't care for Moore, and the way he scowled at me, I figured our feelings were mutual. He didn't say anything to me. We didn't even share nods.

"How come they brought you down here?" I asked Michelle.

"Not too sure," she said, "but I'm glad they did." Her eyes hinted that she may have known more, but that she didn't want to say anything around Moore.

We stood there in silence for about a minute.

"Excuse me, do you need us here anymore?" asked the older of the two deputies still leaning against my car.

Moore walked over to them, and they started talking.

"I take it they're still blaming me for all this," I said.

"I think only at the working agent level. That's Special Agent Gold's brother down there. His name is Jacob. He's a friend of everyone in the local FBI office. I think they looked at you as a nuisance earlier, at worst a possible subject. Now I think they just have a lot of anger to vent, and you make a convenient target."

"So someone thought it might be a good idea for you to come along to protect me?" I said, only half teasing.

"I had that thought, too. They didn't have much nice to say about you in the helicopter. You know, three agents from their headquarters flew in this morning. Apparently the office is going to go through the wringer the next couple of days."

I felt like saying "been there," but I didn't. Someone high up in the FBI had probably linked Myers to the killing of FBI informants in other states. Possibly they even thought he was the alleged international assassin everyone had been looking for, and now they discovered he had an FBI buddy. Well, it didn't matter how clean the office really was, they were going to get a very close and personal look. No field office ever enjoyed that. Unfortunately, they had chosen to blame me for their predicament.

"But we have an interest in this, too. We still have four murders and an attempted one we are trying to close out."

"Wouldn't Bob have come for those?"

"Yeah. It surprised me that they asked for me by name."

I saw Moore studying the crease of white paint on my car. I didn't think it likely that anyone would think that I could run a large SUV off the road with my Mustang. Besides, if necessary, a forensic review of the scrape on my car would verify my story. Still, I felt like Moore studied the scrape in an attempt to come up with a theory to blame me.

"How much damage did he do to your car?" Michelle asked.

"Just the scrape. As he swerved into me, I hit the brakes. We barely made contact. He was going too fast to make the next corner and rolled off."

"I hope he makes it, he's a nice guy," she said. Then, as if her words finally sunk in, "I mean, I always thought he was."

He didn't make it. He died in the ambulance as it rushed to the hospital, his brother by his side.

Chapter 28

The rest of the day proved to be as strange as the afternoon. Before they had cut Jacob Gold out of the SUV, someone in the FBI had made the decision to take me back into Trinidad to get my statement. They transported me in a sheriff's vehicle. Two deputies and Special Agent Moore escorted me. Michelle followed in a separate car. My Mustang remained on the side of the highway.

Getting my statement turned out to be another nasty interrogation by Moore. A local deputy I didn't know sat in on the interview but didn't ask any questions. I assumed Michelle watched from the other side of the one way mirror that covered half of one of the room's walls.

I had no problem handling Moore's leading questions and negative attitude, but I found the whole process frustrating. Just as I started to lose my patience, a person I didn't recognize came in and motioned for Moore. He left and five minutes later the bored deputy left. I sat there for another thirty minutes before anyone returned.

Finally Michelle came into the room. That's when I found out that Jacob Gold had died.

"Before he died he told his brother that he had tried to run you off the road, because he believed that Myers had told you about him."

"I mentioned that to Moore. I don't think he was listening," I said.

"We heard you," she said, referring to herself and whoever else was monitoring the interview.

"What do you suppose it was that Jacob thought Myers would have told me?" It was the same question Moore had asked me. I told him I didn't know and asked Moore the same question. He ignored me.

Michelle glanced furtively at the mirror and leaned in close. "He apparently had fed Myers some info that he had picked up from his brother or other agents. He and Myers had always been close and often talked about ongoing investigations that were in the news. For that matter, Jacob managed a pizza joint that had a lot of cop customers. He probably knew a lot more about a whole bunch of investigations that he shouldn't have had access to. I'm afraid we'll never know the whole truth about Myers' relationship with Jacob, or what information may have been compromised, but he told his brother that he didn't know anything about the killings. Jacob claimed he tried to kill you to protect his brother. He said he had never tried to hurt anyone before, and that he was glad he had failed in his attempt to kill you."

"This whole thing still doesn't make a lot of sense to me. Was Jacob implying his brother was connected with Myers, or that his own involvement by itself would cause problems for his brother?" I asked.

"I don't know. Maybe we'll never know, but I imagine the FBI will look deep into all the relationships."

"You're right about that."

The interview room door opened, and a hand reached in and motioned for Michelle to come out. From my angle I couldn't see who owned the hand.

Michelle left the room, and for another twenty minutes, I sat there in silence. Just as I was getting up to walk out of the place on my own, the door reopened. The older deputy who I had met out at the accident scene took a step into the room.

"Come on, I'll take you back to your car."

"Can I speak to Lieutenant Prado before we go?"

"Fine with me, but she's already gone. She left with everyone else," he said.

He must have seen the question in my eyes.

"Don't ask me what's going on. Nobody's really telling us anything. Whatever this is all about is being backstopped in Denver and D.C. You know, ours is not to reason why, ours is but to do and die."

I smiled at the old quote.

He dropped me off in the dark at the Mustang. A tow crew had a long cable on the SUV and worked it slowly up the slope. Two highway patrol cars were parked close by.

I thought about staying to watch them work, but decided I'd had enough. I jumped into the Mustang and sped off to the first decent hotel I could find just inside the New Mexico state line. I would have preferred my own bed, but the trip would have taken another four to five hours.

I half expected a call from Michelle that night, but I didn't receive one. I didn't call her either, figuring she'd be tied up with work.

The following afternoon, Chubbs and I were playing catch with his favorite Frisbee when she finally called. She apologized for not saying good bye, but her departure had been so abrupt she didn't get a chance. She said Jacob's death and accident had been reported in the paper, but only that he had lost control of his SUV and had died in the accident. There had been no mention of the connection with Myers or me. I told her

I had no problems with that.

She also told me that things were getting back to normal at her office, but she heard it might be a while before the FBI office got back to normal. We both acknowledged that we felt sorry for Special Agent Gold and finally agreed to get together the next time I was in Colorado Springs.

"By the way," she said just before we hung up. "They caught up with Carl and Louise just outside Fairplay."

"They did?" I responded, my curiosity piqued.

"Yeah, and what they told us was true. They have a relative and a doctor they see when they're up there. The doctor vouched for them, as did the relative. I guess they're legit, but I still don't like the chain thing."

I told her I didn't either, but the news was a relief and made me feel good.

I thought about asking her to try to find out if it was Jacob, and not his brother, that had approached me that day in the hotel and told me to go home. I decided not to. There were a lot of questions that still needed answers, like had they figured out who had killed Garibaldi? I had my own working theory that I based on several assumptions, but it worked for me.

If Myers had not arrived in Colorado until after the Garibaldi murder, I pegged Grazzard as Garibaldi's killer. His motive we might never know. It was possible that Garibaldi did, in fact, find out that Lynda Ball was having an affair with Grazzard - a connection that Grazzard may have believed mustn't be made public.

Myers then killed Grazzard and Lynda Ball with Grazzard's weapon. I could think of a few ways he could have gotten his hands on it. Finally, Myers killed Mr. Ball with a shotgun, probably the shotgun later found in the fifth wheeler, and left the semi-automatic pistol he had used on the others at the scene to confuse the police. Grazzard and Mr. Ball were likely Myers' targets all along.

I had less confidence with my speculation regarding the motives for all this bloodshed. I believed it all connected to the Mob cleaning house following the recent compromise of the nationwide Justice Department investigation, but I didn't have a good theory on how the individual murders fit into the bigger picture.

One thing gnawed on my mind that night in the hotel in Raton. It had kept me awake, and I hoped it wouldn't become a nagging concern. Had I done anything to make myself a person of interest to the Mob? I didn't think so. I had become a personal problem for Myers and, through him, Gold; however, I didn't see how any of my actions could pose a future problem for anyone else. I hoped that was true. The last thing I needed was to be seen as a threat by the Mob.

Too many questions that needed answers, but I figured they could wait. I had already tossed enough kindling into the fire that was now going through that FBI office.

Maybe I would make another trip up to Colorado Springs in a few months. I could find out then, if I was still curious. Besides, it would be good to visit the Air Force Academy. I never got a chance to do so on this trip. It would also be nice to see Michelle.

I just wouldn't take Perry with me next time.

- Title: *Dead Men Can Kill*™
- Author: Bob Doerr
- Price: $27.95
- Publisher: TotalRecall Publications, Inc.
- Format: HARDCOVER, 6.14" x 9.21"
- Number of pages: 320
- 13-digit ISBN: 978-1-59095-758-5
- Publication: December 8, 2009

When Jim West, a former Air Force Special Agent with the Office of Special Investigations, moves back to New Mexico, his goal is simple: start an easy going second career as a professional lecturer on investigative techniques to colleges and civic organizations. He never envisioned that his practical demonstration of forensic hypnosis on stage with a state university student would stir up memories of an 18-year old murder mystery. When the student is murdered three days later, West finds himself ensnared in a web of intrigue that pits him and the small town's authorities against a ruthless, psychotic killer.

An aggressive reporter for the town newspaper seeks out West for help with the story, but after one of her co-workers is murdered, she quickly aligns her efforts with West and the Sheriff. As West works closely with her, he begins to wonder if this could be the first real relationship for him since his devastating divorce a few years earlier.

The killer, though, has other plans for the reporter and the story takes fascinating twists and turns, leading to an inevitable, riveting confrontation.

Look out for a new hero on the mystery/thriller landscape! Jim West, retired military investigator, is resourceful, intuitive, pragmatic and always competent. All of West's abilities are tested when he matches wits with psychopathic serial killer William White, a man whose appreciation for murder is surpassed only by his delight in domination. Bob Doerr has crafted a must-read addition to the genre in Dead Men Can Kill, which evolves from absorbing story to absolute page-turner as West closes in on a killer who is supposedly dead. Highly recommended!

--Dallin Malmgren, author of...

The Whole Nine Yards   *The Ninth Issue*   *Is This for a Grade?*

A Jim West™ Mystery/Thriller

- Title: *Cold Winter's Kill*™
- Author: Bob Doerr
- Price: $27.95
- Publisher: TotalRecall Publications, Inc.
- Format: HARDCOVER, 6.14" x 9.21"
- Number of pages: 288
- 13-digit ISBN: 978-1-59095-762-8
- Publication: Dec 8, 2009

Cold Winter's Kill is a fast paced thriller that takes place in the scenic mountains of Lincoln County, New Mexico and throws Jim West into a race against time to stop a psychopath who abducts and kills a young blonde every Christmas...

It was one of those phone calls former Air Force Special Agent Jim West never wanted to receive--an old friend calling to ask if he could drive down to Ruidoso, New Mexico to help locate his daughter who has disappeared while on a ski trip with friends. Jim found himself heading to Ruidoso even though he believed, much like the local authorities, that if she had gone missing in the mountains in December, her survival chances were slim. He didn't want to be there when they found her, but still he drove on.

Once in Ruidoso, Jim discovers a sinister coincidence that changes everything. It appears that someone is abducting and killing one young blond every year around Christmas. The race is on--can Jim locate his friend's daughter in time? But why is this happening and who's doing it?

Jim can't wait for the local authorities to raise the priority of their search, or for the pending blizzard to pass. In his haste he puts himself in the killer's sights. Will he, too, suffer from a cold winter's kill?

"GREAT SUSPENSE! In *Cold Winter's Kill* Bob Doerr grabs your attention from the beginning and holds it until the last sentence. Hard to put down!"

>--*Shelba Nicholson*
>former Women's Editor, *Texarkana Gazette*

Author Bob Doerr Uses his special knowledge to provide authentic details in his novels about how law enforcement agencies do their work.

A Jim West™ Mystery/Thriller

- Title: *Loose Ends Kill*™
- Author: Bob Doerr
- Price: $27.95
- Publisher: TotalRecall Publications, Inc.
- Format: HARDCOVER, 6.14" x 9.21"
- Number of pages: 288
- 13-digit ISBN: 978-1-59095-717-2
- Publication: Oct 27, 2010

LOOSE ENDS KILL **is a fast paced mystery/thriller** that takes place in the historic city of San Antonio, Texas, and throws Jim West into the middle of a police investigation of the murder of an old friend's wife. The police already believe they have the killer in custody – West's friend.

West is drawn into this mystery by a call from the old friend who requests his assistance. West agrees to help his friend and digs deep to try to find another suspect. In the process he soon discovers that he is being followed and targeted for harassment, but by whom?

West quickly discovers that he didn't know his old friend's wife as well as he thought. To his surprise, he learns that she has had a number of affairs dating back for more than a decade. In fact, while investigating the murder, he realizes that his friend and he may be the only two people unaware of her philandering behavior.

Theorizing that one of her lovers could have had just as much motive as her husband, West starts turning over the rocks identifying one lover after another. In doing so, West unintentionally ignites an outbreak of more death and mayhem. The police and his friend's lawyers want West to go back home. The police even threaten to arrest him.

Soon, West believes the real killer wants him gone or dead. Deciding the only way to resolve the case before the outside pressures force him to leave, he sets a trap for the killer using himself as bait. However, he soon learns he may have only outsmarted himself.

A Jim West™ Mystery/Thriller
www.bobdoerr.com

www.ingramcontent.com/pod-product-compliance
Lightning Source LLC
Chambersburg PA
CBHW020354120726
47904CB00002B/559